Praise for

The Summer of Jordi Perez
(and the Best Burger in Los Angeles)

NPR Best Book of 2018
Kirkus Reviews Best Young Adult Book of 2018
Boston Globe Best Children's Book of 2018
Pop Sugar Best Books of 2018
Cosmopolitan Best YA Books of 2018
Autostraddle Best LGBTQ Books of 2018
Buzzfeed Best Queer YA Books of 2018
Paste Magazine Best YA Books of 2018
TAYSHAS Reading List
ALA Rainbow List
YALSA Quick Picks for Reluctant Readers, Nominee
The Amelia Bloomer List, Nominee
Georgia Peach Book Award for Teen Readers, Nomination

"Yes, this book is as fantastic as it sounds."

—*PopSugar*

"The summer's hottest queer teen romance."

—*Entertainment Weekly*

"This book is the queer, fat girl rom-com of my dreams! Plus-size fashion, a fat girl falling in love, nuanced friendships, and cheeseburgers! Did I mention cheeseburgers?"

—Julie Murphy, #1 *New York Times*
bestselling author of *Dumplin'*

"This book is funny, empowering, and romantic, without downplaying the role of platonic friendships. And to the fat girls who are sidelined in almost every romantic comedy? It's a love letter."
—Becky Albertalli, bestselling and award-winning author of
Simon vs. the Homo Sapiens Agenda

"*The Summer of Jordi Perez* is a confectionary delight. From lovely romantic date nights to secret makeout sessions to utterly relatable friend drama, this is the happy queer-girl romance I've been longing for since I knew enough to long for happy queer-girl romance."
—Robin Talley, *New York Times* bestselling
author of *Lies We Tell Ourselves*

"You'll want to go shopping with Abby. You'll obsessively need to sample every cheeseburger in town. You might even plan a foodie-fashion-fun times vacation in L.A. But most importantly, you'll fall in love with *The Summer of Jordi Perez*. Just like I did."
—Gretchen McNeil, author of *Ten* and *I'm Not Your Manic Pixie Dream Girl*

"Amy Spalding is the funniest YA contemporary writer out there."
—*Hey YA Book Riot Podcast*

[★] "Funny, full of heart, and refreshingly free of a weight-loss arc."
—*Kirkus Reviews*, starred review

"Abby's journey is a vehicle for highlighting the dangers of negative self-perception in any relationship or endeavor. . . . Finally able to appreciate her talents, she discovers support and care rather than criticism. Shopping, humor, and summer romance add to the appeal of the story."
—*VOYA*

"Sweet and delightful."
—*School Library Journal*

"A deceptively fun and breezy novel that gracefully delineates the difference between dreaming about a relationship and actually having one. . . . The story moves along effortlessly. This is a book you don't want to miss a word of. . . . A treat with a heroine who's not easily forgotten."

—*Foreword Reviews*

"It's about the painful fizzy joy of a new crush, about the solidity and support we get from platonic friendships, about feeling lost when family dynamics change."

—Leila Roy, feature for *Kirkus Reviews*

"Abby will connect with readers who appreciate the realistic and natural love story between the two girls, and with anyone who's ever struggled to feel comfortable in his or her own skin."

—*Booklist*

"Full of fast-paced writing and just the right amount of romance, this is a happy read that will have you rooting for Abby as she comes to terms with what she wants and how best to get it. Plus, the wonderful queer fat girl rep will leave you with a big smile on your face and an urge to read more just like it."

—*The Mary Sue*

"The plot is as sweet as bubblegum, and probably the lightest, most enjoyable read you'll have all summer. Don't let the bright colors and stellar shopping fool you, this book carries themes like body positivity, following your dreams, and maintaining friendships too."

—After Ellen.com

"Abby's rambling voice is honest, charming, and absorbing. In a story about staying true to one's passions, Spalding (*The New Guy (and Other Senior Year Distractions)*) presents an interesting look at first love, social media, and private and public personas."

—*Publisher's Weekly*

"Amy Spalding's *The Summer of Jordi Perez* bursts with love: for clothes, for burgers (Abby goes on a 'best burger' hunt with a new jock friend) and for Abby's female colleague, Jordi. Abby loves her body too and is comfortable describing herself as fat, with the essential qualification, 'Being fat isn't bad. Acting like fat's an insult is, though.'"

—*Globe and Mail*

Also by Amy Spalding

THE SUMMER OF JORDI PEREZ

(AND THE BEST BURGER IN LOS ANGELES)

THE SUMMER OF JORDI PEREZ

(AND THE BEST BURGER IN LOS ANGELES)

AMY SPALDING

Sky Pony Press
New York

Library of Congress Cataloging-in-Publication Data is available on file.

Cover design by Kate Gartner

Paperback ISBN: 978-1-5107-5184-2
Ebook ISBN: 978-1-5107-2767-0

Printed in the United States of America

In memory of my father, Mark Spalding

Dear Ms. Goldman,

Thank you so much for the opportunity to apply for the internship position at your store. I've been obsessed with Lemonberry since the first time I shopped there! I love buying locally, which luckily in Atwater Village is easy because there are so many great neighborhood spots.

But while I love coffee from Kaldi and pastries from Bon Vivant, Lemonberry is my favorite. You might assume I'm only saying this because I want the internship, but I said this constantly before I even knew about the internship program. I'm so used to walking into adorable clothing boutiques only to find out that nothing fits me since my size falls above the range of "average," apparently.

At Lemonberry, though, that's never the case. I love having just as many amazing and unique looks to choose from as anyone else. Right now, I'm on a budget, so many of the pieces in my wardrobe were bought at chain stores at the Galleria and Americana. But I dream about Lemonberry dresses, and my parents actually got me one for my last birthday.

I don't just dream of great dresses, though; I plan to work in fashion. I'm not yet sure where that will lead; sometimes I want to be a stylist, sometimes an editorial director who revitalizes an old-school magazine, and sometimes a buyer for anything from a teeny boutique to a giant department store. Last week Tess Holliday was my hero, and this week it's Jenna Lyons. What doesn't change is how much I love fashion and style.

I run a blog called +style, *which focuses on plus size fashion but also covers more general fashion news and plenty of subjects (like bags and jewelry) that appeal to people of any size. In the year and a half since I launched, I've gained thousands of followers and even more on Instagram.* +style *has been featured in a variety of online fashion coverage, including being named one of* The Cut's *10 Plus Size Fashion Sites to Read.*

My application is attached. Again, I'm very grateful for this opportunity, and would love to learn and be inspired by you and your store and designs.

Sincerely,

Abby Ives

CHAPTER 1

In modern love stories, our heroines all seem to have something in common. No, not an adorably decorated apartment in the big city, a conveniently timed meet cute with the person of their dreams, or the kind of problem that arises two-thirds of the way through their personal narrative and somehow fixes itself in that last third.

Okay, they definitely have most of those things in common. But the thread binding them all together? It's the sassy best friend. The sassy best friend gets to have witty one-liners, a killer wardrobe, and usually a pretty great job. But it is the best friend's goal to help our heroine fall in love; it is not the best friend's job to fall in love herself.

Therefore, I've just realized that I'm probably doomed at love. Because I'm pretty sure I'm not the heroine. I don't even think I'm in my own story.

Last winter, my best friend fell in love. We live in Los Angeles, so it wasn't over steaming mugs of hot cocoa or whimsically collided skis. Maliah met Trevor in the epic pre-Christmas line at the Apple store at the Grove, which seems to me about as L.A. of a love story as you can get.

Anyway, I did all the best friend things. I looked over his Facebook profile, helped analyze his texts, and—of course—picked out her first date outfit, down to her blue lacy bra and underwear. (He didn't see anything underneath her clothes for two months, according to Maliah, but cute underwear provides loads of confidence and should never be underestimated regardless of the situation.)

I know that I'm obsessing over Maliah's love life right now because I found out last night that Lyndsey Malone has a boyfriend. Okay, sure, I never had official confirmation that Lyndsey likes girls. Zoe and Brooke claim they saw her at a Tegan & Sara concert, but I can't believe I took that as proof of anything! It's not like Zoe or Brooke likes girls, after all, and they were there.

I am seventeen years old. I'm about to be a senior in high school. And while maybe it would be okay at seventeen not to have had an epic love story yet, I haven't even kissed anyone. Not even a *boy*. Last month, I was babysitting for the toddler twins who live next door, and when their twelve-year-old sister got home from her volleyball practice, she made an offhand comment about a boy she liked that made me assume she was nervous about kissing someone for the first time. *Um, I've obviously kissed someone already,* she'd said. *I'm twelve, not nine.*

I want to, in this very moment while I am walking down Glenfeliz Boulevard toward Glendale Boulevard, be fixated on summer looks and vintage reproductions and local designers. But my tween neighbor has more experience than me, and the only real-life girl I've liked has a boyfriend. This is why I keep forgetting to be happy about the dream internship I've landed—and am on my way to right now.

I meant everything I wrote to Maggie Goldman when I applied for the summer position. But I know a lot more than my letter let on; the internet is full of information when you know where and how to look. When I composed my letter, I was well aware that interns tend to get part-time—but *paying*—jobs for the next school year, until college takes you away and opens up space for the next girl. Maggie Goldman believed in giving people their starts; this year that person would be me.

Still, how am I supposed to think about any of this as the true tragic reality of my love life comes into sharper and sharper focus? Once the truth feels like it's physically and literally surrounding you, can you go back to thinking about dresses and accessories?

No more real girls, I decide. Only celebrities and fashion. They can't hurt me.

I'm five minutes early, so when I walk up to the shop, the CLOSED sign is still in the window and the door is locked. A girl is inside at the cash register, but I'm not sure if she has anything to do with my position, and, anyway, I really don't know the non-awkward way of getting her attention. So I just wait.

"Hey," says someone behind me.

I turn around to see a girl who's probably my age. Her look is not Lemonberry's general aesthetic of faux vintage girliness; she's wearing skinny black pants with a slouchy T-shirt, and even though it's June, she's wearing short black boots that come up over the ankles of her pants. I'm not sure what she'd want to browse here once the store's open.

5

"Hi," I say.

"You're Abby, right?" she asks, shoving her wavy dark hair out of her face.

"Yes," I say, even though I probably shouldn't let on to strangers who I am. The moment feels mildly dangerous, but maybe that's just holdover from thinking about my doomed existence.

"We go to school together," she says with her eyebrow raised, and then I can picture her in my geometry class.

"Sorry," I say, and then, "You look different."

"I got a haircut."

I try to think of a nice way to tell her that I'm about to begin the most important professional role of my entire life and that I don't have time to talk right now. Also, I'd love to remember her name because I would feel like less of a self-centered jerk.

The door opens, and Maggie leans out. During my interview, she told me to call her Maggie, so I'm following directions, not being too casual. "Come on in, girls."

Girls?

I walk inside with the girl right behind me.

"It's Jordi," she says.

"What's Jordi?" I ask, though softly.

"*My name.*"

"Oh," I say, and then I smile like that'll keep her from thinking I'm horrible. "Jordi Perez, right?"

"That's me," she says.

"Go on into the back room." Maggie gestures to the door at the back of the shop. "I just made a fresh pot of coffee, so feel free to help yourselves. I'll meet you in a few minutes."

Jordi and I walk into the back room, and even though clothes and designs are all over, Jordi makes her way straight to the coffeemaker.

"Do you want a cup?" she asks me.

"Sure, thanks," I say, even though I think of coffee as a grownup beverage and I'm far from a grownup. When school starts in the fall, I can be someone who carries in a cardboard cup of coffee instead of something like a Frappuccino.

By fall, I'll think of Frappuccinos as *so immature*.

I try to calmly sip my coffee like the adult I'm pretending to be, but it's hot, bitter water and so I sort of accidentally sputter it back into the cup while Jordi's calmly adding Splenda and half-and-half to hers. She smirks and slides the Splenda and half-and-half to me. I tear open three Splenda packets and watch the coffee change from near-black to creamy beige as I pour in half-and-half.

The door opens, and Maggie walks in. I was honestly surprised when I met her, because even though I'd definitely seen her around the shop, she's not who I assumed was the owner and designer. There's a lady who's often working who's always wearing one of the store's pieces, if not a full outfit comprising them. Her hair is dyed the most perfect shade of burgundy and coiffed like a team of stylists or maybe Cinderella's magical mice set it in place each day.

That lady is definitely not Maggie, who today is wearing jeans and a blue T-shirt so faded I can't make out what was originally printed on it. Her brown hair is piled atop her head in a sloppy bun. I try to imagine her designing swingy beautiful dresses and still can't make it work in my head.

"Remind me, which one of you is the photographer?" She looks back and forth between Jordi and me. "And which is the blogger?"

Jordi and I glance at each other but don't answer right away, even though obviously we know what we ourselves are. I don't talk about my blog to anyone at school, though, outside of my closest friends. I don't think anything good would come out of everyone knowing about +*style*.

"I'm the photographer," Jordi finally says.

"That makes me the blogger," I say, even though never in my entire life have I referred to myself as a *blogger*.

"I should have remembered," Maggie says. "I'm not good at details. You'll learn that. I guess maybe you just did. Anyway, you guys might know that we usually only have one intern each summer, but this is a big year for us, and honestly, I couldn't decide between the two of you."

I open my mouth to ask about the part-time job in the fall, because I doubt there are magically two of those, even if Jordi and I are both here. But considering Maggie hasn't brought up the job yet, I probably shouldn't introduce the topic.

"You two will share the duties we talked about in your interviews," Maggie continues. "Filing, some other basic organizing, helping out the staff with certain tasks. But I'd also love for you both to get to use your talents here. So we'll talk more about that once you're caught up on the boring stuff. Okay?"

Jordi and I both agree to that, and Maggie brings us back out to the storefront to walk us around. Even though I've been here what must be at least a hundred times, I've never actually noticed how things are laid out, with the fanciest dresses in the front where they can be seen when people walk by, basics toward the back, and the newest designs in the window displays. You have to walk by everything else to get to the sales rack so that hopefully you'll spend money on something full price, too. And accessories are everywhere, though it seems fairly thoughtful. Little clutches are near the fancy dresses and canvas bags screenprinted with the store's logo are by more casual stuff.

I read online that Lemonberry's interns always end up with free clothes, but now doesn't feel like the right time to ask about that. Actually, I'm not sure there will be a right time to ask about that. Hopefully the clothes will just magically come to me.

Maggie introduces us to Paige, the girl currently working, who doesn't look thrilled but is polite enough to us. I'd hoped the burgundy-haired lady would be here today; Paige's style isn't so precise—her blonde hair is short, though not cut into any sort of specific style, and she's wearing a simple navy dress with shiny tan flats—and my gut says she's less fun to be around than her coworker.

Maybe she would be friendlier if it was just me; two teenagers might be more than she'd counted on. I'd probably feel friendlier myself—or less confused, at least. I thought I would have three months to impress Maggie and earn this forthcoming job. Are Jordi and I competing? Should I ask that? No, I shouldn't, and I know that. Or, technically, Dad warned me that forcing this conversation might seem too overzealous, especially on day one.

I have so many questions for Maggie, though.

"I don't want to overwhelm you guys on your first day," Maggie says, walking us to the backroom. "Do you have any questions for me? About the store, or any general internship questions?"

It does kind of feel like a sign that I'm holding back all these questions and now it's almost like Maggie wants me to have questions. But I want to follow Dad's advice. It's not that I spend a lot of time thinking he's right about things, but my gut tells me he's onto something with this topic. Dad had the same job at the same office for as long as I can remember before his recent career shift, so I guess he did something right.

Oh, great, now for some reason I'm thinking about *my dad* instead of paying attention, and now Jordi's already mid-conversation with Maggie.

"We do have a camera here." Maggie rummages through a cabinet full of random equipment, so her voice comes out pretty muffled. "But if you'd prefer to use your own, that's fine, too. This one's a little old."

She emerges with a camera and hands it over to Jordi, who examines it thoroughly. Photography seems like such a classier and more mature interest than *blogging*. Maggie probably doesn't think that I'm a goober if she chose me for this role, but I hope Jordi doesn't think it either. If there had to be another intern, I'm positive it would be easier if it weren't someone from the same high school, much less someone who I had forgotten existed.

"Abby?" Maggie asks.

"What? I mean, yes?"

"Any questions?" When Maggie's smile is focused on me, it feels so kind and open. I feel like I'm at least momentarily her whole world. By now I've figured out that she smiles like this all the time, so maybe it doesn't mean anything when she smiles at me. Of course I wanted the internship because I wanted free clothes, an eventual paying job, and something great to put on my college applications. But even before my interview, when Maggie called me to set it up, right away I heard in her voice how much I wanted to work with her.

"I'd actually read that usually the internship turns into a job," I say, because Maggie's kind smile screwed up my newly developed business instincts and my guard was down and now the words are out of my mouth.

At least I didn't ask for a free dress, too?

I glance at Jordi, because I assume she'll be bug-eyed at the person who would ask something so unprofessional right from the start. But clearly Jordi is not the type of person who'd react with bug eyes. She's still calmly examining the camera in her hands.

"It often does, yeah," Maggie says. "Any more questions for me? More coffee?"

"More coffee would be great," Jordi says, and I agree

despite that I'm not sure I should add even more caffeine to my body chemistry right now. I've learned that—with all the Splenda and cream—I actually like coffee a lot.

"So, I know this is boring, but if you two want to get started alphabetizing the stack of vendor invoices, that would be great. I'm going to my office for a while to get through some emails, but please come and get me if anything confuses you."

"Like the alphabet?" I ask.

Maggie laughs, thank god, because it's another question I probably shouldn't have asked.

"Well, hopefully you've both got the alphabet down," she says. "I'll see you at lunchtime, okay?"

Maggie disappears into the office at the very back of the room, and I turn to look at Jordi.

"'Like the alphabet?'" Jordi says with a raised eyebrow.

I wait for her to mock me, but her serious expression morphs into something else. Before I know it, she's laughing, and I don't think it's at me. I join in.

"How should we do this?" I pick up the pile of invoices. "Just split it in half?"

"Works for me." She reaches out to take half the papers. We crowd two chairs against the desk and sort through the invoices. I know we're literally just putting things in alphabetical order—basically a job that smart kindergarteners could do—but there's something satisfying about taking piles of chaos and making them orderly.

"Some of these are *old*," Jordi says. "I hope they're paid."

"She said she wasn't good with details," I say.

"Are you finished?" she asks me.

"Almost. I think you're faster at the alphabet than I am."

"Cool, I'll add that to my college applications."

"Best at the alphabet," I say.

She pokes my arm with her finger. "Fastest, not best. Get your application facts right, Abby."

"Oh, sorry," I say. "Maybe I'm bad with details, too."

"Well, you didn't know my name," Jordi says, but then she smiles again. And I realize that having Jordi's smile focused on me feels pretty special, too.

CHAPTER 2

I haven't been into fashion my whole life, which probably isn't possible anyway. (It's not as though there are fashionable babies, unless babies have fashionable parents.) As a little kid, I didn't care about what I or anyone else wore.

But one magical day when I was eleven years old, Mom took my older sister Rachel and me to the Galleria to buy a present for Dad for Father's Day. Obviously, the day was supposed to be about Dad, but then I spotted a bright floral dress in the window of a store, and I became immediately obsessed. Mom wouldn't get it for me that day—I think to make a point about caring about other people—but a few weeks later, she surprised me with it anyway.

So unfortunately the whole thing probably taught me to beg for dresses I was in love with, not to care about other people more than myself. After all, I grew up to be someone who can't even remember the names of people I go to school with.

Oh my god, maybe my epic love story is with clothes and fashion and that's why I'm doomed to never kiss a real person.

No, that can't actually be a thing.

Anyway, it wasn't just that first dress; I kept finding

clothes I loved. More dresses, sweaters, and boots to wear during L.A.'s brief winter—skirts, shoes, tights, and jeans that looked and felt great. No, I wasn't in love with clothes, but maybe I was in love with how clothes made me feel. I was designing how other people saw me, and that felt powerful. I told anyone who'd listen that I'd work in fashion someday, doing anything I could to be part of it.

But then it happened. I was one of the last girls in our class to get my period, and when I did, it was like my body got swapped out with another one. Nothing fit. I was excited to have boobs, but everything else? I felt too big, and I literally *was* too big for my old clothes. I had no idea where to even look for new outfits—and I didn't want to, really, the thought depressed me—and skulking around in baggy stuff made me feel ugly. My future in fashion felt more than over; it felt like it never even had existed as a possibility.

And of course, this just had to be around the same time I was figuring out that I didn't dream about kissing the boyband members Maliah did because we had different tastes in music. Because all of a sudden, I was dreaming about kissing girls.

It was a weird year.

I started spending way more time on Tumblr. There it didn't seem to matter that only recently I didn't even know who I was anymore. I became obsessed with one particular plus size fashion Tumblr because the girl who ran it was just a little older than I was and put together the kinds of outfits I used to wear, back when I was pre-period and skinnier than Maliah.

15

The only problem was that the clothes were *expensive*. And most of them were only available online, and my parents said I was not mature enough to be trusted with their credit card, much less my own. I started printing out all my favorite looks and taking them shopping with me. It turned out that knowing where and how to look meant I didn't have to spend a million dollars putting outfits together, even if I was too big for a lot of the stores I used to shop at.

And I felt like myself again. My style defined me again, not my size.

But I also felt sort of selfish. Maybe there were other girls like me, or even a little like me, who also lusted after designer outfits and felt like they'd never be able to afford to look good. Not before they were out of school, at least. So I started my own Tumblr and typed up a short entry about the sweaters I'd found that day at the mall. I posted photos of my finds, though not me in them. That felt too personal. I linked to my new site in the comments of others that I loved, but once it was just *out there*, I worried. Maybe it wouldn't seem personal enough, or too personal? Maybe no one would care about my shopping finds! But only a couple days later, I started getting comments and reblogs, and girls messaged me to ask other shopping questions.

So I kept doing it. My mom blogs for a living, at least in part, so I stole all the tips I could from her. I kept commenting on similar blogs and invited them to visit mine. I reblogged and retweeted and Tumblr'd and liked and faved and hearted all over social media. I wrote custom posts geared toward anyone who commented with something they wanted to see next, like formalwear or boots.

It, sort of magically, worked. And then the more I wrote, the more followers I gained, and it made me want to write even more. Now it's just a regular part of my life.

I keep Tumblr Abby and real-life Abby as separate as I can, though. I don't post pics of myself, even when I'm wearing the exact same looks I'm recommending. Maliah is my only friend who knows about +*style*, and I only told her because she wanted to know why I was always checking my phone. Maliah doesn't believe in secrets, so holding anything back is a bit of an exhausting yet pointless pursuit. The effort doesn't feel worth it for a freaking blog.

Once Jordi and I have combined our stacks of invoices, we give Maggie a few minutes to come out of her office. When she doesn't, I decide to creep close to her closed office door to see if I can guess how we should proceed.

"Can you hear anything?" Jordi whispers.

"No," I say, but I forget to whisper. The office door opens almost immediately, and I try to back away subtly. I don't make eye contact with Jordi, but I can hear her snort.

"We finished the invoices," she says calmly to Maggie, who's emerged from behind the door.

"Great. Are you guys hungry? Let's go grab lunch. I don't want to overwhelm you on your first day."

17

Considering we've been here for a couple hours now and the only thing we've actually done is put a stack of paper in alphabetical order, I'm not exactly feeling over-whelmed. Not by the internship, at least. By the uncertain state of the fall job, sure. By feeling like maybe I've lost out on something special by splitting things with Jordi, definitely. By thinking of Lyndsey Malone kissing Blake Jorgensen—*of all people*. Blake Jorgensen who, *twice last year*, interrupted our World History teacher because he felt like he "could explain the Ottoman Empire in a more relatable way."

Yeah, I'm definitely overwhelmed.

"Abby?"

I look to Maggie, who seems like she's awaiting some-thing from me. Possibly an answer to a question she asked while I was thinking about how Blake Jorgensen's hair is blonde in one section and he claims it's from the sun but we're all sure he bleaches it. Oh, god, I am for sure now missing probably another vital question.

"Lunch?" Jordi says. "Viet Noodle Bar?"

"Oh, sure, great," I say. And it is great, not just because I like the restaurant, but because Maggie wasn't doing some-thing like offering one of us the fall job while I was get-ting angry at a boy I barely know for being with someone who'd never see me that way anyway. Why am I taking it so hard when I can't imagine *anyone* seeing me that way?

We walk down the block to the restaurant, which isn't one of my regular spots, because in our family, going out to dinner is tantamount to cheating on Mom. And maybe someday I'll be the kind of girl who has regular lunch spots and favorite places for bringing dates, but right now all my extra money goes toward shopping (and obviously occasionally Frappuccinos). Also, I'll probably never have dates; I'll just need cool brunch places so I can meet up with Maliah and guide her through the travails of her love life.

"Not everyone knows their major yet," Jordi says, with a look to me.

Oh, crap, I stopped listening *again*.

Even though we've gone to school together for at least all of high school, Jordi's voice isn't familiar to me at all. I don't know her tone, and she definitely sounds more serious than anyone I hang out with. Up until today, Jordi and I have probably never exchanged more than a few words.

I know Jordi's friends, though—well, I know who her friends are. They all wear lots of black, but not in the stoned-skateboarding-slacking way. They stand out in Glenfeliz High School because in Southern California, most people choose to wear colors that complement the near-constant sunshine. I feel like Jordi's group is artsy and cultured and serious, but maybe I'd think that of anyone so enamored with the color black. If I switched to all-black clothing, I wonder if everyone would suddenly think that of me.

Maybe I should try it out, at least for a week. No! I'd miss colors way too much. Today, for example, I'm wearing a yellow floral dress with a tiffany blue belt and gold sandals, with a tiny jeweled barrette in my shoulder-length cotton candy pink hair. I was doing my best to go for a

Lemonberry vibe without making it seem like I was trying *too* hard. It's funny how trying hard is supposed to be the very last thing you seem like you're doing in fashion, when, come on, no one just *throws on* an outfit that has the least bit of style to it. Trying hard shouldn't be seen as a crime.

Anyway, I really do think that when the school year ended, Jordi didn't quite look so cultured or bad-ass or intimidating. But I've never *just looked* so much at Jordi before.

"What about you, Abby?" Maggie asks, and I manage to remember I'm in the midst of a conversation.

"I don't know about college yet," I say, even though part of me feels like it already knows so much. I see myself in New York, or even still here, but downtown and no longer living at home. My parents want me to focus on something serious in college—which is pretty crazy considering Mom makes her living *blogging about food*—and refuse to believe that fashion can be serious. It's as though they've forgotten binge-watching whole seasons of *Project Runway* with me while I choked up at all of the emotional moments.

"You have so much time," Maggie says with a wave of her hand. I wonder how old she is. Honestly, I have no idea how to judge adults' ages unless they look really visibly old. Maggie's probably younger than my parents, but by how much, who knows. "Not everyone has to have as much sorted out as Jordi does."

Oh, no. Jordi must have had such a good answer about college, and I wasn't even paying attention. I seriously spent most of last year dreaming about making this internship mine, and I actually have it—well, half of it, anyway!—but instead of soaking up as much knowledge as possible or impressing Maggie with my passion and social media savvy, I'm daydreaming. And while daydreaming *sounds* like a wispy, romantic thing perhaps done by the heroine in a romantic comedy, considering my daydreams aren't romantic or wispy, I don't think it counts.

And now I'm literally daydreaming *about daydreaming.* And all the while, Jordi is sitting next to me, looking serious in her all-black clothes and having some sort of genius answer about her future.

"So I want to be honest with you both," Maggie says after our waiter takes our drink order. My stomach clenches while I await news of my fate. Our fates, I guess. There are a lot of fates hanging in the balance right now.

"I'm going through a divorce right now, and I feel a little more scattered than usual," Maggie continues, and I find myself exchanging a split-second look of *oh dear god, what do we say now?* with Jordi.

At least, that's what I presume Jordi's thinking right now, because I definitely am.

"I still want to make sure you two get tons of experience this summer," Maggie says. "So hopefully everything will be great. Business as usual."

"I'm sorry," I say. "About your divorce, I mean."

"Me too," Jordi says, and even though she has one of those vaguely monotone voices, I can hear her sincerity. It's funny how things like that can be apparent.

21

"Girls," Maggie says, and she laughs softly. "I wasn't telling you to get sympathy. But thank you."

I'm trying to figure out what to say next, and then I'm surprised when the waiter shows up because I've been so busy thinking about a billion other things that I haven't even considered my order. I just sort of point to something and hand off my menu. Of course, it's not even mildly concerning that I wasn't ready to order a bowl of pho (or whatever I just asked for), but I can't ignore the fact that I feel less and less prepared to get through this day—a day that's so far included walking through a store, alphabetizing some papers, and ordering lunch for myself. When I've pictured myself post-college, no matter what part of the high-stakes fashion world I saw myself in (stylist, editorial director, department store buyer, designer), that part of that world was high stakes.

I firmly believe I can be plus size in the rail-thin world of fashion, but not if I'm also getting flustered about *food* at a restaurant *in my own neighborhood*. Why can't I be more like Jordi, who—despite that she was clearly as surprised by Maggie's divorce announcement as I was—looks calm and pays attention and probably has more than a vague idea of what she just ordered? I didn't even know I had this side, this panicky daydreaming Abby who'll never make it in fashion. How can you go seventeen years on Earth and not know all your sides?

"While we're being honest," Maggie says, and I feel a shift in that moment, the way the smell of the air changes right before it rains. "It is true that I normally hire the summer intern on a part-time basis, and while I definitely have enough work for the two of you this summer, I won't be able to bring both of you on this fall."

Jordi and I exchange another look. This time, even though I'm pretty sure that we're again thinking the same thing, it doesn't feel so united.

"I'm hoping that it'll sort itself out organically," Maggie continues. "So let's not focus on that. I just want to be open with you two. Okay?"

"Okay," I say quickly. Hopefully it makes me seem agreeable, the kind of person you'd want to hire for a paid job.

"Okay," Jordi says, and I try not to analyze her exact same barely-a-word response for proof that she handled even that better than I did. I'm seized with the urge to cry, but I push it down because that would be seriously ridiculous.

Still, it's very hard to ignore that *sort itself out organically* couldn't mean anything but *one of you will be right for the job and the other very obviously won't.*

CHAPTER 3

After lunch is a redux of before lunch: filing and worrying about Jordi's high competence level. Unfortunately, I seem to be way more adept at the latter than the former.

Summers are my favorite. They used to be, at least. Summers were when my sister, Rachel, and I were free from school and extracurriculars (her: yearbook, me: drama club costumes) and could do whatever we wanted with our time. And once Rachel, three years older than me, got her license, we *really* could do whatever we wanted.

But two months ago, Rachel texted to say she wasn't coming home. She got an *amazing internship* near campus and also *her boyfriend* and it just makes more sense financially and also *her boyfriend*. I have met her boyfriend, Paul, and I can't imagine wanting to be around someone *more* who has an old-timey twirly mustache and a thousand opinions on avant-garde films from the 1930s. Paul is a guy I'm convinced that Rachel and I would have made fun of together before he became *her boyfriend*.

"How was the big internship?" Mom asks almost as soon as I walk in because now it seems she's always about two feet from the front door. Our house is a little bungalow that was always the right fit for the four of us, but even with Rachel away at college—and I guess maybe forever from now on—it's gotten way too small. Mom's food blog turned into a monthly morning news segment, and then a weekly one, and now Eat Healthy with Norah! is *a brand*. It's also the thing that takes up most of the living room, dining room, and my parents' bedroom. Only my room and the bathroom still feel safe, and that's only sort of true given that, right now, there's a pile of Eat Healthy with Norah! reusable tote bags on Rachel's unused bed. The other week Maliah spent the night, and it ultimately ended up being easier for her to just sleep underneath the bag-covered comforter than move anything.

"It was great," I say.

"Oh," she says, and then, "good," which is fine, because if I'm lying to her, I can't be annoyed she's pretending to be happy for me.

"You'll be running the place before long, kiddo," Dad says, looking up from a pile of paper samples. I decide not to correct him because even interns with less sad prospects aren't exactly next in line to run places, and so he's probably not being literal.

"I'm going to hang out with Maliah," I say, because by the time I left Lemonberry, I had three texts from her about hanging out poolside at Trevor's. My friends Zoe and Brooke had checked in with me to see how my first day went, but they're not nearly as forceful as Maliah is. The thing I didn't really learn from rom-coms is that after the happily-ever-after, your collective friends are often forced to co-mingle. This is why I have more than a casual knowledge of lacrosse bro lingo now.

"Be home for dinner," Mom says. "I'm trying something very exciting tonight."

When other moms say things like this, they're probably referencing tacos or delicious sandwiches, but the last time my mom made tacos, it was just chicken wrapped in pieces of lettuce. She kind of made it look like tacos, which is the sort of thing she features all the time on Eat Healthy with Norah!, but I more than occasionally just want to Eat Normally with My Family.

What's so bad about a few tortillas anyway?

"I'll be home," I tell Mom before sidestepping her and Dad to get to my bedroom. Maliah texts again while I'm changing, so I tap out a quick reply before switching to a bright blue casual dress and my matching Converse. They can't make you get into a pool if you're not equipped with the right wardrobe, right?

It takes me about twenty minutes to walk to Trevor's house. I ring the front doorbell a few times, even though I can hear everyone yelling and splashing behind the house. I haven't fully worked out the etiquette and customs of the rich, preppy, and athletically inclined.

I text Maliah that I'm there after my repeated doorbell rings result in absolutely nothing. She opens the gate to the backyard and sticks her head out.

"Come on back, weirdo," she says, which is how she's referred to me for forever, but forever ago it didn't feel like it does right in this moment. Forever ago, Maliah wasn't wearing a sparkling bikini with all the confidence in the world while I actually worked out a backstory on why I didn't bring a swimsuit. And Maliah would have definitely managed to get through a day at Lemonberry less awkwardly than I had.

"Did you ask Brooke or Zoe?" I ask as we round the corner and step out into the backyard proper. There are a few girls—though none I know—but it's mainly dudes running around and leaping ridiculous cannonballs into the pool. Maybe if I liked guys, I would understand all of this—find it cute, even—but I don't think so. It hardly seems like a key selling point, especially when plenty of other guys at school seem funny and smart and interested in things besides sports and beers.

Not that I'm *not* going to take a beer. It's here, after all.

This has been a new world for me, though, since Maliah and Trevor became *serious*. This group of guys could be pulled straight from a movie about rich jocks partying their summer away. I think it's safe to say I never thought I would be even an extra in a scene from that kind of story.

"I wanted to see *you*," Maliah says, and even though I'd love for a higher percentage of people I know to be here, I like being someone special to my best friend.

"So how was your first day?" she asks me.

"It was . . ." I shrug. "I don't know."

"Did you get any free dresses yet?" Maliah asks.

"No." I pop open a can of PBR, because even rich boys in fancy houses have cheap beer. "There's another intern."

"Did *she* get any free dresses?" Maliah makes a face. "Unfair."

"No one got any free dresses," I say. "I thought that this would be . . . just mine. The way it's always been."

"One girl in all the world," Maliah says in a dramatic voice.

"Well, in all of the Eastside, at least," I say. "Now I probably won't get the job in the fall. Which I was really counting on, you know. Money and my college applications."

I texted all of this to Rachel already, but she hasn't gotten back to me yet. I guess she's too busy with her own internship to give me the internship pep talk I so desperately need. Well, I *want* a pep talk. Maybe what I *need* is a cold dose of reality.

"Why wouldn't you get the job?" Maliah asks, and I feel it. I did need a pep talk. "You're great at all your fashion Tumblr stuff. You were on *The Cut!*"

"I felt like such a goober today," I say. "Guess who the other intern is."

Trevor bounds over to us straight from the pool and wraps his arms around Maliah's bare stomach. She squeals as he drenches her with cold pool water, and that almost immediately turns into making out. Okay, it's just kissing, but it's kissing with a lot of contact, and I'm standing *right here*, so it's fair to qualify it as making out.

Seriously, I couldn't be happier for Maliah, living out her real-life love story. I just occasionally or maybe *slightly more than occasionally* wish it affected my life slightly less. Also, is this an inevitable part of love, or even of *like*? It's a horrifying thought. But since I'm going to be alone forever, at least I won't become one of them.

Though will I just be surrounded by squealing and PDAs? My future is doomed.

"What were you saying?" Maliah asks as Trevor runs back toward the pool releasing some kind of warrior yell. Boys in big groups remind me of babysitting our next-door neighbors' twin toddlers. There's so much chaotic yelling and wrestling—and the sinking feeling that maybe nothing less than full adult supervision is required.

"Wait, what suit are you wearing?" Maliah grabs the skirt of my dress and starts pulling it up. I let out a full-on scream. Even the warrior-yelling boys look over.

"What the *hell*, Abby."

"I'm not wearing a suit," I say. "And I don't want anyone seeing my underpants. That was a normal reaction for underpants-seeing prevention."

"It's a pool party!" she says. "I told you to bring a suit!"

"There was a problem with our washing machine last night," I say. "So I couldn't get it ready because I was at my internship all day. And, anyway, speaking of my internship, guess who—"

"You okay over here?" One of Trevor's buddies makes his way over to us. "Sounded like something violent going down."

"I'm fine," I say. This is the one I don't dislike, because he bought me a Diet Coke once, and didn't laugh the other week at the girl whose bikini top fell off when she dove into the water. For a lacrosse bro type, I guess he's harmless enough.

29

"Be safe," he says with a smile.

"Jax," Maliah says with a grin. "You know that hitting on Abbs is hopeless, right?"

Oh my god, that's right. His name is actually Jax, like he's an action hero or a for-dudes-only line of deodorant.

"I still need to talk to you about something," Jax says with a little head nod. I feel like he knows this gesture works on girls and so he's worked out the intricacies of exactly how much to tilt his head and squint his eyes.

Somehow it even sort of works on me.

"Leave her alone," Maliah says, though with a smile.

"I'll text you later," Jax tells me while walking off.

"Good luck without my number," I mutter to Maliah, who snorts.

"He'll probably get it from Trevor," she says. "Fair warning."

"Why does *Trevor* have my number?" I take another sip of beer. It's not good but it's cold and free.

"You know," Maliah says with a little shrug. "Emergencies and stuff. If he can't get in touch with me, he can try you."

See, it's great that I'm doomed to my spinster existence—I literally don't understand anything that couples do.

"So what are you talking about?" Maliah hops up to sit on the little stone wall that sections off the pool area. "The other intern? Someone exciting?"

"No," I say. "Jordi Perez. From school."

Maliah squinches her eyebrows, nose, and mouth all at once. "Jordi Perez? I thought she was in juvie."

"Juvie?" I burst out laughing. "Is juvie even real? I thought that was something that happened to bad kids in movies from the 1950s."

"Abby, juvie is completely real, and I can't believe she's not still there."

"She seems fine," I say. More than fine. Professional! Inspiring! Fashion-serious in all black! Well-spoken! Beautiful!

"I heard she burned down a building. *Arson*, Abbs."

"You are my best friend and I love you," I say, "but that doesn't sound like something that could have really happened."

"Be careful." Maliah grabs my arm and forces me to stare into her eyes. "Promise me."

"Um, okay. Sure."

"What's it like otherwise? Can you use a computer? Then you could still work on your blog."

"I don't think so." I feel a twinge of guilt that in today's weirdness, I haven't yet come up with my next post idea. "I don't even know what I'm writing about."

"Swimsuits," she says, forcefully. "And you should take pictures in them. At least in the nautical striped one."

"Is it too clichéd to write about swimsuits for my second post of the summer?" I ask. "And you know how I feel about putting pictures of myself online that aren't severely locked down. Why would I start with *me in a swimsuit*?"

Maliah pokes me in the shoulder. "'Cause you'd look *smoking* and maybe this is how you find a girlfriend, finally."

"I don't want a girlfriend," I say, because it's what I

always say. It feels good and consistent and right to stick to a story. After all, it's not embarrassing not to have something you don't even want.

The thing is, even if I wasn't already doomed to never know love, it would still seem impossible. I don't know how to find girls—Lyndsey is proof of that—and I don't know how, if I managed to, one of them would be even interested in me, and then even if *all of that* magically happened, I don't really know what it would be like. Watching Maliah with Trevor is a little like watching my best friend but also a little like spying on a stranger.

"My dad's on his way home," Trevor yells. "Everyone clear out."

"Can you give me a ride?" I ask Maliah as I chug the last of my beer.

Trevor pops up next to us and slings his arm around Maliah's shoulders. "'Everyone' doesn't mean Mal."

"I'm sorry," she says. "You'll be okay, right? It's still light out."

"I'll be fine," I say, because it's not about safety! I just wanted to hang out with my best friend. "What are you doing tomorrow? I don't work on Tuesdays or Thursdays."

"Maybe Thursday, then? I already have plans tomorrow." She looks so cozy wrapped up in Trevor's bicep.

"Okay, Thursday then." I wave and walk toward the gate.

Jax jogs up beside me. "Did I hear you need a ride?"

"I guess you did," I say. "Which is weird because I thought you were all the way over there."

"I have excellent hearing," he says. "Ask doctors."

"Which doctors?" I ask. "Any doctors?"

"Any doctors that have tested my hearing," he says. "They're always impressed. Come on. Where do you live?"

I barely know him, of course, but when you don't drive, you get used to jumping in cars with friends of friends. I give Jax directions to my house and follow him out to his silver BMW. Boys from Westglen Preparatory High School always have nicer cars than my parents do. At this point, I expect it.

"So you like burgers, right?" Jax asks me.

"What? Burgers?" I shoot him a look. "Because I'm fat?"

"No! You're not—"

"I am," I say. "It's fine. Being fat isn't bad. Acting like fat's an insult is, though."

"Uh, okay then," he says, though pleasantly. Of course, then he cuts off two cars as he swerves around a line of traffic backed up to turn on Riverside Drive.

"You're terrifying," I tell him.

"Just answer the question, Abby."

"Yes," I say. "Like most intelligent people, I like burgers."

"I have to do this project," he says. "It involves burgers. You in?"

"*Am I in?* To a project you haven't explained at all? And also, I barely know you?"

"We're like, friends-in-law," he says with a grin. "The couple's two best friends."

"That's not a thing."

"It's completely a thing—"

33

"You missed my street," I say, and he screeches the car around in almost a U-turn. Somehow we're both still alive as he pulls up to my home. I haven't seen Jax's house—I mean, why would I?—but I assume it's like Trevor's, tucked into hills with its own gate. Our bungalow is all but mere inches apart from the houses on either side of it. It's the sort of difference I didn't know was a thing for a long time, but then you're in a BMW post-private pool party with a lacrosse player, and your house that you very recently thought was normal is actually a teeny toy home.

"Thanks for the ride," I say. "Though it nearly killed us both."

"That was nothing," he says. "I'll text you more info later."

"I still don't know what you're talking about."

"I gotta get home," he says. "But time will answer all questions, friend-in-law."

"Seriously," I say as I get out of the car. "That's not a thing."

CHAPTER 4

The house smells delicious when my beeping phone wakes me the next morning. By now I know not to expect breakfast in the kitchen, but a food photographer. When I tiptoe out in my pajamas, I see that I'm right.

"Look how great your mom's burgers look," Dad tells me. Until last year, Dad worked at a media agency, but now he's managing all the non-Norah Eat Healthy with Norah! business, like scheduling and publicity and accounting. He used to come home and tell us funny stories about the grumpy old executive vice president he reported to. Now he reports to Mom, so even though I'm sure there are funny stories, he's stopped sharing them.

"Sure," I say, but for two big reasons they don't at all. Mom's food always *sounds* like a good idea, if you don't hear the details. It's a cheeseburger! What could go wrong? Well, first, there are no buns but fake "bread" made out of grilled mashed cauliflower. And it seems unfair to call it a *cheeseburger* when instead of cheese, the ground turkey meat is sprinkled with nutritional yeast.

Also, of course, there's kale instead of a piece of lettuce.

But that's not even the worst of it. That stuff's just *healthy* and so I can get behind that. But food photography is actually really disgusting. The burger's grill marks would be good enough for real life, but to make sure they really show up on camera, they're touched up with dark brown eyeliner. Everything's brushed with oil to make it shinier, and this burger is actually in perfect stacked order because little pins are holding it together. The kale has been misted with plant food, but that's not as bad as it could be. The other week there was a photo shoot with a bowl of fruit, and it had all been sprayed with *deodorant*.

"Abbs." Dad sighs while smiling. I can tell he thinks this will make me feel guilty, but it's only mostly effective. "You have to forgive her at some point."

"I should get dressed." I glance at Mom and then at the woman standing next to her who's holding a much fancier-looking camera than Maggie gave Jordi yesterday. My pajamas might be cute—a pink tank top with cupcake-printed shorts—but I'm still wearing pajamas in front of a stranger.

And you don't have to forgive anyone you don't want to.

It didn't feel like this when Rachel was still here. It was easier for Mom to forget how disappointed every facet of me made her when the perfect daughter she would have picked out from a catalog was standing right beside me. The Ives aren't supposed to be a three-person unit; we only function correctly at four.

After I take a shower and put together a couple of outfit options, I grab my phone. Jax has texted a third time, which astounds me. Aren't fratty types unable to wake before noon due to residual post-partying effects?

can u meet me or not??

At least his texting style meets his stereotype's expectations.

I decide to wear my shorts printed with lemons and flowers with a bright white sleeveless shirt Maliah gave to me for my birthday this year that I've somehow managed to keep in spotless condition. Sometime between hanging up my towel and adding a bright pink enamel necklace to my outfit, I must have decided that even giving in to Jax's text demands is a better use of my time than sticking around here.

Plus this is clearly a going-out look.

Normally, I understand my own motivations a little more. Everything seems a little fuzzy since yesterday's daydreaming and distractions in Lemonberry, though. Am I bored? (Possibly.) Do I miss Rachel? (Absolutely.) Am I jealous that Maliah has another person to spend her time with this summer? (Obviously, even if that makes me a baby.)

And so Jax and I meet outside of the overpriced juice place on Glendale. He's wearing a Westglen T-shirt with baggy basketball shorts and worn-out flip flops. He looks like he put less effort into getting ready than I even realized was possible, but even a lesbian can admit that it all still sort of works because he's tall and in really good shape and clearly goes to a barber who knows exactly what to do with his sun-bleached light brown hair.

"Man, I am *hooked* on these things," he says, holding the door open for me. "Who the hell knew beets could be good to drink."

I groan without even meaning to. "You sound like my mom."

"That's flattering." He orders some fruit/vegetable combo that would make Norah's heart sing. "What'd you want? It's on me."

"I'm good," I say. I think it should be illegal to pay double digits for freaking *juice*. "I'll get a coffee next door."

"I bet you're curious," he says while we're exiting The Juice and walking into Kaldi. "*What is Jax up to? Burgers sound intriguing!*"

"That doesn't sound like my inner monologue at all," I say before ordering a blended mocha from the barista who seems like he's trying too hard to look like Che Guevara. "Oh wait! I like coffee now. Regular coffee."

"So . . . just a coffee?" the barista asks.

"You heard the lady," Jax says. "Get her a coffee!"

He does, and then I spend a few minutes getting the coffee to the same consistency as yesterday. I think of Jordi when I taste it, and I know that I should probably hate the competition, but I smile anyway.

"Cool fruity shorts," Jax says.

"Is that sarcastic?" I ask as we sit down at a little table with our beverages.

"Do I seem sarcastic?" He grins, and I have to admit that I'm not sure Jax is even capable of sarcasm. "So have you heard of the Best Blank?"

"I have not."

"It's my dad's thing," he says. "It's an app. Kind of like Yelp but instead of reviewing places, it's all about finding the best stuff. So if you're in New York and you want the best lobster, it'll tell you where to find it."

"Okay," I say. "Could it tell me the best overpriced juice in Atwater Village?"

"Yup," he says. "It will, at least. Dad's still working out all the kinks, getting investors, all that. So he needs some people testing it this summer, and I volunteered for burgers."

"Why am I involved in this?" I ask.

"Uh, because you're cool and we'll have fun eating a shitload of burgers and ranking them?" He shrugs. "Also, I need girl advice and you're my best possible source."

I laugh aloud. "That cannot be true."

"You're a girl and you date girls. You have all the girl knowledge someone could possess."

"I'm a girl, sure," I say. "And in some magical dreamland, maybe I'd date girls. But in this one, the one we're actually living in? I just get crushes on celebrities and then one real girl who turned out to be straight. You should really, really not be taking any advice from me."

"Which celebrities?" he asks. "Last week I had this really weird sex dream about—"

"No," I say. "I do not need to know how that sentence ends."

"But you'll eat burgers with me?" he asks.

"I seriously don't understand why you're asking me."

"Friends-in-law!" he says. "Seriously, doesn't it bum you out sometimes? Last summer I totally would have gotten Trevor in on this. Now he's tied up with Maliah sixty percent of the time and then the other forty he's talking about eating right so he's ready for next season."

"I'm sure you have other friends," I say.

"Yeah, and so do you, and you're still here with me in your fruity shorts."

He grins, and I realize he's right. I could have made plans with Brooke or Zoe. And instead I'm here.

"C'mon," he says. "Did I mention my dad's company pays for everything?"

"You didn't, and . . . fine."

"You'll do it?" He holds up his hand for a high-five. "Hell *yeah*."

"I have an internship Mondays, Wednesdays, and Fridays," I say. "So I can't just eat burgers nonstop. Also, I'm not planning on having a heart attack at seventeen, so I *really* cannot eat burgers nonstop."

"We'll get it worked out." He holds up his juice and tips the last of the bottle into his mouth. "We can start today. You in?"

I may have already hit my Jax limit today, but the only burger I can get at home is full of pins and eyeliner. It's not hard to make the decision.

That's the thing about Jax; somehow, he, a guy I barely know, already feels like a forgone conclusion.

We walk to the Morrison, even though Jax has his BMW. It seems ridiculous to me to drive less than a mile, especially in June when it's still fairly cool out. L.A. might have the reputation for being summery year-round, but usually the heat is still ramping up when June rolls in. Clouds and light fog hug the city, especially early in the day, and this is so predictable that it has a name: June Gloom. It might not be cheery, but it's good to take advantage before the brutal heat of August and onward envelops us.

"You should learn to drive," Jax tells me as we walk inside. The Morrison is technically a sports bar, but since they serve food, you don't have to be twenty-one to get in. "L.A. sucks without a car."

"I do fine without a car," I say. "Learning how to drive seems like more trouble than it's worth. And not everyone's parents will just buy them a BMW when they turn sixteen."

"Oh, come on," he says as we're led to a booth and given menus. "Making fun of people with BMWs is more clichéd than actually driving one."

Sadly, I think this is a good point. Also, my mom's old Honda is sitting in the driveway. Rachel drove it in high school, and now it's mine, if I want it. Since driving sounds terrifying, though, I don't want it at all.

"Do you know this girl, Gaby Manzetti?" Jax asks while I'm reading through all my burger options. The Morrison's menu is extensive. "I think you guys go to the same school."

"She's a junior," I say.

"I'm the age of a junior," he says. "I skipped a grade. So it's okay."

"It'd be okay anyway, it's only a year," I say. "And, wait. *You*? Skipped a grade?"

"Bam," he says. "I'm smart."

"Oh, god," I say.

41

"Give me your phone," he says. "I need to put the app on it."

Against my better judgment, I hand it over. "So are you going out with Gaby?"

"Shit, I wish," he says. "That's why I'm glad you're a girl expert."

"I don't know her personally," I say as he taps on my phone. "I have no pull."

"I'm not saying you do," he says. "You'll know stuff, though. Girl stuff. I'm sure of that."

"Hmmm." I take my phone back from him and investigate the newly installed app. "I'm not sure if that's girl stuff to know," I say. "Every girl is different."

I say it with authority because I'm a girl and I have a bunch of friends who are girls. And yet there's still part of me that feels like a phony expert. Maybe Jax can't make headway with Gaby, but he's obviously a guy who normally gets what he wants. I'm too much of a lost cause to even formulate what I want. It's possible there is some fairly accepted standard for girls in the want division. Maybe there's *girl stuff to know* after all.

"Yeah, yeah," he says. "Every girl's different."

"Don't say that like it's horrible."

"Fine," he says, but with a grin. "C'mon. Let's order some burgers."

Best Blank isn't complicated. You enter the restaurant's name and what you ordered. Jax assures me that by the time the app actually launches, most of this will auto-fill for you, but even as it stands now, it's not difficult. You just rate the burger—or whatever else you're eating—on five scales: taste, quality, service, value, selection. It takes no time at all, and I can totally see how people will want to do this on a regular basis. One thing I've learned from blogging is that people *love* giving their opinions.

"Did your dad invent this?" I ask.

"Sorta," Jax says. I expect him to elaborate. "Seriously, let me tell you about this dream I had last night. Taylor Swift was—"

"Stop," I say. "Let's agree to keep our dreams to ourselves this summer."

The photoshoot has ended by the time I'm home. While I'm glad not to deal with strangers in our house, it does make it hard to get past Mom and Dad working in the living room.

"You're supposed to let us know where you are," Mom says. "You know that."

Last year, Rachel would have filled in Mom and Dad for me. I'm still learning how to function as an only child. "Sorry. I was just out with a friend."

"Maliah?" Mom asks.

"Just this guy," I say.

Mom and Dad exchange a look. I'm so afraid it's a look of hope that I escape to my room without another word. I have a post to write about tank tops anyway.

CHAPTER 5

On Wednesday morning, I wear my favorite skirt—printed with peppermint candies in various states of unwrap—with a soft and fitted T-shirt. I pull a loop of beads around my neck—an accessory I recommended in yesterday's post—and apply lip gloss before heading out.

I'm positive Jordi already has the real job locked down, but style I can handle.

While I'm focusing on untangling my earbuds, a person falls into stride next to me. Our neighborhood is fairly safe these days, but I still find myself on instant Stranger Danger. Mom says it never hurts to be suspicious.

"Hey," says a familiar voice, and I realize that it's Jordi. We've just passed a slate-gray house. It's small, like mine, but I think the color makes it much cooler, as does the smooth and polished wooden gate surrounding it.

Jordi's dressed similarly to how she was on Monday; today she's in a long draped black shirt over black leggings and the same short black boots. She looks thoughtful, professional, the kind of girl you'd want as your intern. Maliah's rumors couldn't be true, except that there's something else about Jordi. I'm sure there's something different about her beyond the haircut. She looks tough, or tougher, at least. I imagine her punching someone, but someone who deserves it.

"I like your Christmas skirt," she says as we walk off toward the shop.

"It's not a Christmas skirt," I say, looking down at it. "Wait, is it? Are peppermints seasonal? I thought they were year-round."

"Maybe so." She pauses her Jordi pause before I get another smile. Each one feels like a reward I've earned.

Oh, no.

Oh, *no*.

I couldn't *like* Jordi, could I?

Oh, no.

"What'd you do on your day off?" she asks me, and suddenly it's as though I'm walking way too fast for a normal person. I slow down. Now I feel like I'm walking too slow, but when I speed up it's like I've lost the ability to judge what normal walking speed is.

"Are you okay?"

"Oh, fine, sure." I try to match my pace with hers. Why is this so difficult? "I ate burgers. It's a long story."

"Burgers can be a long story?" she asks.

"I mean, anything can be, I guess," I say. "Under the right circumstances?"

"Sure."

"What about you?" I ask as we turn onto Glendale Boulevard. A breeze lifts her hair off her neck and I think about its gentle curve and, oh no, oh no.

"I took my little brother to the library," she says.

AMY SPALDING

Immediately it seems right that Jordi is someone's big sister, but then that feels like the most ridiculous thought that could come over a person.

I don't like this at all.

Today, Maggie walks up to Lemonberry as we do and lets us in right away. Next to Jordi, I can't help but worry I look too bright, too big, too literally candy-coated, but Maggie smiles at me. She looks just as disheveled as Monday, but I can see in her eyes that something's different today. I think something's better.

"Great skirt," Maggie tells me. "Vintage?"

"Thanks! It's old but I'm not sure it's old enough to be vintage. I got it off eBay." I glance at Jordi and bite back going into more of my internet shopping techniques. When it's only you and an adult, it feels safe to share lots of yourself and all of your enthusiasm. It's weird how the truth can feel so fake in front of someone your own age, though.

"You can both head to the back," Maggie says. "I'll catch up in a minute."

We walk to the back room, and Jordi reaches into the black bag still strapped across her, takes out a lunch bag, and leans past me to shove it into the refrigerator. I scan the open spaces to figure out if there's a spot for my bag. I'm sure my tostadas will survive until lunchtime if they don't fit.

"Be bolder, Abby," Jordi tells me, and grabs my bag from me to shove it in next to hers. It feels like something metaphorically romantic is happening, seeing our lunch

46

bags leaning against each other, but then I realize I am thinking—metaphor or no metaphor—about refrigerated fabric bags, and I let it go.

I let Jordi get coffee first so that I can copy how she mixes hers. It isn't like a crush thing; it's just that, even after Kaldi yesterday, pouring myself coffee seems like way too adult an activity for me. And maybe I don't even have a crush; maybe Jordi's just really cool. I mean, Jordi *is* really cool, so why can't that be it? That's probably it.

"Why are you staring at me?" Jordi asks.

Oh my god. "No reason."

She smiles. "You're staring at me for no reason?"

"I'm trying to learn how to mix coffee."

Jordi takes another mug out of the cabinet and takes care of everything before passing it to me. It feels like such a warm gesture—not just literally—that I can't help grinning at her and taking a huge sip.

"Oh my god!" It's the second time this week that I spit out a mouthful of coffee. "It's so—"

"Hot?"

"It's really hot."

Having a crush makes you an idiot.

"Jordi!" Maggie pops in from the front. "Grab the camera and come on out. We have a few new boxes arriving from the other designers we carry, and I'd love you to take a stab at photographing them."

"If it's okay . . ." Jordi reaches into her bag and takes out a smaller bag, which turns out to contain a very sleek camera. "I brought my own today."

"Of course it's okay! Come on." Maggie smiles at me. "We'll get you logged in on all our social media later, okay, Abby? For now, do you want to see the new shipments?"

Do I!

Maggie introduces us to the burgundy-haired employee whose name turns out to be Laine. Even as she's slicing open giant boxes, her hair is in place, her blue floral dress doesn't even seem to rumple, and she's wearing four-inch heels.

"Abby, you can help take off the plastic bags and put everything on hangers," Maggie tells me. "We might have to steam the wrinkles out of some of these dresses before you take any photos, Jordi. And feel free to use Laine—she models a lot of our looks for us."

"'Use'?" Laine laughs. "Thanks, Maggie. That's flattering."

I watch Jordi watch Laine through her camera, and I wonder what she's thinking. And then I wonder what it's like to be looked at through Jordi's lens.

Today's shipment is of two new styles of dresses—a fit and flare dress in blue polka dots and an A-line look in bright pink—and a variety of cardigans. Layering is very important to Los Angeles fashion. The city has a reputation for constant sunshine and warmth, but once the sun is down at night, LA remembers it's secretly a desert under its newer identity. The cool night air doesn't care what midday was like.

"Oh, I love this," I say, even though I was trying to stay quiet and professional like Jordi. A bright fuchsia cardigan is too much for my resolve.

"Try it on!" Laine says.

"Yes," Maggie says. "I'd love to see it on you."

"What size?" Laine asks me, because the thing about thin people is they always seem to take sizing really casually. "Medium?"

The other thing about thin people is they always guess low for your size, as if that's a kindness, or maybe they can't comprehend a size beyond that. And I wish it didn't bother me because, honestly, I don't think there's something wrong with how I look. And when I do sometimes hate what I see in the mirror, it's never my body. Well, not the *size* of my body, at least. I worry my nose is weirdly pointy, and I hate how my hair looks without dye, and I find it disturbing that sometimes in photos my posture is just like Mom's.

I worry about how other people see me, though.

"Probably not a medium," I say, trying to riffle through the sweaters from the back because that's usually where the largest sizes are. Cute brands that make fake retro clothes always tend to run small, so it's a safe bet.

"That's huge on you," Maggie says as I pull on the biggest sweater. "You look homeless. I mean, chic, but homeless."

"Maybe that's what I was going for," I say, which makes everyone laugh. Even Jordi.

Ugh, if I thought Jordi was just cool and not—oh, god—*hot*, I'd probably be able to stop noticing the curve of her upper arms. If I don't want to have a crush on any more real people, why do I still have one?

The human condition is bullshit.

"Hold still." Maggie pulls the cardigan off me and checks the tag before exchanging it for another in the pile. This one fits perfectly, even if it clashes disturbingly with my peppermint skirt.

Laine grabs a bright patterned scarf from a display and wraps it around my waist like a belt. I somehow manage to simultaneously clash even more but also look better. "Are you using Abby as a model?"

"No," I say, and then to make sure everyone knows I know it's a ridiculous thought, I laugh a bunch.

"Abby's here to help us out with social media," Maggie says, thank god. "But that's a great idea."

"I'm . . . really not the model type," I say, and it feels like it's for the millionth time even though of course Maggie and Laine are new to me. Maliah's convinced +*style* would be even more popular if I didn't just talk about looks but posted photos of myself wearing them, but the last thing I need are photos of myself out there where anyone could say anything about them. About *me*.

"Think about it," Laine says. "I never thought I'd do it either."

I find it hard to believe that someone who looks like Laine wouldn't at least think about it, but I let it go because there are more cardigans to unpack. I learn how to check a packing slip as well as add to store inventory in the system. Maggie sends me to the back to steam the blue and white dresses, which I pretend I know how to do.

The steamer turns on easily, and before long seems to be, well, *steaming*, so I pick it up and point it at the first wrinkled dress. It seems like real magic to watch the dress smooth out before my eyes, and I tip the steamer just enough to get the last bunched bits of the hem.

"Aaghh!" I yell. Apparently you aren't supposed to tip steamers, and now there's hot water all over my side, hip, and thigh. It's not hot enough to burn me, but it definitely doesn't feel *good*.

"Hey, are you okay?" Jordi walks into the backroom with her camera in her hands. "We heard you yell."

"I'm okay," I say. "I don't know how steamers work, I guess. Everyone's going to think I wet my pants."

"You're not wearing pants," Jordi points out. "And no one wets their pants in that . . . direction."

"Don't take a picture of this."

The corners of her mouth twitch. "Sure."

I manage to get through steaming the rest of the dresses without further steaming myself, and by the time I bring them out to Laine, Jordi's already taking photos of the sweaters hung against a plain backdrop. I don't have further orders from Maggie, so I just stay quiet and watch Jordi work. I hear the *click click* of the shutter, and it feels safe to study her because she's so focused on the sweaters. It's hard to believe she's my age and not a professional.

Maggie lets us break for lunch once all the new clothes are hung up and inventoried, though Jordi still has photos left to take. While I'm assembling my non-tostada tostadas, Jordi microwaves a Pyrex container of something that makes the whole backroom smell like—and this is no exaggeration—heaven.

"What's going on back here?" Maggie asks as she walks into the room. "It smells like—"

"Heaven," I say. "I figured it out. It's definitely like heaven."

I don't even know where I get the things that come out of my mouth. Should that concern me?

"Leftovers," Jordi says. "My dad made pollo verde last night."

She squeezes in next to me and glances over at my pile of veggies and tempeh on jicama.

"You're so lucky," I say, eyeing her pollo verde. "I think my mom's morally opposed to making anything that good."

"That's sad," Jordi says, completely deadpan. I like waiting for her smiles now; they always come eventually. This is only the second day I've spent with her, and I know this about her already. I like how in the span of less than a hundred hours you can know a thing about a person.

Oh my god. I am really doomed.

After lunch, Jordi goes back to taking photographs, and Maggie brings me to her office for all the social media login information. I have a pretty good following for +style, but I'm excited to contribute to a store's accounts, where there will be so many more people to hopefully engage with.

I'm well aware that for some reason people think social media is one of those things, like selfies and reality TV, that's bringing about the downfall of civilization. But I can't complain about being able to talk to people all over the country, and even the world, about things that matter to me. I love my friends and I love Rachel, but there are things about me they could never relate to.

"Sorry," Maggie says, sorting through a pile of papers on her desk. "I have everything written down somewhere."

"It's okay," I say, hovering near the doorway.

"Sit down, Abby," she says. "It might take me a few."

"Sorry," I say, and she looks up abruptly from her paper-sorting.

"Don't apologize," she says. "That's my business lesson for you. If you haven't done anything wrong, don't apologize."

"Oh, okay," I say, though I'm not sure how that's a business lesson. Should I ask for more elaboration? Should I just understand this? I was really hoping I'd just be making cool posts on Twitter. That much I am sure I can handle.

Maggie keeps looking through piles of crap. I wish I could do something to help, but I have at least enough business acumen not to start pilfering through her paperwork.

"This is embarrassing," she finally says. "I feel terrible that I'm wasting your time, Abby."

"I'm okay," I say.

"And I feel bad about the whole . . ." She shrugs. "I'm thrilled to have you and Jordi here this summer, but I never wanted it to feel like a competition. I hope you two can work together and not feel like you're fighting it out. You know each other from school, right?"

"Uh, sort of."

"Ah, here we go!" Maggie pulls out a piece of notebook paper with scribbling on it. "You can use the computer out there. Take a look, get acquainted with the accounts, and then we can talk Friday about any of your initial ideas, okay? And if you want to take more time and wait until next week to chat, that's okay, too. I don't want to throw you in before you're ready."

"I'm sure I can be ready by Friday," I say, not because I'm actually sure, but because Jordi rolled in today with her fancy, shiny, professional camera. I can manage some thoughts about Instagram.

I spend the rest of the day looking at Lemonberry's social presence. Considering I've followed them everywhere that's possible since the first time I shopped here, it's weird there can be surprises. But somehow they have fewer followers than *I* do and hardly any interaction at all.

For the first time since I was a daydreaming mess at the noodle restaurant, I feel like I might be able to accomplish something here.

Maggie finds me a little notebook, and I spend the rest of the day jotting down ideas. Jordi's still out front taking pictures, so I don't see her again until the day's over and we're heading out together.

"Where do you live?" Jordi asks.

"On Brunswick," I say.

"Just past me," she says, like—and I could be making this up and not actually hearing it, to be very fair—like that realization pleases her.

My phone buzzes in my hand, and I look down to see I've missed a lot of texts. The first is from Maliah (*You're free tomorrow . . . right???*), and there's one from Zoe (*Let's hang out SOON!* ♥), and then the rest are all from Jax and all about going out tonight for more testing of the Best Blank app.

Jordi nods at my phone. "Everything okay there?"

My phone buzzes again right there and then. *juicy burger on vermont. i can give u a ride. say yes!*

"I guess I have to go eat a burger," I say to Jordi.

"So, burgers really are a long story," she says.

"It's just this thing this guy Jax is doing," I say. "I'm helping him out."

"*Jax?*"

"Don't get me started," I say.

"Is he your boyfriend?" Jordi asks.

"Oh god, no," I say. "I don't have a boyfriend. I wouldn't have a boyfriend."

"Not one named Jax, at least."

We've somehow already arrived in front of Jordi's sleek gate.

"See you Friday, Abby," she says. "Have fun with Jax and the burgers."

"Have fun with . . . photography," I say.

"Uh, sure."

Have fun with photography?? Oh my god.

CHAPTER 6

Maliah promises to pick me up at noon for whatever we're doing on Thursday. Even though, obviously, I've been obsessing over everything at Lemonberry, I'm still hoping we'll go to the Glendale Galleria, which is right next to the outdoor shopping plaza, the Americana. While Maliah and I have very different styles, we're good at shopping together, and between our different taste and different sizes, we never fight over anything.

Well, occasionally we fight over jewelry and shoes. That sounds like the most clichéd girl fight ever, but I can't deny that it's true. Even so, my shopping trips with Maliah—especially now with Rachel out of town—are some of my favorite times.

Even if they're just best friend shopping montages in the love story that is Maliah's life. I'll take what I can get.

The text that shows up from Maliah at 11:30 is concerning, though.

We're leaving now to get you! So we might be early! Be ready!

"We"? Okay, I'm sure there's a possibility that she separately contacted Zoe and Brooke. But lately "we" only means one additional person.

Trevor's car pulls up, and I take a moment before I leave the house to let my face look as disappointed as I feel. Jax had asked me to hang out and eat burgers today, but I'd turned him down for one-on-one time with Maliah.

Once I can manage a smile—or at least a neutral expression—I head outside. I start to get into the backseat behind Maliah, but the seat is already taken.

"Hey!" Jax greets me as I get in from the other side. "We're hanging out after all. Your dress is cool."

One year ago, Rachel and I took a class at Sew L.A. so we could learn how to make clothes from all of the crazy fabrics you can get at crafts stores. Rachel picked one with mermaids and I chose one with parrots. It turned out we were both terrible at sewing, so our instructor helped us correct our mistakes and strongly advised we take a class on the basics next time instead of heading straight into dress-making territory. That sounded boring, but at least we each got a dress out of it.

"Only Abbs could make parrots look cool," Maliah says.

"You got something against parrots?" Trevor asks her.

"Well, people act like they can really *talk*," she says. "They just *mimic*. It's not that impressive."

Trevor cracks up. "You think parrots are overrated?"

I still don't feel like I know Trevor, really, so it makes me feel good that he's laughing. He must feel something real for Maliah if he's amused by her parrot opinions.

"Where are we going?" I ask.

"Santa Monica," Maliah says. "The beach and the pier."

To be fair, it doesn't sound horrible. When you live on the Eastside, going down to the beach can take forever, so it doesn't happen as often as non-L.A. people think. Plus, I know Maliah will have over-prepared. We'll have beach towels and sunscreen and bottles of water. And thanks to Trevor and Jax, we'll probably have beers.

God, I'm spending a lot of time with Jax lately.

I'm right about all of it: Maliah lays out two giant towels when we arrive, and Trevor has sneaky beers in a Nordstrom bag. Of course they sit together, which relegates Jax and me to the other towel. I can't blame him for this; he probably has no idea that I expected a best-friends-only day—that I felt like I *needed* one. I'm not even sure if a best-friends-only day is something I can expect at seventeen years old.

"We're going to get snacks," Maliah calls to us. "Watch our stuff, okay?"

"On it," Jax says.

Maliah walks off, hand-in-hand, with Trevor. My phone beeps only a moment later. *Sorry, Abbs. Jax was in the car when it pulled up. I'll make it up to you! XOM*

"I saw Gaby this morning," Jax says. "She was getting juice from Juice, too."

"Congratulations," I say.

"Man." Jax hands me a beer from the bag. "She does not find me charming."

"You can't expect everyone to," I say. "Can you?"

"C'mon, Abbs," he says, and even though Maliah's the only one of my friends who calls me that, I don't mind it. "*You* even find me charming, and you're all about the ladies, too."

I sip my beer instead of admitting he's at least partially right.

"Why do you like her?" I ask.

"What do you mean?"

"What do you mean, what do I mean?" I ask, even though I'm not sure I could put my feelings for Jordi into words. What's the word for her hands clutching her camera, her slow smile, the angles of her neck and shoulders?

Oh my god, I sound bananas. I feel bananas. Liking someone is nothing but bananas.

"I don't know. Do I have to have a reason?"

"*Yes*," I say. "People want to be liked for real reasons."

I didn't even know that was a thing I knew or believed, especially because I can't imagine what about me anyone would like. It's not that I'm horrible—I'm definitely not horrible! I just don't feel special enough. I'm a supporting cast member, not a lead. There's nothing about me that could sway a girl from disinterest to love, or even to *like*.

"Do you just like her because she doesn't find you charming?" I ask, looking out to the ocean. On June afternoons, it's fairly crowded, but the sound of the waves creates some sort of magical white noise that makes it feel like Jax and I are in our own world.

"Shit," he says. "I hope not."

I laugh and sip my beer. Cheap beer is really mostly water. It takes a few of them to get you drunk, so one at a time always feels safe. Right now, Jax feels safe, too.

"This is a dumb question, probably, but . . . what do you do when you like someone?" I ask. "I mean, I'm *positive* that she doesn't like me, but—"

"You stalk her Instagram yet?" Jax asks.

"No . . . ?"

Jax gets out his phone. "What's her name?"

"No."

"C'mon."

"Fine," I say. "Jordi Perez."

He types it in. "She's cute."

"*Too* cute?" I ask. "Do you think? For me?"

"Shut the hell up," he says, still scrolling. "Yes. Hell *yes*."

"What?" I'm embarrassed that I didn't already think to look for Jordi on Instagram. My crush is at least twenty-four hours old at this point. I've wasted so many of those hours. "What did you find?"

"She went to a Tegan & Sara show," he says. "Bam. You're set."

"Bam? Lots of people like Tegan & Sara," I say. "People who aren't queer. *Trust me*."

"I'm calling it," he says. "You're in."

"You're crazy." I take his phone from him. Jordi's profile photo looks like a professional black-and-white photograph, and it's as if light and shadows clung to all the right places so that the picture is the most absolutely Jordi possible. I barely know her, but I can tell that much.

Oh my god, I have completely lost it. *Light and shadows??*

"Add her," Jax says.

"Wouldn't that be weird?" I ask. "We're just interns together. We're not friends."

"Add her," he repeats.

"What if she thinks I'm weird?"

He sighs loudly and grabs my phone from me. "What's your passcode?"

"Uh, no." But for some reason, I unlock my phone and let him take it.

"Done," he says after a couple moments. "If she asks you why you added her, you can blame some asshole at the beach and it'll be true."

"You're not an asshole," I say. "Well, maybe you are. You're really comfortable with other people's phones."

"That *is* the definition of an asshole, sure."

I unlace my Converse and dig my bare feet into the sand. I'll regret it later, considering I wasn't told about the beach and therefore didn't bring flip flops, but right now it's all worth it to feel the warm sand between my toes.

"So what's your next move?" Jax asks me.

"What do you mean? What was my first move? Oh, adding her on Instagram? Technically I didn't do that; that was all you."

"She's gonna add you back, clearly," he says. "Then find a recent photo, nothing too old or you look like a creep, and leave a nice comment. Then find another one, and don't comment or anything, but bring up something similar next time you see her. Like if she takes photos at the park or whatever, mention that you like going to the park or whatever too."

"This is your big advice on girls?" I ask. "No wonder you need my help."

"Look, this shit normally works," he says.

"But not with Gaby."

"Nope. But normally, oh yeah. You're right in. I swear on . . ." He looks around. "That seagull."

The seagull immediately flies away.

I laugh again. "Nice try."

The thought of Jordi liking any girls, much less me, still sounds like fiction. But it's a good piece of fiction.

When we pile back into Trevor's car later, I notice I have a new notification on my phone. I know that it means very little that Jordi added me back—not even "very little," it means nothing at all.

But I still nudge Jax and hold up my phone. He grins and holds out his hand for a high-five.

CHAPTER 7

I have a notification when I open my computer that evening. Well, I have two—Maliah tagged me in a photo she took in Santa Monica, and my hair looks like fancy cotton candy and my dress is vibrant, so I don't untag myself. But I digress, because the other notification is a direct message from Jordi.

A direct message from Jordi!

don't bring your sad tostadas tomorrow, abby.

I start typing back immediately. I delete every sentence as it appears on the screen. *I won't ha ha ha!* looks deranged. *Are you serious??!* sounds potentially combative. *I don't know what's going on but it's cool you're thinking of me right now!* is just clearly not okay on any level, as I sound both clueless and majorly creepster.

I message Jax instead. *Does having a crush always make you feel bonkers? Is it just me? Do you regret talking to me so much? Were you prepared for so many questions? Did you hope it would just be burgers and Gaby?*

He messages back right away. *feeling bonkers can come w the territory. no regrets, but unprepared 4 sure. ur like a weird onion.*

I laugh aloud. *A weird onion???*

His response is almost instantaneous, as though he was waiting for me to ask. *lots of layers of weird. i dig it.*

Okay, it's vaguely possible—and so hypothetical that it doesn't really matter—that if I liked boys, I might like Jax after all.

The next morning I magically arrive at Jordi's exactly when she's walking through her gate.

"Hi," I say.

"Did you get my message?" she asks. "You didn't respond."

"Oh, I ..." ... *was afraid I'd sound unhinged.* "Sorry. I did get it, though. There were more leftover faux-stadas, but I left them for my parents."

"Good girl," she says and smiles.

I wait for details on the lunch we're going out to together, or whatever I'm apparently eating instead of piles of sad vegetables and tempeh. We just walk quietly, though.

"Did you have fun at the library?" I ask when I can't take the silence any longer. Probably it's only been a few seconds but in certain situations a few seconds can be an eternity.

"That was Tuesday, but we did," Jordi says, and I realize out of nowhere how desperately I hope that "we" just means her and her brother. Jordi could have a boyfriend. Even if Jordi—miraculously—likes girls, why wouldn't

Jordi already have a girlfriend? How could I be the only person who's noticed her?

I wish it worked another way in my head. If only I found her silences maddening instead of intriguing. If only I thought it was boring or predictable or silly that she's in all-black every day, even in the warm June sunshine. If only I didn't think that whatever she did to end up in juvie wasn't justified, no matter what it was.

If Jordi had wanted to burn down a building, I believe that structure should have rightfully gone down in flames.

Once we get to the shop, Jordi takes her lunchbag out of her black bag and nudges me. "Dad gave me extra caldo de pollo for you."

I don't know what that is, but Jordi's dad gave her food *for me*. Jordi's dad knows I exist. I already love caldo de pollo.

"You're so lucky your dad cooks," I say. "I mean, my mom makes . . ."

"I saw," Jordi says as we pour our coffees.

"No . . . well, have you heard of Eat Healthy with Norah?"

"Nope."

Maggie walks out from the back room. "Oh, no, are we talking about Eat Healthy with Norah? One of my friends is obsessed with her. I, on the other hand, find her incredibly irritating."

"Me too," I say with a sigh. "Norah's my mom."

"Oh, Abby, I'm sorry," Maggie says. "I never would have said—"

"It's really okay," I say. "Trust me, I understand."

"So . . ." Jordi says. "It's a website?"

"It's a website, and a segment on the local NBC affiliate, and other shows bring her on as a healthy eating expert all the time. It's wraps with cucumbers instead of tortillas, and sandwiches with lettuce instead of buns, and a grilled cheese except that the bread is actually made from cauliflower. And everything's tiny little portions."

I wonder if I just seem like a fat girl complaining about not getting to eat enough.

But then Jordi's neutral expression turns into a frown.

"I'm glad I rescued you, then," she says. "Extra glad, now that I know about the cauliflower."

"I'm not even sure how you'd make bread out of cauliflower," Maggie say. "I mean, I understand I could look it up, but I think bread is great."

"Bread *is* great," Jordi and I chorus, and then we exchange a tiny grin. Well, Jordi's grin is tiny. I'm pretty sure that mine is somehow wider than my face.

Maggie gets Jordi started on downloading her photos from her camera to the computer in the back room before taking me into her office to chat about social media, or at least that's what I assume we'll talk about. I have my notebook of ideas ready to go.

"I really am sorry," she says. "I had no idea she was your mother. I never would have—"

"No, seriously," I say. "She *is* incredibly irritating."

"Anytime you want someone to buy you real bread," she says, "just say the word."

"Deal." I open my notebook. "So I just wrote up some preliminary ideas for different social media platforms, just sort of based off of wanting to get people excited about new arrivals, but also maybe to get more followers?"

As the words come out of my mouth, it's almost as if I can hear myself as someone else. And I sound like I know what I'm doing. I sound like someone who can compete with Jordi.

Ugh, why do I have to compete with Jordi?

"First, I saw that—"

Maggie's iPhone buzzes on her desk, and she frowns at the displaying number. "Let's talk about it later. I've unfortunately got to handle this and it might take a while. See if Laine needs your help."

So instead of sounding like a professional, I spend my morning learning the right way to fold sweaters for a display. At first it feels like a waste of my time, but as we organize by color and size, it feels like something's come alive. Who wouldn't want to pull a sweater from this organized rainbow?

The morning flies by, and I try not to look too eager when I follow Jordi to the breakroom and wait as she takes two Tupperware containers of soup out of her lunch bag.

"Thank you," I say. "It's really nice that you—your dad—"

"It's nothing," she says, but she smiles as she sets the containers in the microwave. I stare at the *caldo de pollo* as it rotates. Soup of love! Well, probably not, but I've decided that's what *caldo de pollo* translates to.

After the microwave beeps, Jordi unceremoniously takes the containers and two spoons over to the table for us. I feel sorry for the soup because it's come to represent all my current hopes and dreams, and that's a lot for soup to live up to. But it is *delicious*, and not just because of its potential meaning. It's full of huge pieces of zucchini, potatoes, carrots, chayote, and chicken; if any soup could make me believe, this is it.

"This is incredible," I tell her. "Thank you. And thank your dad."

"Sure," she says. "We have this all the time but . . . Yeah. It's really good."

"Do you know what people like my mom call meals?" I laugh even though maybe no one else thinks this is funny. "Solutions. *Here's a great solution for eating pizza!*"

"Man," Jordi says. "Poor pizza."

We eat in silence for a few moments.

"What are you doing after work tonight?" she asks. "Stuff with burgers?"

"I . . ." I take a big spoonful to buy some time to work on my response. "No. Nothing, honestly. I should lie so you don't think I'm a loser, but, nothing."

She laughs as she elbows me. "I was going to take some photos tonight, if you want to come with me."

I think of Jordi's profile picture, of the light and shadows sweeping over her face. "It's so amazing you're a photographer."

"Ehhhh." She eats a few spoonfuls of soup. "I'm still working on what I am. I like taking pictures, but I also like painting, and I like sculpture, and I like street art. I like everything I try. But I think photography's my favorite."

"That's amazing," I say, and then I laugh because I sound much more enthusiastic than I mean to. It is, though. "I think it's great you like everything. Yeah, I have fashion, but it's nothing big like art."

"Fashion can be art. And art doesn't have to be big," Jordi says. "It can be just for you."

"It's okay if I come with you?" I ask. "It's not like, a private thing?"

"I wouldn't ask if it wasn't okay, would I?"

I have no idea if this means anything, but I agree regardless. As if there was a chance I wouldn't.

Maggie ends up leaving right after lunch, so instead of looking like a social media badass, if there is such a thing, I continue helping Laine. She ends up sending Jordi and me home early because, without Maggie there, there aren't really any new projects to take on.

We walk to Jordi's house together. I expect to go in with her, or at least wait here by the shiny gate so she can do whatever she needs before taking off for photography.

"Meet back at seven?" she asks instead.

"Sure!" I say and force myself to walk home without enacting some kind of grand farewell. I'm seeing her in less than three hours, and even if I wasn't, that would be unnecessary.

"Big news!" Mom says when I walk inside, and for just the splittest of seconds, I think my parents know about my photography non-date. I come back to reality very quickly, though.

"A publisher wants your mom to write a cookbook." Dad grins and wraps an arm around Mom's shoulders. They look like a stock photo for happy middle-aged couples; blonde and sunny and fit in that way Californians are expected to be. "How exciting is that?"

I'm not entirely sure. She's on local TV at least once a week and has been on the Food Network more than once. Is a book more exciting than TV?

"Everything's paying off," Mom says, and I nod. "How's the internship?"

"It's great," I say. "Anyway, I'm going out tonight, if that's okay, and I need to get ready."

"Have fun," Dad tells me. "I'm taking your mom out to celebrate."

Their last celebration dinner was at a raw food restaurant, so I find it unlikely the celebration will be too . . . celebratory.

I review myself in the full-length mirror in my room. I wore a really basic yellow dress to work today—and if Jordi doesn't like me—and why would Jordi like me?—changing would be really weird. This isn't a date. You can't make something a date by just hoping it's a date and wearing a good dress.

I settle for applying mascara and lip gloss.

Jordi's waiting outside when I arrive back at her house.

She's also wearing the same thing as earlier, though she's layered an army green jacket over her outfit and switched out her boots for black Vans.

"Hey," she greets me.

"I'm still thinking about that soup!" I say, even though I mean to just respond with a similarly chill *hi*. "Also, hi."

She smiles. "Let's go."

"Where are we going? Do you have one place you like to take pictures? Or just all over? Is something happening tonight you want to specifically photograph?"

Oh god, so many questions. How can I know it's too many questions but ask them all anyway?

"I don't have anything specific in mind." Jordi lifts her camera out of her bag and takes off the lens cap. "I like not having anything I'm after."

Then it happens before I can react: she points the camera at me and snaps a few photos.

"Agh!" I fold my arms across my chest, and that feels awkward, so I tuck them behind my back, and then I worry my hips look big in this dress, so I just let my arms hang straight down. Now I feel like I have monkey arms.

"Sorry," Jordi says. "But this is why I don't ask."

"Because I have monkey arms?" I ask, except that's a term I came up with in my head and not aloud, so Jordi's confused look is more than fair.

"Because no one looks like herself when she knows she's being photographed," Jordi says. "But before you knew, you did. And you don't have monkey arms." She holds out her arms to her sides. "My arms are way longer than yours."

"But you're taller!" I step closer to her and hold out my arms. "No, yours *are* way longer."

We're standing face to face, inches apart, and Jordi automatically knew what monkey arms were. My face feels warm, and my lips are suddenly something I feel very aware of. I've known of the general feeling of wanting to kiss someone, but I've never felt the specific wanting to kiss someone *right in this very moment* before.

Click.

Jordi smiles at me. "Got you."

"When you take a picture, can you tell what a person is thinking?" I ask. "Does it show in the photograph?"

"Why?" Jordi asks. "What are you thinking?"

"Nothing," I say. I say it more quickly than I've said anything in my life. Speed can be very suspicious, I realize.

"Too bad." Jordi turns from me and continues down the sidewalk. I try to predict when she'll hold up her camera as I turn those two words over and over in my head. I think some graffiti on the curb might interest her, but it doesn't. *Too bad.* I don't even notice a patch of flowers emerging from dry grass, but Jordi does. *Too bad.* I think the sunset might be a cliché, but Jordi's camera clicks while it's pointed at the horizon.

Too bad.

"You're quiet," she says.

"So are you," I point out.

"I don't count," she says.

"I didn't know if quiet people knew they were quiet," I say. "The way loud people know they're loud. People

72

sometimes think I have no idea, but it's not that I don't know, I just can't help it? Words come out of my mouth all the time."

Jordi turns onto Los Feliz Boulevard. "I never assume someone doesn't know herself."

"Oh my god, no, I didn't mean that I thought you didn't, I—"

"Abby," she says. "Chill. I meant that I know that you know you're loud. Louder than me, at least."

"You'll have to say *chill* a lot," I say. "If we keep hanging out. Because I am bad at it and I'll need reminders."

Jordi takes a photograph of the tagged billboard over the Chevron gas station. The graffiti artist's work looks crisper and better designed than the supermarket ad it's covering.

"That'll be a good shot," I say. "Not like the others won't be. I'm sure you're really talented. Well, maybe not the ones of me, but that's not your fault. You can only do so much."

"What's that supposed to mean?" she asks me.

"N—nothing." I lose track of how to stand normally again. "I'm not a model."

"Are you asking me to stop taking your picture?" Jordi asks. Her voice is a little softer. "If you want me to stop, I will. I didn't mean to make you feel weird."

"I always feel weird," I say.

She grins as a breeze pours in around us and her wavy hair flies out around her. "Me too."

"You can keep taking my picture," I say.

And she does.

73

CHAPTER 8

Jax picks me up on Saturday afternoon so we can go to Pie'n Burger in Pasadena. Getting there requires the freeway, but since it's the weekend, traffic is light and Jax vrooms his car easily to our destination. Today he has music blasting slightly beyond what I'd call listenable. I'm not sure what I'd have guessed his taste would be, but I would not have picked indie folk guys whistling and hand-clapping.

"Can we turn this down?" I ask. "I can barely hear you."

"Man," he says. "This shit's my jam. But fine."

"So I sort of went out with Jordi last night," I say. "I mean, not really. Not like a date."

"Nice," Jax says. "Didja hook up?"

"I said it wasn't like a date."

"You can hook up on not a date," he says. "You can pretty much hook up anywhere."

"Maybe if you're you," I say. "She wanted to take pictures in our neighborhood, since she's this amazingly talented photographer. So I went with her."

"So she's like an artsy type," he says. "That's what you're into?"

"I don't know what I'm *into*," I say. "I like her, specifically."

74

"Why?" he asks. "Remember, you have to have real reasons. I can use your rule against you."

"How is that using it against me? Because . . . she's smart in this really calm and thoughtful way. And she takes photography seriously like it means the world to her. And . . ." I picture her and smile. "She'll be super quiet and then say something kind of funny and sly."

I'm not sure I've ever thought much less spoken the word *sly* before.

"And hot," he says.

"Well, yeah." I think about Jordi standing perfectly still and snapping picture after picture, and about being the one to see it all happen. "Did you ever come up with an answer for why you like Gaby?"

"Of *course* I did," he says as he parks the car next to the restaurant. "Come on, let's do this."

"And?" I ask as we walk inside. "So?"

Pie'n Burger is an old-fashioned diner that's been here more than forty years, and it's like time has mostly stopped inside. We sit down at the counter and quickly decide that even though we've been trying to diversify to add as many options as possible to the Biggest Blank, we'll both get the regular hamburger. Our only other options are a veggie burger or a turkey burger, so we feel secure in keeping things simple.

"Okay, so here we go." Jax leans back in his chair. "She's cute and smart."

"That's barely specific," I say. "That's almost vague."

The waitress clunks our sodas down without a word or

a smile, but I don't care because even these are old-fashioned here, syrup and soda water poured over crushed ice.

"If we were reviewing sodas," I say, "these would win."

"Save it for the full app launch," Jax says.

"So what else?" I ask. "How do you even know Gaby?"

"Our moms are in some alumni group together," he says. "I see her around at these events I get dragged to."

"Aren't you too old to get dragged to events?" I ask. It's been years since I was seen at anything branded Eat Healthy with Norah! Though that's probably as much my mom's choice as mine.

"You don't know my mom." He polishes off his last bite of burger. "So what's your next move with Jordi?"

"Why are you always asking me that?" The Thousand Island dressing on the burger has seeped through enough of the bun that I give up on holding it and surrender to the fork and knife.

"Because you need a next move."

"I doubt that I do," I say. "It all feels . . . I don't know how it feels. Like it's hopeful but also crazy and impossible. It's like you told me I could fly."

"Man," he says. "Your self-esteem . . ." He mimes a plane with his hand and then makes the hand-plane crash.

"I'm just realistic," I say. "Why do people treat realism as pessimism?"

"You're fucking cute," he says. "You know that. You wouldn't wear all your weird fruity clothes if you didn't think that."

"It's two separate things," I say. Isn't it? "Also, it's just a weird coincidence you saw my lemon shorts and this pineapple shirt."

"It's not a weird coincidence you own all of it," he says. "So what happens if you like some hot girl? The worst possibility?"

A vision of Lyndsey flashes in my head. Lyndsey hand-in-hand with Blake. Lyndsey's Facebook status *in a relationship*. And I do my best to relay all of this to Jax, even as he's also tapping at the Biggest Blank app at the moment. I prefer to get fully through the meal before giving my feedback, but that's hardly the biggest difference between Jax and me.

"Wait." Jax stops messing with his phone and stares at me. "Your biggest fear is they might hook up with someone else instead? That's basically *nothing*."

"It feels awful," I say.

"Lots of shit feels awful," he says. "Life feels awful."

"Uh huh." I take the last sip of my soda. "It must be awful for you. In your big house and your car and as many girls as you want."

"One, my house isn't that big," he says. "Ya know my parents are divorced, right? The big house is up in San Francisco, along with my dad. Two, not the girl I actually want. Three, okay, fine, my car's awesome."

"Your life's basically perfect," I say. "I'm sure your parents aren't humiliated at the mere thought of your existence."

Jax's jaw tenses. "You'd be surprised. You done? You input your rating yet?"

"Give me a second. Aren't we supposed to take this seriously?" I scan the menu board to check the price. We're supposed to rate the value, but it's been tough adequately judging that with Jax paying for everything. A free burger always seems like an excellent value.

"Do you think we'll be sick of burgers by the time the summer's over?" I ask once Jax has paid and we're on our way outside.

"Nah. How do you get sick of burgers? They're perfection." He unlocks the BMW. "So how'd you know you were gay?"

"How'd you know you weren't? It was probably the same way."

He laughs as we get into his car. "Touché."

My phone dings with a text that night, and I hope it's Maliah even though I know she's out with Trevor, but I assume it's Jax because that's way more likely these days. However, the name on my phone isn't one I've seen recently, and I smile before I even read the contents of the message.

I heard about Mom's book. Therefore I assume she's more annoying than usual. Sorry!

I type back as quickly as I can. My last three messages went unreplied—and the texts before that were too brief to even count—but Rachel must be still holding her phone at this very moment, so I reply immediately. *I don't understand how a book is a bigger deal than TV??*

The little dots appear to show that Rachel's typing, and I feel something loosen in my chest.

Local TV and low-rated Food Channel stuff . . . this is a bigger deal, she responds. *This is a whole book of Norah. Just imagine that.*

The dots show up again. And then: *Sorry I've been out of touch. Things are so busy. How's your summer?*

Weird, I type, *but fun. I guess. How's your internship?*

It takes her a while to type. I fill the time by looking at all of Jordi's photos on Instagram again. I search for signs, though of exactly *what* . . . I don't know. I know there won't be a photo where I can suddenly see that not only does Jordi like girls, she likes *me.*

I keep looking anyway.

Rachel finally responds: *It's great! How's yours?*

What the heck was all that typing about then?

Obviously, since Rachel is halfway through college, it's been nearly two years since she left for Boston University. I cried when we dropped her off at LAX (and most of the drive home, which is no small journey when you're going back to the Eastside) but then my sophomore year started, and somehow I got used to her not walking with me or waving to me in the halls or, of course, being around at home. Before then we were a team. Mom could spend all her energy coming up with healthy alternatives to things we used to like eating, and Dad could turn over all the free time to Mom's assistant work instead of using it to take us on night hikes in Griffith Park and walks around Silver Lake Reservoir like he used to. We still had each other.

Her freshman year, at least, Rachel still texted all the time. She'd send funny posts to me on Instagram, and we'd FaceTime whenever possible. She was home for the whole summer after, and it was almost as though her year away hadn't happened. It was almost like nothing had changed.

But then she started her sophomore year, met Paul, and everything's shifted.

Mine's great too, I type. And then that feels like enough so I move my phone to my desk to charge it and go back to my careful research of Jordi. I don't learn much that I don't already know. When she's tagged in photos it's with the same group of friends I've seen her with at school. The bands she follows seem local and obscure, which I would have guessed, and I don't look any of them up because there's nothing wrong with liking pop music and I'm afraid Jordi's cool music will make me feel silly.

I mean, not that I don't feel silly with about a million tabs all devoted to Jordi Perez open in my browser right now. I remember doing this with Maliah, many months ago, analyzing Trevor for any possible defects. It would definitely feel less creepy if I were doing this with my best friend, but there are two huge obstacles: mainly that Jordi has no real interest in me, and also that Maliah thinks Jordi is some hardcore criminal.

I guess it's also fairly creepy to not care if Jordi is some hardcore criminal. But I really, really don't.

The four of us—Maliah, Zoe, Brooke, and me—are some-how magically all free to go shopping on Sunday after-noon. We take Maliah's Mini Cooper even though if we do any serious buying there'll barely be enough room for the four of us plus bags. Maliah always seems vaguely offended if Brooke offers to drive us in her banged up old Nissan, which, true, is not an adorable mint-colored British car, but does have plenty of room for friends *and* shopping bags.

"Did you hear there's a party at Denny Nuckles's on Friday?" Zoe asks as we stop off at Starbucks on our way to the mall. I'm not sure I need to prove to my friends that I'm now sophisticated about coffee, so I do order a Frappuccino.

"And what else did you hear, Zo?" Brooke asks her with a very knowing smile. We're basically a team of two sets of best friends. Just like Maliah and me, Brooke and Zoe have known each other since childhood. And also just like us, they're sort of physical opposites. Maliah's dark-skinned with perfect ringlets of sun-kissed hair (it's whatever chemical mix they use at her salon but it looks sun-kissed) and fits into sample sizes, while I'm one of the palest people in southern California with cotton candy hair and a plus size dress size. Brooke is tall and blond in that all-American natural way magazines say is in most seasons, while Zoe is just under five feet tall with a pouf of bright red hair—also natural even if *Vogue* would never refer to that shade as such.

"Okay, fine," Zoe says, as her whole face flushes. I've

never seen someone whose *forehead* even turns red. "Brandon's going to be there."

Zoe has nursed a crush on Brandon Salas since high school started and they ended up in the same algebra class. He's quiet and therefore supposedly sensitive, and all of us are used to dissecting the small morsels of conversation he's shared with Zoe for clues about his potential interest level.

There's a chance I'm getting ahead of myself, but if Zoe and Brandon are at the same party, it seems hugely probable that they'll fall in love. Then two out of three of my closest friends will be in relationships. And considering how pretty and confident and smart Brooke is, she can't be far behind. I'll be the only forever alone one left standing.

I was hoping that wouldn't happen until college, and by then I'd be having my cool single fashion life in New York anyway and I wouldn't care.

"I'm in," Maliah says. "Trevor's going out of town this weekend."

Why does she have to say that? She could just say she's coming to the party without making us feel like we're her second choice.

"Tell them how you know about the party," Brooke tells Zoe, poking her with her Frappuccino straw when she doesn't answer immediately.

It turns out that Brandon messaged Zoe to see if she was going. We make her read the texts aloud as we head through and past the mall to the Americana, which is the outdoor shopping center next to the Galleria. The two-story Forever 21 is always our first stop, but we're in less of a hurry today as we comment on each of the messages Brandon sent. There is no doubt to any of us how much he likes her, from the first greeting (*Hi!*—exclamation point use always seems very positive) to the most recent (*Hope I see you on Friday.*—sure, not definite plans, but heavily hinting at them).

With three of us, plus Zoe, analyzing these messages, it feels like there's a science to it. Brandon's interest seems without question, and I'm, I realize, *jealous*. I have no such confirmation of Jordi's interest, unlikely as it may be. There were things she said on Friday night I know we could spend the rest of our shopping trip turning over and over.

"What?" Maliah asks as I drift in her general direction inside the store. "And do you think I can pull off like a long drapey dress? Like I'm one of those hippies over off of Laurel Canyon?"

"Yes," I say. "Not that you know any actual hippies."

"Like you do either!" She laughs and flips through a rack of dresses. I point out two that are prettier than the rest. "Something is up with you. Are you still sad about Lyndsey?"

"Nothing's up with me," I say. "This summer's just . . . weirder than I expected."

CHAPTER 9

The best thing possible happens on Monday morning at work. No, Jordi doesn't declare her eternal love or even bring me any delicious leftovers. Okay, she does tell me to relax when we arrive and makes me a cup of coffee, but that isn't the point.

The point? Maggie brought in the new fall line!

Sketches of all six new dresses, as well as samples of each. And by samples, I mean beautiful actual dresses that I get to look at and touch. Maggie didn't just have the teeny tiny sample size made, either; she has plus size samples for each dress, too. I might actually wear Lemonberry's plus size sample size, but I try to only casually mention that fact. I'm sure Maggie has a lot to do with these dresses right now and isn't ready to hand them over to one of her interns.

Oh my god, but how great would it be if she was?

"These are incredible," I say. "I'm so jealous you know how to design dresses. I wish I had that skill. Or making dresses! Once my sister and I tried to take a class over at Sew L.A. It didn't go well."

"Abby, you're only seventeen, give yourself a break," Maggie says with a smile. "I didn't learn any of this until I was in my twenties."

84

I run my hands over a floral dress with three-quarter sleeves, a flared skirt, and a matching belt. "I love this fabric design. It's so tropical. Like my parrot dress but . . . more restrained."

"You have a parrot dress?" Maggie and Jordi ask together.

I nod.

"I demand you wear it on Wednesday," Maggie tells me. "Please."

Jordi and I spend the rest of the morning studying the dresses. Jordi's making notes for the kinds of photos she'd like to take, while I'm thinking about how these six dresses comprise the fall line. There's one that's almost casual, with a lighter weight fabric and a less streamlined cut, all the way to a fuchsia taffeta with a voluminous skirt. Someone like me—well, like me with more money—could easily want all of these dresses. But I can see how someone who only wanted formalwear could stop in for the fuchsia dress, or someone like Maliah who's trendy but not into strictly retro looks would look amazing in the casual bright white dress.

I can't wait until a full selection of the dresses is actually in the store and people can buy them.

"Hey, what did you bring for lunch?" Jordi asks me. "Can it wait until Wednesday? Do you want to go out? I have cash if you didn't bring any."

"I have cash, too," I say. "Sure. I don't even care if it can wait until Wednesday. It has, like, a disturbing amount of yucca."

Jordi pulls her bag over her shoulder and neck. "What's yucca substituting for?"

I grab my purse and follow her outside. "Croutons. Isn't that sad?"

"So your mom's big enemy is carbs, huh."

"I mean, I get that you shouldn't have carbs nonstop," I say. "But never seems like . . . it's extreme. But I guess Norah's extreme."

Jordi looks up and down our block of Glendale Boulevard. "Where do you want to go?"

"BonVivant?" I ask. "They have really good sandwiches."

"Yeah, let's get you some bread," Jordi says.

We walk down the block and get into the long line. I grab menus for us, and there's a moment as I hand one to her that our fingertips graze. It's intense, like one time I touched a wire on a broken radio.

"The dresses were cool," Jordi says. "I hope Maggie gives all of them to you."

"I was hoping that, too," I say. "Is that selfish? I feel like you probably don't want any of the dresses."

"Nah, I'm not really a dress type," she says.

Does that mean something? Please let it mean something. Lots of girls, regardless of whether they like girls or not, aren't into wearing dresses. I'm into wearing almost nothing *but* dresses and I'm as gay as heck. But please, please, *please* let it mean something.

"Your look is so defined," I say. "Which I love."

Why did I say *love?*

"'Defined'?" she asks with a smile.

86

"You know, like Laine. You could pick out an outfit for Laine without her having to get involved. It's the same for you. I think having a really defined look is a really key part of having great style."

"But you have great style," Jordi says, "and I never would have known to pick out a parrot dress for you."

"Maybe once you see it, you'll feel differently," I say. "And, thank you."

The people right in front of us are taking forever to deliberate between soups, and I shoot Jordi a look.

"It's a tough decision, Abby," she says.

It's finally our turn to order, and we both get sandwiches like people who aren't the least bit afraid of bread. Since Jordi orders first, she offers to find a table for us, and there's something about making my way over to her that feels really good.

Oh my god. Like, I really cannot ever again make fun of Maliah in my head (or otherwise) for how doofy she can be over Trevor. I'm literally finding enjoyment in walking across a restaurant and locating a coworker at a table.

"So, hey." Jordi leans toward me a little. "I have a proposal."

A proposal.

Okay, I don't need to hear anything else she says to know it is not that kind of proposal. We are only seventeen, and we are not dating. But the word, oh my god. I can't help but picture it. My dress is stunning and designed by Maggie. Jordi's in something white and fancy that isn't a dress. We're the Ives-Perezes and we laugh whenever anyone screws up our names on Christmas cards.

Seriously, what is *wrong* with me? All people with crushes can't get quite this wacky, can they? Society would cease to function.

"I know that we both want to get the job in the fall," Jordi says. "And we probably both read everything about it we could find. But . . . I don't want to fight over it with you, Abby. If I get it, I just want to . . . get it."

"Same," I say as quickly as I can manage. "Yes, of course!"

Please let this mean something, too.

"Also, I know we're supposed to get free clothes, and obviously if I do, I'll tell Maggie to give more to you instead."

"That's . . . that's really nice. Thank you, Jordi."

Our sandwiches arrive, and I notice that the table next to us contains the people ahead of us in line. They've finally gotten their soups and still seem to have a lot of questions, mainly about cilantro.

"I sorta feel like they've never ordered food in a restaurant before," I say, and Jordi snorts.

"I'm proud of you for getting through your sandwich-ordering so quickly."

"You too! It was a tough job."

Jordi spots something across the restaurant and lifts her camera out of her bag. I can't figure out what it is that she's shooting, but that mystery makes it even more exciting to watch.

"Sorry." Jordi caps the lens and puts the camera away. "My friends hate when I do that without warning."

"I don't mind," I say. "You can't help when inspiration strikes you."

I make a face because it's the cheesiest thing I may have ever said, and I need Jordi to know that I know it. But she only smiles in return. And the truth is that even if nothing ever happens with Jordi and my weird thoughts about her electrical fingertips are all in vain, I'm still really glad I'm getting to know her.

The house is, magically, empty when I wake up on Tuesday morning. There's a note from Dad in the kitchen that he and Mom have "a thousand" errands and they'll see me later. I get dressed as quickly as I'm capable of; I don't really believe in not putting time into a look. It's not that I'm worried I'll see someone I know and look terrible—not that I wouldn't hate that—but my clothes are for *me*. When you're making your way through the world in a look you feel confident about, everything feels easier.

I zip my laptop into my bright pink bag and walk over to Kaldi. I order coffee—yes, a regular coffee—and a bagel—yes, Mom would cry—for sustenance as I work on my next blog post. Honestly, I feel a little guilt toward +*style*. I'd figured my Lemonberry internship would keep me constantly inspired, but it's almost like I get it out of my system and then have less of it when I sit down to write. Also, to be fair, I'm not really doing much of sitting down and writing, period, between the internship, the burgers project, and using my computer time to stare at Jordi's Instagram on a bigger screen instead of doing, well, anything less creepy.

Maliah drops by after texting to see what I'm up to, and so this means two times in one week I get to see her without Trevor. I manage not to say that, though.

"What's today's post?" she asks, hovering behind me with her iced coffee. I do a quick inventory of open browser tabs to make sure there's nothing incriminating or even just weird. There is an article called *How to Find the Best Underwear for Your Butt Type* but I decide that's universally relatable for most girls.

"Midi skirts? Come on, Abby. No one looks good in midi skirts."

"Untrue, you just have to put together the right outfit," I say. "And that's totally the point of my post."

"You should post a photo of your black-and-white skirt," she says. "When you wore it with the yellow belt and the button-up shirt? So cute."

I agree that it's one of my better recent outfits, but Maliah should know better, and I tell her so.

"I just don't get it," she says. "You are all about fashion. Every day. Why not let people see it? Real examples, instead of just talking about stuff and posting pictures from online stores?"

"I reblog photos of street style all the time," I say. "And people who do OOTD posts! That means 'outfit of the day'."

90

THE SUMMER OF JORDI PEREZ

"I know what it means by now, and you should be the one doing those posts." Maliah sits down across from me and lets out a growly sort of sigh. "You look amazing, all the time."

"Can you imagine my mom's reaction?" I ask. "'Eat Healthy with Norah!'s Norah suspected of having a fat kid!'"

Maliah rolls her eyes very forcefully. "No one would say that."

"A photo goes up of a teeny tiny actress who has, like, *the hint* of cellulite, and people line up to call her a cow."

"It's not the same," Maliah says. "You aren't famous. You're a regular girl. And you know you look great."

"Me thinking it is different than other people thinking it," I say.

"Fine, fine, fine. Anyway, there's no way your mom would have that kind of reaction."

I don't push it because Maliah doesn't know the whole story. No one but Dad knows the whole story, and it's much better that way.

"I just want your blog to be as popular as it can be," Maliah says, and then we both laugh.

"Oh, yes," I say. "The universal wish every girl has for her best friend. Tumblr popularity."

"Seriously, though, Abbs! Can you at least work toward it?"

"I still don't know why it matters to you that the internet knows what I look like," I say as I type up a description of a striped midi skirt similar to mine. "The internet couldn't care less."

"That isn't my point," she says. "It's that you think there's something wrong with you."

AMY SPALDING

"No," I say more sharply than I mean to. Everyone around us looks up from their laptops. "Sorry. I don't think that. I just feel like . . . everyone else will. People who don't know me. In person people get, you know, all of me. When it's just a photo, it worries me they can't see past how I look."

"But how you look is . . ." Maliah sighs and shakes her head. "Never mind. I don't want to have this fight again, and I really don't want to have it in this coffeeshop."

"Good," I say. "Ooh, here's a skirt with apples and pears print!"

"That definitely sounds like something you'd own," Maliah says, and I realize Jax's theory about me and fruit clothes is absolutely on the mark. Is that bad?

"It's three hundred and seventy-five dollars," I report. "So definitely not."

"So I have to go." She gets up even though I feel like she literally just sat down. "I'll pick you up Friday for the thing at Denny's, yes?"

"Sure." Don't ask, I tell myself. You already know the answer. "Plans with Trevor?"

"We're going to a Dodgers game," she says.

"Ugh, really?"

She laughs. "Shut it. It's our national pastime, Abbs. See you Friday."

So I spend the rest of the day alone. The good news is I do eventually find the apples and pears skirt on deep, deep discount on another site and give in to my fruit wardrobe destiny.

92

CHAPTER 10

The party's already loud and overflowing onto the front yard when the four of us arrive at Denny's house on Friday. Club-type dance music—well, what I'd expect clubs to play while people do the sort of dancing that seems more like fully-clothed sex—filters out into the night air, and I can't help but shoot Maliah a look.

"It'll be fun," she says. "I need a night out with my girls."

Maliah never said things that sounded like deleted dialogue from old episodes of *Sex and the City* until she fell in love with Trevor. Considering how stupid just a one-sided relationship in my own head with Jordi has made me, I really can't judge anymore.

I mean, I will, of course. But it no longer feels fair.

I follow Maliah in, with Zoe and Brooke behind us. We have to walk through a narrow hallway to get to the kitchen, where we assume the drinks will be. As soon as we emerge from the squeezed space, I see a whole pack of kids in black. Artsy, thoughtful, purposeful black. Except Jordi. Jordi's wearing a white tank top and army green shorts. I've never seen her bare legs before, and it's honestly a lot to process.

"Hi, Jordi," I say in a squeaky voice I barely recognize as my own. Maliah whips her head around and gives me a look.

"Hey, Abby," Jordi says with a nod.

"I didn't know you were coming," I say. "Not that you have to tell me. Why would you? There aren't intern codes of conduct for parties."

Then I nervously laugh for, let's just say, longer than necessary.

"Abbs." Maliah forces a red Solo cup into my hand. "Let's go outside."

The four of us escape into the crowded backyard. I spot Gaby Manzetti almost right away, and I give her a tiny wave. I think we know each other well enough that it isn't weird, and later I can report back nicely to Jax and look like a good friend.

"So what's going on, Abbs?" Maliah asks me. "You can't hide anything from me."

"Nothing's going on," I say.

"She likes Jordi," Brooke says very matter-of-factly. "That's all. You do, right, Abby?"

I sigh. "Was it that obvious? Was it, like, embarrassingly obvious?"

"It was obvious but cute," Brooke says. "And it's only obvious because we know you."

"I don't know if Jordi realizes," Zoe says. "But Jordi should realize; I want her to realize!"

"Jordi probably doesn't like girls," I say. "No girls do. It's like a whole school full of girls who only like boys. Plus me."

"Oh, Jordi's definitely gay," Maliah says, though she isn't smiling. "But she's also *a criminal*, Abbs."

I take a big swig of whatever's in my cup. It's horrible, somewhere between Hawaiian Punch and what I imagine sadness might taste like. "How do you know?"

"Everyone knows," Maliah says. "I told you. She went to juvie or something. It's basically public knowledge."

"I didn't mean about that," I say. "How do you know she's definitely gay?"

"Hey," someone says, and I look over to see that Gaby and her friend Marji are joining us. We all greet each other even though I really want to get back to the conversation we're in the midst of. However, I owe this to Jax, and also maybe it's good to take a break. I don't want Maliah to be right about juvie, so is it fair to hope she *is* right about Jordi liking girls?

"How's your summer been?" I ask Gaby. "My friend Jax said you were doing a really cool volunteer thing."

Gaby rolls her eyes and laughs. "Aren't you too . . . not horrible to hang out with Jax?"

"Jax is actually a . . ." What even *is* the word for Jax? "A good friend. He seems like more of a bro than he is. A super douche wouldn't hang out with a fat girl with pink hair, right?"

"You can do better than Jax Stockton," Marji tells Gaby, which makes Brooke and Zoe laugh, and I also see how from some angles that might be true. He still wears his ugly flip flops and is keeping his hidden depths, well . . . hidden.

"He really is a good guy," I say, and I feel that whatever's in this cup is already making my cheeks flush. "Sorry, am I talking about Jax too much?"

"Yes," Marji says.

"I doubt he actually likes me," Gaby says with a big smile. I swear that I understand in a flash why Jax is crazy about her. "He's just a flirt."

"Flirts can't be trusted," Marji says.

"I'm glad you guys are friends or whatever," Gaby tells me, "but I just don't really take him seriously."

I'm about to respond with whatever I can come up with to refute that when I catch a glimpse of Jordi out of the corner of my eye. Her group's moved into the backyard, too, and we lock eyes for just a moment before Marji starts complaining about Jax more and I have to do my best to defend my friend.

Ugh, how is Jax my friend? This summer so far has ceased to make sense.

Somehow the subject gets turned to Brooke's family's upcoming trip to Hawaii, and we're all offering swimsuit opinions instead of viewpoints on Jax when there's a burst of noise across the yard.

"Jordi," I hear, and I may visibly perk up. I'm only so strong.

"It's not a big deal," someone else says.

"*Shit*," Jordi mutters, but loudly. I didn't even know Jordi's voice could be that loud. "*Shit*. They'll kill me."

It sounds like a half dozen people chorus back again that whatever it is isn't a big deal.

"You have no idea," she says and pushes her way through the crowd. Nearly every single partygoer stares in her direction, but then the song changes from one hip-hop song to another and dancing is remembered and Jordi's forgotten.

By everyone but me.

I try to trace her path, and end up catching up with her in the bathroom that's connected to what appears to be Denny's parents' bedroom. I'm sure we aren't supposed to be in here but rules don't seem to matter right now.

I make my way over to Jordi and see that she's splashing water from the sink onto her shirt. "Are you okay?"

"Some asshole spilled a beer on me," she says. "No, not some asshole. One of my friends, and it was an accident, but . . ."

She keeps splashing and dabbing at her shirt with hand soap in a very un-Jordi-like manner.

"It's easy to get stuff out of white clothes," I say. "You can just bleach it once you're home. It'll look fine then."

Her face crumples and she sinks to the tiled floor. I'm not sure what to do, but it seems impossible to top the awkwardness of towering over her, so I sit down, too.

"I have to be perfect this summer," she says. "Which doesn't include coming home smelling like beer."

"It wasn't your beer, though," I say. "Will that matter?"

"Would it matter to your parents?"

"I guess not."

She sniffs and leans over so that her face is completely hidden from me. "I got into huge trouble the last week of school. My parents almost made me turn down the internship as a punishment, but I promised they could trust me."

"You seem really trustworthy," I say. "I'll vouch for you. Will that matter? Do I seem trustworthy?"

I hear, amid more sniffling, a little snort. It's a relief that she sounds like herself again, though I guess the tears are also her being herself. No one's only their happy side, even if that's all we show the world whenever we can help it.

"Do you like Gaby Manzetti?" she asks.

"What? I mean, I don't hate her? We're not really friends." I shrug and wonder why so many people this summer want to talk about Gaby Manzetti. She's a nice person and all but doesn't really seem like someone who should be a hot topic.

"I saw you guys talking," she says.

"It's a long story," I say.

"Like everything with you," she says, but she looks up and smiles. "Gaby and burgers."

"They're actually related," I say. "My friend Jax likes her. I'm supposed to . . . be his hype man or something. And I'm pretty sure I'm terrible at it."

"I can't believe you're terrible at anything," she says.

"Oh my god," I say. "Seriously? So many things."

Her smile fades. "Did you drive here? Could you maybe take me home?"

"I don't have my license," I say. "Maliah brought all of us. But if you don't mind waiting until later, you can totally catch a ride with us. And maybe if you use enough soap, your shirt will just smell like lavender or basil or whatever that is."

Jordi sighs. "I hate this. My whole life has been *fine* and then *one thing* . . . I'm practically on probation."

She totally went to juvie, and I totally do not care.

"They'll understand," I say, because Jordi's dad makes her extra food for me, and the food doesn't taste like Mom's crisp and sterile *solutions*. Jordi's dad's food tastes like love. How couldn't he understand a spilled drink?

"I was looking at sample portfolios online," she says. "I want my photography portfolio to be as good as possible for my college applications. And a guy had this image of fire at the horizon and . . . I was obsessed with it."

Arson, Abbs, I hear Maliah say.

"There's this house a few streets behind yours," she says. "It's been for sale for months, and it has a tiny pool. It felt like a safe place to burn something. There's water *right there*."

I realize I'm holding my breath.

"I even bought my own fire extinguisher," she says. "It felt really safe. So I lit some dried out grass and weeds, and . . . I got some good shots. It was starting to look like I'd imagined it would. And I was completely aware of how much was burning, and the extinguisher was literally leaning against me."

"But then it spread too quickly and the house burned down?"

Jordi laughs. "No! Jesus, Abby. A cop showed up and accused me of trespassing and arson. The fire kept burning while he yelled at me, so by the time he took the extinguisher from me and put it out, it looked worse than I would have let it get. And even though I showed him my camera, I don't think he believed me. He kept saying things like *a cry for help* and *heartbreak is hard*."

"What?"

"I don't know. So he made me get in the back of the cop car and I was sure I was getting arrested. But he just took me home and told my parents his version of what happened. And they completely believed him, even though I had the photos, and even though of course I'd shown them the portfolios I thought were good examples." Jordi is sniffling again. "It was like they couldn't even see me anymore. I was just the girl some cop dropped off at their front door."

"I'm so sorry." I hate that she's crying and that I don't know what to do about it. I touch her shoulder and then her hand. "That cop's an idiot."

"Maybe," she says. "Maybe I'm the idiot."

"Don't even," I say. "You're the smartest person I know. At work you're this total professional."

"So are you," she says, and I realize our hands are still touching.

"I'm an idiot, too," I say. "If it makes you feel better."

"Definitely," she says, and we're making eye contact again. And still hand contact.

"So I was convinced I wouldn't get the Lemonberry internship," I start because it feels unfair to have Jordi's words out there and not mine. "I know Maggie had a ton of applicants, and as I'm sure you can guess I was kind of goofy and rambly in our interview. My mom was being extra understanding about it—which isn't really her thing—and said she had a big project for me with Eat Healthy With Norah! And I honestly think I'm better at social media than my mom is, but, you know. She's on TV. She has a lot of followers. So even though it's not fashion, I started to get excited. I'd get a ton of experience with a huge audience, and maybe that would lead to . . . I don't know. Something actually involving fashion, or a job, or just something really good to put on my college applications to make me stand out."

Jordi sighs loudly. "That's all every advice site says. *Find a way to stand out.*"

"Right? If we're all standing out, aren't we all just . . ."

"Blending in?" She smiles at me. "I don't think you could blend in if you wanted to."

"I feel like you could, because you're stealthy," I say, and I laugh because it sounds so silly and so honest at once and somehow our hands are still touching. I'm afraid to over-think it or even look at my own right hand, but I'm pretty sure our hands might be doing more than touching. There is a very real chance we are holding hands right now, but I don't want to jinx it.

"Anyway. I come up with all these ideas for my mom. I even wrote sample posts for her and developed these stupid hashtag ideas about nutrition. '#NoCarbsNoProblem'? '#BetterDeadThanBread'? But Mom looked . . ." I have to give myself a moment while I remember Mom's expression.

"She looked like I was an adorably stupid puppy who'd peed on a rug or something. Her big idea was that I'd be the *before*, and then I'd document eating her food all summer—which obviously I do anyway because that's all we have at home—and then I guess I'd theoretically keep a food diary on her blog, and it would all be about me *documenting my weight loss journey*. And Mom said . . ."

Great! Great. Now I'm crying, too. Except Jordi's stopped crying, so I'm just crying on my own.

"She said I'd finally be happy *and pretty*."

"Abby." Jordi slides her arm around me and squeezes me, and I can't believe the words are actually out of me. "You know that's bullshit, don't you?"

I nod through my tears. "Sure. I'm happy enough. And being pretty's . . . it's not my goal anyway. And it's not about *my size*."

"Shut up," she says but with a smile. "You're beautiful."

"You shut up," I say, laughing even though my nose is all snotty and I'm sure I've smeared mascara down half my face and *Jordi just called me beautiful*. I don't want to think about it—about anything.

I don't even decide to do it.

I just do it.

I lean in and kiss her.

CHAPTER 11

I convince Maliah to add another person to the carload home and also to leave in time to get Jordi home at a semi-reasonable hour. It's a tight fit. Jordi's in the middle, but only sort of, because Mini Cooper backseats barely have middles, and one of Jordi's legs is propped up over mine. It's ostensibly to save space for Zoe on the other side, but also we spent an indeterminate amount of time kissing on the floor of Denny Nuckles's parents' bathroom and it doesn't feel fair not to be touching at all right now.

Jordi threads her fingers through mine, and I think of how only minutes earlier her hands held my face the way her hands hold cameras. There's strength and concentration in her grip.

She just had me in her grip.

"Where am I going?" Maliah asks. "I have no idea where Jordi lives."

"Just down the street from me," I say. "On Glenfeliz."

I think Maliah sighs in a huffy manner but I don't care because Jordi's head is on my shoulder. *Jordi's head is on my shoulder.* Her hair is soft against my jawline.

"I feel like you have to pull back on pushing Jax on Gaby," Brooke tells me from the front seat. "You need a new

103

tactic. Or—and I'm saying this with love—Jax needs a better hype woman."

"Is Jax even real?" Jordi asks.

"Oh, he's real," Brooke says. "A real piece of work."

We all laugh because it sounds like something someone's mom would say. Also because it's true.

"You can pull over here," Jordi directs Maliah just as I have a genius idea.

"Mal," I say, "switch shirts with Jordi. Your parents won't notice it smells like beer."

Maliah's parents are both doctors, and when they're home, they sleep like the dead.

"What? No."

"You don't have to," Jordi says.

"You're the only one who's the same size," I say. "Please."

Maliah huffs a bit more but takes off her seatbelt and maneuvers out of her lacy white shirt before tossing it behind her.

"Close your eyes," Jordi tells me, and I obey even though I want to peek. I'd do anything Jordi asked. "Okay. You're safe."

I climb out of the car so she can get out.

"Thanks for the ride," she tells Maliah.

Maliah slips into the beer-stained tank top. "It's fine."

"I'll have your shirt dry-cleaned and give it to Abby to give you."

"God, it's *from Forever 21*. Just get it back to Abbs."

"Text me tomorrow," Jordi tells me as I get back into the car.

"I don't have your number!"

"Well, get it." She leans in and smiles. "Kidding. I'll message you."

"Okay. Good night."

"Good night, Abby." She closes the door and waves as Maliah peels out.

"Oh my god," Brooke says.

"Oh my god, Abby!" Zoe leans over and pokes my leg. "Hours ago you said no one is gay at all and now you have *a girlfriend*."

"She just hooked up at a party," Maliah says quickly. "She doesn't have a girlfriend."

"Mal," I say. "I think it's more than that."

"I told you to be careful," she says. "She's going to corrupt you."

"She can corrupt me all she wants," I say, like I'm a new person who goes around saying everything I think *on purpose*. "I want to be corrupted."

Zoe giggles. "You have it *bad*."

Maliah parks in front of my house. "See you."

My best friend loves honesty and details, and so I know the right thing to do right now is to lay some of this out for her. If she knew more about Jordi, and if she knew more about how *I felt about Jordi*, maybe she wouldn't be barely bothering to make eye contact with me.

But it doesn't feel like the time (past midnight) or the place (a tiny car filled with other people), so I just wave and let myself into the house. Mom and Dad must be in bed; the house is silent and dark. There doesn't seem to be a right thing to do with myself. I pace around our tiny living room, I get a glass of lemonade from the refrigerator, I walk into the backyard and sit on the grass. It's hard to see stars in Los Angeles—the kind in the sky—because of streetlights and billboards and pollution, but I look for them anyway.

And right at this very moment, for maybe the first time ever, I feel like I'm in my own story.

In the morning, it all feels like a dream. I'm the sidekick. I'm the goober who rambles at work. I am not the one who takes a beautiful girl in her arms and kisses her.

Except that last night, I was.

I grab my phone from my nightstand and see the alerts. It seems as though everyone I've ever known wants to talk to me.

Brooke: *Tell me everything.*

Zoe: *Tell me EVERYTHING!!!* ☺ ♥

Maliah: *Don't forget to get my shirt back for me.*

Jax: *brgrs? 2day? whut up?*

Seriously, why would he take the time to write *whut* when it's literally the same amount of effort to type the word correctly?

Most importantly, I know that I didn't dream anything because there's an Instagram message from Jordi containing only a number, which I add to my phone immediately.

Hi, I text her.

hey abby, she replies almost immediately. *are you free tonight?*

I am, but also who cares if I was already? I am now! *Yes! I'm free!*

It's so nice to stop caring about looking cool.

can i take you out? proper date.

I'm finding new records for how quickly I can tell someone *yes*.

Maliah is maybe not my favorite person right now, but I still text her once I've taken a shower and put on my afternoon interim pre-date outfit. *Need help with perfect first-date look. Can you come over?*

She doesn't respond right away, but I remind myself that maybe she's just doing something. Maliah's allowed to have a life that doesn't permit constant texting. I suppose. If Rachel were home, I'd get her help, but the truth is I'd still want Maliah here. Some jobs require your best friend. Though of course it'd be nice if my big sister were here, too.

I walk down the hallway and find my parents in the kitchen with an array of recipes spread out on the counter. "Is there breakfast?"

"She finally arises!" Dad says with a biblical intonation to his voice. "There was breakfast a couple hours ago."

"Why didn't you get me?" I ask, except that I know why. My sister's always been an insanely early riser, and she'd be the one to drag me from slumber to the table. Mom and Dad haven't had to worry about me in ages.

"I can make you something, sweetie," Mom says.

"I'll just have a yogurt," I say, and then take a deep breath as I turn away toward the refrigerator. "So . . . I have a date tonight. That's okay, right? I'm seventeen."

"Of course it's okay!"

I can hear Mom's smile even with my head in the fridge in search of the best yogurt varieties left.

"Is it with Jax?" she asks, and I nearly hit my head on the refrigerator's shelf. "You two have been spending a lot of time together."

"Mom," I say, as Dad says, "Norah."

"What?" she asks.

"I told you last year that I'm gay." It hadn't been a big speech. It was just weird keeping part of my identity a secret—especially when back then I never could have imagined it would have led to something like kissing the most beautiful girl I've ever seen at a high school party *as if I'm someone cool enough to do things like that* . . . except now there's a chance I am? So one evening at dinner I'd just said it.

"Well, I didn't know if you'd still feel that way," Mom says. "Feelings change."

"It's not a feeling," I say. "It's . . . never mind. I don't know why I bother."

"I'm sorry," she says, though in the kind of tone that doesn't completely feel like an apology. "You've just been spending so much time with Jax lately."

"I could spend all the time in the world with Jax," I say. "It won't make me straight."

"Of course you can go, Abby," Dad says in his let's-all-just-get-along voice. "What's her name?"

"Jordi," I say, and it turns out that even when I'm extra annoyed with Mom, I can't speak Jordi's name without smiling. "I'm taking my yogurt to my room."

"Don't throw out the container there," Mom says, because she has nothing to say about her gay daughter but plenty about where it's appropriate to dispose of dairy products. "And remember to bring your spoon back to the kitchen."

Eating yogurt alone in your bedroom, by the way, feels sad even when you're about to have your first date with your dream girl.

Maliah stops by a couple hours later without having responded to my texts. I'm so happy to see her I don't even bring it up.

"I want to start by saying that I still don't approve of this," she says once we're back in my room. "And I don't think you need my assistance. You have the best style of anyone I know. But I'm your friend and I'm going to help you pick out what you're wearing."

"You're wrong about Jordi," I say. "She never went to juvie and she's a really good person."

Maliah sighs and sits down on my bed. "I know you have this weird, sad fantasy that you're going to die alone, but that doesn't mean you have to date just anyone who comes along."

"Mal, I *like* her," I say. "A lot. I just hadn't told you because . . ."

"'Because'?"

"Because of exactly this. Because you have something against her." I want to say that I'm too annoyed to flip through my closet, but I'm not sure there's a level of annoyance high enough for that to actually be the case. "Anyway, before it didn't matter. I thought it was impossible."

"I didn't come over here to listen to you to insult yourself," she says. "Wear the dress that looks like tie-dye and your pink wedges. Everything goes with your hair and you'll look really soft and pretty."

"Ooh, that's good." I pull the dress out of my closet. "I haven't worn this to work yet."

Maliah gets up to sift through my jewelry box. "Don't wear any complicated necklaces."

"Do you think it's too much look?" I ask, and she finally laughs.

"No, you dork, you just don't want to make it harder to access your neck."

"Oh! That's actually good advice."

"Don't say *actually*! All my advice is good." Maliah takes out my strand of white ceramic beads I found for dirt cheap at a yard sale. "Can I borrow this?"

"Sure."

She slips them over her head and examines herself in the mirror. "How'd Norah take it? The big date?"

"I think she's still out there hoping I'm secretly dating Jax."

Maliah laughs. "Gross. You and Jax would have the ugliest babies."

"*Maliah!*"

She fluffs her hair. "What? It's true. I can see things like that. You both have round, pale faces. Your baby would look like the moon."

"What about me and Jordi?"

"That's not scientifically possible." She walks to my doorway. "I have to get home. Mom and Dad are making me go to this boring benefit tonight. Some disease needs money."

"Sorry. Have fun?"

"Sure." She rolls her eyes. "And, yes. In a more technologically advanced world, you and Jordi Perez would have cute babies."

CHAPTER 12

The doorbell rings at seven sharp.

"Punctual," Dad says. "That's good in business, and it's good in relationships, too."

"Dad, that's the weirdest thing you could say right now. Please don't say anything like that in front of her."

I walk past him to open the door, but he stops me.

"Let me do this. It's a dad job."

I'm not sure that's true but I let him. And then Jordi Perez is standing in my doorway. She's wearing a slouchy gray T-shirt with black jeans, and—a detail that makes my style-craving heart explode—suspenders.

And, strangely enough, she's holding a basket of tomatoes.

"Hi," Dad says. "Jordi? Come on in."

She steps inside and glances around until we make eye contact and then looks back to Dad. "Hi, Mr. Ives. I, uh, I know this is weird but my parents insisted I brought these tomatoes. We have plants and there's just been this ... overflow of tomatoes. I'm sorry, this is—"

"It's great, my wife and I love homegrown tomatoes." Dad takes the basket from her as Mom walks into the front room. "Norah, Jordi brought us tomatoes from her garden."

"Thank you," Mom says and then looks to me. "She's actually pretty."

Oh my god.

Dad looks toward the front window. "What are you driving?"

"My dad's Prius," Jordi says. "It just had an oil change."

"Sounds good," Dad says.

"Don't stay out too late, girls," Mom says.

"Okay," I say. "Let's go."

I rush Jordi outside before things can get any more embarrassing. "I'm so sorry about them."

"I'm the one who came with *produce*." She takes my hand. "Hey."

"Hey." I smile at her. In these shoes, I'm a little taller than her. "I'm so glad you asked me out."

"I'm glad you said yes. Come on. Let's go."

I get into the car. "Where are we going?"

"You'll see," she says with a smile. "I planned the whole night."

"I feel bad! That sounds like a lot of work." I don't actually feel bad at all. Jordi planned a whole night for us. Who cares if it was a lot of work!

"You can plan our second date then," she says. "Deal?"

Second date? "Deal."

She reaches across the console to take my hand again. It seems unfathomable not to be holding hands constantly when now this is a thing we've done.

"Give me a hint," I say. "About tonight."

"Abby," she says and laughs. "We'll be there in about ten minutes. You'll survive."

"I might not," I say. "The suspense might literally kill me, and then you'll feel horrible."

"All right," she says. "If you start displaying any symptoms of death, I'll fill you in."

"Was everything okay last night?" I ask. "When you got home? If I can ask?"

"Of course you can ask. And, yeah. It was fine. My mom walked into the living room without her glasses, asked if I had fun, and went back to bed. There's no way she could have known I had a different shirt on. Oh, and speaking of, Maliah's shirt's in my bag. Remember to get it from me."

"Sorry about her, too," I say.

"Abby, it's cool."

"I can't believe this is actually happening," I say, and then I sort of hear myself in my head and laugh. "I know I sound silly, but . . . I liked you so much."

Oh my god, is that too much to confess? Do most people know the level of confession appropriate for date one?

"I liked you too," she says. "I wanted to kiss you last week."

"I wanted to kiss you then too," I say, and then I think about how we haven't yet kissed today. It's nearly been twenty-four hours since we've kissed. "I kind of want to kiss you right now."

"*Kind of?*"

We both laugh, and then we're at a conveniently red light at San Fernando and Fletcher, and we meet midway over the console. It's crazy how just yesterday this would have only been fantasy and somehow right now it's my whole world. My hands in Jordi's hair, her eyelashes brushing my face, Jordi's lips, Jordi's lips, Jordi's lips.

"Can I have a hint?" I ask as she pulls the car onto the 2 Freeway.

"You're getting your hopes up too high," she says. "It won't be that exciting."

My face feels tight because all it's doing is smiling and kissing. My face has never had a better day. "I bet it will be."

"God," she says, "you're cute."

Neurons must be firing or creating new pathways or whatever happens in my brain; I've never before had the sensation of someone else thinking I'm non-platonically cute.

Jordi ends up driving us to Highland Park, which is only a couple neighborhoods northeast, though not somewhere I hang out often. Living in LA without driving isn't that hard as long as you don't expect to venture much out of your neighborhood.

But with Jordi, I want to explore the whole city.

"This was always my favorite restaurant," Jordi tells me once she's parked and we're walking down the sidewalk. The street's lined with restaurants, bars, and old-fashioned shops. I love the feeling of being somewhere so new to me that's also so close to home. It makes the world feel bursting with possibilities. "Mom and Dad always let us choose where we go out to eat for our birthdays, and I'd always pick this place."

"That's so exciting," I say, and she laughs.

"I'm potentially overselling it. It's little and it's not fancy. But I was trying to think of the best place to take you, and I felt like it had to have lots of carbs. So Italian made sense."

"Yes," I say, as Jordi holds open the door to a place called Folliero's.

"Actually, wait." She gently lets the door close and then takes her camera out of her bag. "Your hair in this light . . ."

"It's good?" I ask.

"It matches the sunset." Her face is completely serious as she snaps photos, of me, the building, the sky. "Sorry. Is this annoying?"

I shake my head. "I like watching you work."

"We can go now." Jordi puts her camera down but not away, and opens the door once again. "Let's go have a meal that would make your mom cry."

It's funny how something about my mom can also be romantic.

The restaurant's tiny with brick walls. Jordi and I are seated at a table in the back, and I sit next to her instead of across because I don't want to stop holding her hand.

"What color is your hair really?" Jordi asks while I'm browsing the menu.

I look up from the list of pastas and grin at her. "How do you know it isn't this color really? Maybe I was born with pink hair."

"A pink-haired baby sounds adorable."

"My hair's blond," I say. "Kind of like my mom's, but not quite so light. But it's easy because I don't have to bleach it to add the pink. It just shows up."

"I tried to do that once," she says. "But I think I did the bleach wrong, because the tips of my hair turned orange, and the next time I brushed it, a bunch fell out. I took it as a sign to just leave it like this."

"I like it like this," I say, and I start to touch her hair, but then the waiter shows up to get us drinks, and then somehow Jordi's taking photos again. The walls, the table, me.

"How do you know?" I ask. "If something's a picture?"

"Sometimes I'm just guessing," she says. "But the thing I love about photography is that for just a moment, you can make everyone else look at the world the way you see it."

I smile at that before having an idea. I take my phone out and take a picture of Jordi. If anyone saw this photo, they'd know what my whole world looked like right now.

After we split a tiny pizza and attempt to split a giant slab of lasagna, we head back outside to Jordi's car. I'm pretty sure she intends to actually drive somewhere right then, but I study Jordi's thin silver necklace glimmering in the day's last rays of sunlight with Maliah's necklace advice in my head.

So I don't buckle my seatbelt right away. Instead, I lean in to kiss Jordi, and not midway over the console like before. At a red light we'd kissed sweet, restrained, almost fully in accord with traffic laws.

I don't care about traffic laws now.

Literally mere days ago, I didn't even know if I knew how to kiss. But kissing doesn't feel knowable; kissing is something you *do*. It's like breathing. Jordi's lips are soft but they're also rough and it's gentle except when it's hungry.

Hunger—this kind of hunger—is another feeling I didn't know I was ever going to have.

"We should go," Jordi says as I'm kissing the space between her necklace and her t-shirt collar. "Abby. We're on a strict timeline."

"Are we seriously?" I laugh. "You're such a nerd."

"Well," she says, "it's not *that* strict."

"Good." I focus my attention back on Jordi's collarbone. I could lose myself here. Jordi probably doesn't care too much about her timeline because her hands trace lines down my arms and across my shoulders. Her breath sounds heavy and full of the promise of *us*.

"Wait," I say as her hands grasp my waist, and this new world we've entered dissipates. "Sorry."

"It's okay," she says but with a question mark in her voice.

"You're so tiny," I say. "I could probably put my hands around your waist. Well, I couldn't, I have little hands, but someone with big hands could."

"What are you talking about?" Jordi asks.

"When your hands are there, you know exactly how much space I take up," I say, and I feel silly and also worried and how did I think I could continue to make out with a girl without thinking about my size?

"You take up the right amount of space," Jordi says, and her hands are back on my waist. "Don't say things like that. Please."

"Okay," I say, but I feel out of breath and not in a good way.

"Why would I be here right now if I thought something wasn't right about you, Abby?" she asks. "I'm sorry if your mom's making you crazy with all of her solutions, but you know that's not how it really is."

"I guess."

"No," she says and holds my face so that I look right at her. "I mean it."

"Okay." I'm not sure if I sound any more convinced, but we start kissing again so I guess Jordi believes me.

Eventually Jordi says we're at the far end of our timeline, and so she drives through and past Downtown LA to a part of town in a neighborhood I don't know.

"Have you ever been to Pehrspace?" Jordi asks me as she searches for parking on a narrow, curving street. "I probably missed getting a really good spot because you distracted me."

"Oh, sorry you'd rather park than get kissed," I say, and she snorts. "I'll try not to be hugely offended. And, no, I've never been here. Where's here? What are we doing?"

"You're really impatient," Jordi says. "It's pathetic how cute I think that is."

She takes another couple turns and finds an open spot on the curb. "Pehrspace is this all-ages art space and venue for bands. Right now there's a photography show of street style up, so I thought you'd like it."

"Oh my god yes," I say, as we walk down the sidewalk. Jordi slides her arm around my waist and I think she's trying to make a point. Maybe I'm already a little used to it, though. "You're good at planning dates. You must do it all the time."

Oh my god, no. Not a thing to say.

"No, I . . ." Jordi smiles and looks down at her black Vans. "This is, in full honesty, my first date."

"Mine too!" I almost jump up and down. My wedges keep me from making any more of a fool out of myself. "We're totally on the same page."

Jordi looks right up at me. She's still smiling. "Good."

We take a turn off the street into a dingy strip mall, and if I didn't trust Jordi, I'd think I was about to be murdered. But then our destination becomes clear; in the furthermost corner is a crowd of people in a haze of beer and pot and clove cigarettes. It looks like an extended version of Jordi's crowd from school. I'm a little concerned I'll stick out in my candy-colored outfit, but two girls stop me on my way in to ask where my dress came from.

(I try not to sound too enthusiastic about my internet shopping habits, but it turns out I can only dial that back so much.)

"Hey, Jordi," the guy in the front room greets her. "You can just go on back."

"What about Abby?" Jordi holds up a five-dollar bill. "I'll pay for her."

The guy stamps our hands, and I follow Jordi into the next room, which isn't as crowded as it was outside. The walls contain photos of people downtown, of all ages, in outfits ranging from shredded jeans and old T-shirts to sparkly handmade gowns. The subjects are young and old, white and brown and black, conventionally beautiful and just normal.

"I get what you were saying about having defined style," Jordi says. "Some of these people just *do*, even if I've never seen them before. You can tell."

"This is amazing," I tell her. "I'm so glad you knew about this."

"Do you want to stay for a while?" she asks. "Some local bands are playing."

"Are they good?" I ask. "Should we?"

"Let's stay for the first one," she says. "I think you'll like them."

I'm pretty sure that Jordi is just trapped in some kind of first date fog that makes me seem cooler than I am, but then kids our age are setting up their instruments and launching into a song that sounds like a fuzzed out hissy version of something I'd listen to. The sound pounds in my chest, and I can't tell the bass drum apart from my thudding heart.

CHAPTER 13

My beeping phone wakes me on Sunday morning, even though I could lie in bed dreaming about Jordi for potentially an infinite amount of time. The texts are all from Jax, and I realize I haven't responded to him since before yesterday. *Whut up abbz* it starts, and by now has turned into *r u dead?* I reply with the news that I am still in fact among the living, and we quickly make plans.

After getting ready, I wave good-bye to Mom and Dad while calling out the vaguest information about Jax and lunch on my way out of the house. Jax's BMW is in the driveway, and it's funny how happy I am to see him. The morning after Maliah's first date with Trevor, Maliah and I walked to the restaurant called Home, which we normally avoided because the wait to get in was so epic. But standing in the line outside didn't even matter because there was so much to discuss. I always figured it would be Maliah who'd hear every last detail if the miracle of miracles happened and I actually had a first date. So it's funny that— now that we're living in miraculous times—Jax is the one I'm out with now.

"Did you die yesterday?" Jax asks over the banjo or ukulele or whatever other hipster stringed instrument is blasting from the speakers. "Twenty-four hours with no Abbs. It was rough."

"Sorry," I say, but I doubt he buys it because I'm smiling so wide.

"Shiiiiiit," he says. "Somebody got some."

"I did not *get some*," I say. "Wait—*get some* is sex, right? I did not have sex."

"I like to think it has a more fluid definition than that," Jax says, and I make a face. "What?"

"'Fluid'? Gross."

"Mature, Abbs. C'mon. What's the haps?"

"First, I should tell you that I tried to talk to Gaby for you and . . . honestly, Jax, I am not a good hype man. Hype woman. Whatever. I'm sorry."

"It's fine," he says. "Stop withholding important info."

So I tell him. The spilled beer and the bathroom floor and the kissing. The Italian restaurant and the photography show and the band and the gelato afterward. Being walked to my doorway like I'm old-fashioned and special.

To Jordi, I think I'm special.

"Hell *yeah*," Jax says.

"She's so great," I say. "Like, I can't believe how great she is. I feel like . . . how am I the only one to figure it out? There should be a million girls fighting me for her."

"That sounds incredible," Jax says. "Describe the fighting and the girls."

I elbow him. "You're a cliché."

We end up at The Fix on Hyperion, which we seriously could have walked to from my house. Jax's car love will kill the planet and his physical fitness, I swear. Playing lacrosse can only do so much, right? The constant car-driving and beer-drinking and burger-eating must outweigh it.

Honestly, I'm not even sure what lacrosse is.

I'm still really glad Jax is my friend.

I'm outside of Jordi's gate early on Monday, but she appears almost as soon as I arrive.

"Hi," I say but only partially because she covers my mouth with hers. It is a perfect greeting.

"So I've been thinking about it," she says, taking my hand and starting down the sidewalk. "We can't let Maggie know. Or anyone else at Lemonberry."

"Why not?" I ask, because how can I not talk about this? How can I sit near her without my hand in hers? How can I not look at Jordi like I'm poisoned and she's the only antidote?

"Abby, it's work," she says with a little smile. "We're professionals."

"Ugh, that's right, we are." I let go of her hand. "I'll try not to smile too much."

"You smile all the time," Jordi says. "It won't be suspicious."

"Jax said I was smiling extra yesterday," I say. "He totally figured it out."

"When do I get to meet Jax?" she asks. "I still have doubts about his existence."

124

"Jax would be the weirdest imaginary friend ever," I say. "I'm sure you'll meet him soon. He can be tough to escape. So, are you free Saturday? This coming Saturday? Five days from now?"

"Abby, I understand how days of the week work. And, yes. Second date?"

"Second date!" We round the corner, and Lemonberry comes into sight. "Okay. I'm taming back my happiness."

"Just outwardly, Abby," she says, and I laugh.

"Hey, girls." Maggie walks up from the opposite direction. "I'm exhausted. Mondays are terrible. Let's go get coffee before we go in."

We walk down the street to Starbucks. My hand bumps Jordi's a few times but I manage not to hold on. I'm also fairly certain that I have a normal smile on my face and not an obnoxious one.

It's tough judging that about yourself, though.

"So I got some fun news this morning," Maggie says while we're in line to order. "There's a sort of pop-up fashion show for local designers happening downtown this week, and Lemonberry will be part of it."

"Oh my god, that's amazing," I say. "It's so cool that fashion is happening outside of fancy upscale places in non-traditional—sorry. I'm geeking out."

"Abby, you have no idea how much I love that you're geeking out," Maggie says with a huge smile, but then turns to Jordi. "Would you happen to be free on Saturday? I'd love you to take photos of the show."

Jordi makes eye contact with me and I nod, and then

worry I'm relaying the wrong info, so I shake my head, and I can see in her eyes that she still has no idea what I'm trying to communicate.

"You'll get such cool shots," I say. Jordi smiles, in this very understated way I am not sure how to duplicate. "Maggie, I'm free too, and I can totally be there to post stuff and—"

"Abby, you're a doll to offer, but I can only bring so many people, and, anyway, you should enjoy your night off. I feel terrible enough I'm dragging Jordi in on the weekend. I'm not going to ruin both of your nights. And, Jordi, you can take one day off next week to make up for it. Sound good?"

No, none of it sounds good, but I nod anyway. Of course, Maggie's talking to Jordi and not me so it's even weirder that I'm lie-nodding.

"I'm sorry," Jordi murmurs while Maggie steps up to order a complicated latte. I hadn't realized a latte could have so many specifications.

"It's fine," I say. "We can reschedule."

"Not just that," she says. "You'd love being there, probably more than me."

"It's really okay," I say, even though I'm not sure I'd feel the same way if I wasn't now going out with Jordi. It's an opportunity I'm not getting, and of course Jordi's going to shine. She'll impress the hell out of Maggie and whoever else sees the photos. She'll impress people merely by shooting photos in front of them because she's such an obvious professional. How couldn't anyone see that?

But Jordi didn't ask for special treatment, and also it's not Maggie's fault that Jordi's so good at what she does. There's just really nothing tangibly impressive about tweeting. And that's probably a good thing for society, but right now it's a pretty lousy thing for me.

I finally *finally* hear from Maliah on Tuesday. *Pool at Trevor's. Wear your freaking suit. Bring my shirt if Jordi gave it back to you. See you soon.*

Sure, this sounds fun.

I want things to be okay and normal, so I do pull on my new nautical-themed one-piece, a fluttery yellow cover-up, and step into my gold sandals before leaving my room. Mom and Dad are sitting side by side and looking at Mom's laptop in rapt interest.

"Kiddo, look at this," Dad calls to me. "Your mom was listed on HuffPo as one of the top ten nutrition Twitter accounts to follow. Her follower count's going through the roof!"

"Oh . . . cool. Anyway, I'm going to Trevor's. Maliah's demanding it. See you later."

They sort of mumble good-byes to me, but at least I'm free to leave without any further questioning. The walk takes a while, but the June Gloom has finally turned into, well, just plain June. It's sunny and the sky is bright blue and I'm happy to be out in it.

I walk up to Trevor's just as Jax is. This is great news

because now I don't have to awkwardly figure out how to get in without bothering Maliah. It really feels like it's not the day to bother Maliah.

"Finally," she greets me as I walk in behind Jax.

"I literally got your text, changed, and walked over," I say. "I paused for about ninety seconds so Mom and Dad could tell me a thing about Twitter."

"Why don't you learn to drive?" she asks.

"Because anywhere I can't walk usually someone will take me to," I say. "Also, it's scary. It doesn't seem like the kind of thing just anyone should be allowed to do. Like, seriously, can you believe someone said that legally Jax should get to operate a motor vehicle?"

Maliah laughs. "You're way more responsible than Jax."

"How did I get dragged into this?" He tosses me a beer and runs off to join a circle of bros. It's only ten-thirty in the morning, so I walk the beer back over to the cooler and trade it for a can of fancy blood orange soda.

"I have your shirt," I tell Maliah.

"Good." She takes a sip of lemonade. "How's that going, anyway?"

"Jordi, you mean?" I want to appear exhausted with Maliah's attitude, but the problem is that I haven't mastered saying Jordi's name without smiling. "It's good. Really good."

"Be careful," she says.

"You can say that a thousand times, but it's still going to sound stupid to me."

"Abbs, I care about you." She gives me a look I think

she thinks is wise and knowing. "I just don't want you to get hurt."

"Well, I don't want you to get hurt either," I say. "But I never said anything when you first started going out with Trevor. I was like, a thousand percent supportive."

"Trevor didn't have *a record*," she hisses.

"Neither does Jordi," I say. "Why won't you believe me? When have I ever lied to you about anything, Mal?"

"Well," she says, "you apparently had a crush on Jordi and didn't even bother to mention it to me."

"Oh my god," I say. "Seriously? That's a thing you think is reasonable to say after how you're acting?"

She's wearing her hugest pair of sunglasses but I can still feel her eyes on me. "Okay. That's fair."

"Did I just win an argument with you?" I ask. "For the first time in the history of anything?"

"Oh, Abbs, shut up," she says but laughs. "That benefit was terrible, by the way. They had pictures of people with whatever this disease was, and by the time we left, I was convinced I had it, too."

"Your parents should know better than taking you at this point," I say.

"I know! They love to look like the perfect family—"

"You *are* the perfect family," I say, because, oh my god, the Joneses. They're all good-looking and fashionable and smart. Once Mr. Jones played tennis with George Clooney, and the paparazzi snapped pictures of him. A gossip blogger posted a pic with the caption *Who cares about Clooney?*

I want to hear all about this bangable hot black doctor, and I tried to show Maliah but she says she'll never look at anything related to her dad that contains the word *bangable*. And Mrs. Jones had her photo in *Los Angeles* magazine for being the first female cardiologist to perform a particular surgery. (I'm sure she was also written about in medical journals, but my family doesn't have a subscription to any of those.)

"Then I went home and Googled—"

"Mal, you know better than to ever Google," I say. "Please tell me you didn't go on WebMD."

"I'm only so strong," she says, and we both laugh.

"I don't want things to be weird with us," I say.

"I know." Her tone is easy. "Me either."

CHAPTER 14

The week goes faster than I want it to. I would have been living for Saturday, but now instead of carefully planning our second date, I'm home with my parents while Jordi's in the midst of the world of fashion. Maybe by next week, we'll work into each other's schedules better; organizing time isn't a romantic or sexy activity but I guess it's weirdly important when it comes to dating. But Tuesday I hung out with Maliah and Co. for most of the day, and Thursday Jordi had to entertain her brother.

Work's off-limits but also it's funny how it isn't. Maggie might step into her office and then I get to gaze at Jordi for a moment or she might run her fingertips down my arm. And then on the way home, we'll turn off Glendale Boulevard where it's quieter and shadier and I'll just say that there are approximately five thousand more spots to stop and kiss from that intersection to Jordi's gate than I could have guessed.

But tonight's not about kissing. Tonight is about counting out stacks of twenty-five promotional Eat Healthy with Norah! postcards to be sent to some sort of LA food event.

Well, tonight is also about checking all of Lemonberry's

social media feeds to see what's happening at the fashion show.

"How did that date go?" my dad asks, and I can't remember if I'm on twelve postcards or thirteen, so I start over.

"Greg," Mom says, and I hold my breath for what's coming next. "Girls don't like to talk to their dads about dating."

Considering how much of what my mom has to say is about eliminating delicious foods from your life, this is maybe the smartest thing she's said in years.

"I thought kids hated it when their parents weren't involved in their lives," Dad says, and I laugh.

"Yeah, Dad, that's what all the kids are sitting around talking about." But I feel bad for him with this stupid assistant work and his confused expression. "It was good. It was a good date."

I recount a stack and wrap a rubber band around it before refreshing everything on my computer, which is open next to me on the couch. Photos are up, and I can tell right away from their angles and sharp focus that they're Jordi's work. Laine is one of the models, and then there are two other models in Lemonberry dresses who are just as beautiful and well-coiffed. I am doing intern type work *for my parents* while Jordi is shooting pictures of beautiful women.

"This is harder than I thought it would be," Mom says from her computer. I have no idea what she's working on, but a Word document is up on her screen while Dad and I are counting out our stacks.

"Take a break, Nor," Dad tells her. "Abby and I can finish this."

"I might take a walk," she says. "If you really don't mind."

As soon as Mom's out the door, Dad says "Hey, go check my filing cabinet."

"What? Why?"

"Just do it."

Dad has this beaten-up gray filing cabinet that looks like it stored death records or something even more depressing in the 1950s. When he left his ad agency job, he loaded it up with his old files "just in case."

But now it looks like the bottom drawer is full of snacks. "Oh my god. Dad, you're a hoarder!"

"I'm a proud carbs hoarder," he says. "Look, I love your mom, and her food, but . . . a life without Chex Mix? It's not a life I want."

I grab a bag of Chex Mix for him and take a bag of Goldfish for myself. "Dad? Seriously, don't you hate this? Not the food-hoarding, but . . . being Mom's assistant? I swear I do more exciting things at my internship, and I'm only seventeen."

"It's not always that simple," Dad says, before scarfing down a few handfuls of Chex Mix. "I liked my job fine, Abby, but it wasn't my life."

"What did you want it to be?" I ask. "Like, you weren't seventeen and dreaming about media planning or whatever, right?"

"Kiddo, my life is your mom and you girls," he says. "So when it looked like it would be possible for your mom's career to really expand, I wanted to do anything I could."

"But didn't you used to do, like, big things at work?" I

ask, even though I'm not entirely sure what Dad's old job had consisted of. "And now you're counting postcards."

"I wasn't doing big things," he says. "I was working on spreadsheets and PowerPoint decks, and feeling like more of an order-taker than someone pitching big ideas. If I'd been fulfilled by it, I wouldn't have left—hell, your mom wouldn't have wanted me to leave. Believe it or not, I'm much happier now."

"Oh," I say, because this all feels like breaking news to me. Could stacking postcards actually somehow be Dad's life's work? At least he's making Mom happy. And I might be far from her biggest fan, but I can't deny their relationship is sort of admirable. Maybe even romantic, though I don't want to think about that. I might just feel weak because I'm home alone on a Saturday with my dad and promotional postcards and Goldfish crackers while Jordi's taking photos of models.

Oh, god, Jordi and models. I refresh my feeds again. There are more photos and, somehow, everyone gets more beautiful. I go back to the postcards. By the time I go to bed, the professional fashion show photos have stopped, and there's a casual one clearly snapped from someone's phone. The models are there, but so is Maggie, and so is Jordi. A model's arm is around Jordi's shoulders.

Obviously I don't actually think Jordi is hooking up with a gorgeous older model, but also it is not exactly the best thing to look at when you're me right now. And then my phone buzzes but it's just Jax, who seems to be mildly drunk and stuck at a party.

But luckily while I'm working on my blog the next morning, a text arrives from Jordi. *are you free today? my family's making empanadas and they're insisting i invite you.*

Oh my god, I get to hang out with Jordi, meet her family, *and* eat empanadas? This might be the best day ever.

I get permission from Mom and Dad, and then figure out a casual but cute outfit (my lemon shorts and a blue V-neck with pink sandals) before walking over. Should I be nervous about Jordi's parents? Yes, they're *insisting* I come over, but they don't trust Jordi after her fire photography. Maybe they're insanely strict with her. Maybe they don't even know that Jordi's gay and just think that I'm some girl she works with. I mean, I *am* some girl she works with, but what if that's all they know?

Still, for the first time, I don't wait at the gate. I walk in and then ring the doorbell.

"Hey." Jordi opens the door and smiles at me. "Come on in, Abby."

Jordi's house is *perfect*. I don't mean that in an *I like Jordi and therefore this house is perfect to me* way. Just like the shiny gate and the slate gray exterior, people have put thought into this house. Of course Jordi understands light and shadows and framing. The living room has olive green walls and then furniture in shades of blues and browns with framed artwork and photos scattered throughout. There's even a perfectly calm gray cat curled up on an orange ottoman like it was placed there by a stylist.

"That's Frankenstein's Monster," Jordi tells me. "Which

is why you should never let cat-naming fall to the young-est family member."

"The cat seems okay about it, at least," I say, and she smiles.

"Thanks for coming. I know this isn't the coolest way to spend today. My dad's really into honoring his family's recipes, or whatever, so we get roped into it sometimes, too."

"I'm super glad to be here," I say. "Though I feel bad because you planned our first date and now this is all you, too."

"No," she says. "Our second date is still ahead of us. My parents are involved, so this does not count as a date."

"Did you have fun last night?" I ask. "Your photos were amazing."

"It was . . . interesting. I'll tell you more later." She cocks her head to the side. "Are you wearing lemon shorts?"

"Be honest with me: do you think I have too many pieces of clothing that have fruit on them? Bear in mind an apples-and-pears skirt should be shipping to me this week."

"I think you have exactly the right amount of fruit cloth-ing," she says. "Come on. If I don't bring you in to meet my parents, they'll get demanding."

I'm about to ask what they know, but then she takes me by my hand and I guess they know the truth.

"Guys, Abby's here," she says as we walk into the kitchen where a couple around Mom and Dad's age is sitting at the kitchen table. The air is fragrant with a savory doughy smell, like someone was just baking, and ingredients have been set out along the counter like ground beef, onions, bright bell peppers, cans of tomato paste, and jars of spices.

Jordi's parents are, of course, cool, like they came as a matched set with this house. Jordi's dad has bold glasses and a very precise haircut, and he's wearing a James Perse T-shirt with jeans, which is the sort of look I should demand Jax investigate. Her mom has wavy hair like Jordi's, but it's longer and highlighted perfectly and completely goes with her flowy boho look.

"It's great to meet you." Mr. Perez stands up to shake my hand, and then Mrs. Perez does the same.

"I love your hair," she tells me. "It's like strawberry gelato."

"Oh my god," I say. "I *love* strawberry gelato. Thank you."

"Jordi says you're a genius with social media," her dad says.

"I'm . . ." I smile at Jordi. "I'm okay. It feels like a goofy thing to be good at."

"In this day and age? Not at all." Jordi's mom walks to the refrigerator. "Can I get you some juice or coffee?"

"Not so fast," Jordi's dad says. "We don't seem to have enough onions. Can I send you girls to the store?"

"For a fee," Jordi says, and her dad hands over some cash from his wallet. "Can we take Mom's car?"

"You can take my car," he says. "And go to Gelson's. Trader Joe's has garbage produce. See you in a few."

I follow Jordi into the garage and see why she wanted to take Mrs. Perez's car: it's an old Mustang. I'm sure I never want to drive, and I don't really care about cars, but *oh my god.* We get into the Prius, and Jordi turns down the volume on the blaring NPR.

"Hey," she says, and we kiss softly, like it's a secret between us. "I'm sorry I didn't text you last night. After the show, they brought me to this afterparty."

"Was it cool?" I ask as she backs out of the garage.

"I guess. It wasn't really my thing, but Maggie and Laine made it fun." She shoots me a look and then goes back to paying attention to the road. "We're not found out, but . . . we need to be extra careful."

"Why? What happened? Are there rules about dating? Is someone homophobic?"

Jordi squeezes my hand. "One question at a time. First of all, I accidentally drank, because one of the models, Aliyah, didn't know I was seventeen and gave me what I thought was juice. And I never drink so I was . . ."

I grin. "Drunk?"

"What's between normal and drunk? Tipsy? Anyway, they said some guy was checking me out, and then that turned into all these questions about if I had a boyfriend or not, and to get it all to stop, I told them I have a girlfriend."

A girlfriend.

"If that sounds like too much, just remember there were something like five women chanting *he's cute* and I didn't know what to do," Jordi says as she turns the car into Gelson's parking lot.

"It doesn't sound like too much," I say. "The girlfriend part, I mean. The chanting part sounds terrible."

"Okay," she says. And she smiles.

"What did the guy look like?" I ask. "Who was checking you out? Was he cute for a guy?"

She laughs. "No. Come on, let's get some onions."

We head to the produce section, but I forget that you can't get there without seeing an in-store display of their featured and semi-famous nutritionist.

"Oh my god," Jordi says. "I never noticed this before."

"I hate it," I say. "It's like my mom can watch me buy an orange."

"Well, today she can watch you help me pick out onions that my dad won't deem garbage," she says.

"Your parents seem really nice," I say, and then I'm not sure if I should take that opinion back. "Sorry, I know there was the whole thing with . . . it's none of my business and—"

"It's okay." She hands me an onion. "Seem good to you?"

"Jordi, this is *not* my area of expertise."

"My parents are . . ." Jordi sighs and runs her hand through her hair. "They're great. They support all my dreams and it was never an issue that I'm gay and they know I want to move to New York for college—"

"Oh my god," I say, even though I am well aware it isn't the right time to interrupt. "Me too!"

"That's really good news for me," she says. "Anyway. It makes it better and worse. My parents are normally the best. We never had fights like my friends seem to have with their parents. So when they didn't believe me . . ."

I squeeze her hand but it's holding an onion so I accidentally squeeze that instead, and we both laugh so hard that other people look.

Jordi feels secure that the onions we select aren't

garbage, and we head back to her house. A boy who looks a lot like Jordi but with glasses is in the kitchen with her parents, and he waves when we walk in.

"I'm Christian," he says. "I'm thirteen. I know I look younger because I'm short, but I'm thirteen."

"I'm Abby," I say and wave back.

"Okay, guys, let's get started," Mr. Perez says and directs us all to different parts of the counter and island. Mrs. Perez brings me coffee, fixed exactly how I like it, and then brings me an apron.

"You look too pretty to spill anything on your clothes," she tells me, and the compliment is so unexpected I just stare at her. "Everything okay?"

"Everything's really good, yeah." I try to look less awkward and tie the apron around my waist. It's longer than my shorts, and the top is wide, so I sort of look like I'm not wearing anything underneath. I turn to show Jordi, and she laughs.

"That's the shortest apron we have," Mrs. Perez calls.

Jordi snaps my photo.

"Hey," her dad says. "Be careful with that camera, Jordana. Your mom and I didn't let you combine Christmas and birthday gifts so you could get beef all over it."

"I'm nowhere near any beef," Jordi says, but I'm too hung up on something else to know whether that's true.

"Jordana?" I ask. "Is your actual name Jordana?"

"I should have never invited you over," she says but she's smiling.

"Have you ever made empanadas before?" Jordi's dad

asks me, and I shake my head. "Great! I can't wait to walk you through everything."

Jordi and Christian simultaneously groan.

"This takes long enough as it is, Dad," Jordi says. "Can you work and talk at the same time?"

Mr. Perez smiles but doesn't move to do any cooking. "Guys, this is your abuela's recipe. It's important to do it right."

"*Dad*," Christian says. "Do it right. Not talk about it all night."

"It's daytime," he says, smiling like he's gotten one over on his kids. Okay, maybe he isn't actually that much cooler than my dad.

"So I made the dough this morning, because it needs time to chill in the refrigerator," Mr. Perez continues. "We'll make the filling now. Jordi won't chop onions because her eyes are too sensitive—"

"*Dad*," she says.

"—so do you two want to split chopping the peppers? Jordi, show Abby how we like them."

"'How *we* like them'?" she asks, but I can see the smile in her eyes. "Come on, Abby. Also, Dad, please, can you blast anything but NPR while we work today?"

Yeah, he's definitely not actually that much cooler than my dad.

Jordi shows me how to chop the peppers to the desired size and we get to work while her mom chops onions, Christian chops hardboiled eggs, and her dad organizes the ingredients and heats oil in a giant sauté pan at the stove. Everyone compromises on a classic rock playlist that Christian calls *cheesy* but is full of the kinds of songs you wouldn't necessarily choose on their own but make you want to sing along.

Mr. Perez cooks the beef and then sautés the onions and peppers. He hands this duty off to Jordi at a certain point and directs Christian to add spices while Jordi stirs the pan. Mrs. Perez asks me to assist her, and we get out five glasses and a couple different beverages from the refrigerator.

"This is actually my favorite part," Mr. Perez tells me. "Help me divide up the dough."

We divide it into five chunks, and then Mr. Perez shows me how to roll it into little balls. Jordi and Christian, in the meantime, have stirred together all the ingredients, and then it's time to seal the filling inside the dough. The Perezes make a contest out of who can do it the fastest—seriously, their lemonades and iced teas are almost immediately forgotten—but I'm slow and methodical instead. The Perezes all swoop in and steal my remaining dough, and Christian is declared the winner. His empanadas are the sloppiest, but as he points out, speed was the goal, not precision.

We're released from our duties while the empanadas go into the oven so Jordi shows me down the hallway to her bedroom.

"Oh my god." I take in the sight of a bedroom that's much, much pinker than I expected. "You love Hello Kitty."

"Yeah," she says, smiling. "So?"

I look at the Hello Kitty stuffed animals on the bookcase, the Hello Kitty headphones on her desk, the Hello

Kitty-dressed-up-as-other-characters postcards stuck on a bulletin board. "It's a surprise. Hello Kitty doesn't seem very bad-ass. She's so *cute*."

"You can be cute and bad-ass at the same time." Jordi smirks at me. "Like you."

"Well, you do have sensitive eyes," I say, and she snorts.

"I should have never let you meet my parents."

I look at the framed certificates on the wall. "You won awards!"

"It was art camp," she says. "Everyone wins awards at art camp."

"'First Place in Photography,'" I read. "That doesn't sound like just a participation trophy."

Since she doesn't seem to mind, I keep exploring her room. I inspect a few framed photographs: the downtown skyline, the dry LA riverbed, a block full of brightly painted walls.

"Are these yours?" I ask.

She turns to see what I'm asking about. "They are."

"You're so good," I say. "Like, really good. I can't wait to see how your pictures from the other week turned out. When will they be ready?"

"Hang on." She sits down at her desk and opens her MacBook. "I can show you."

"What about this?" I gesture to a canvas that's been brushed over roughly with countless shades of red and textured bits of other items, like feathers and torn papers, captured within the paint. "Did you paint this? Or . . . create it, or however I should say it?"

"I did," she says.

"Jordi, seriously, you're *so good*."

"Sit down," she says with a smile, and we somehow perch together on her desk chair. The photos from the other week load in thumbnails, and then Jordi scrolls through each one, letting it fill the screen. The street, the sidewalk, parking lots, and me.

"That's cool," I say, because in the third photo of myself she shows me, my hair is caught in a breeze and extending horizontally across the frame. "I look like I'm magic."

She pulls gently on a lock of my hair. "You *are* magic. Do you want me to send you all the photos?"

"Maybe not all of them," I say. I'm still getting used to looking at myself like this. When you take a selfie, you control the angle and the frame and how much you reveal. I was out of control for these photographs. "This one, for sure."

She continues scrolling, and it feels like more and more of the photos are of me. There are angles of me I've never seen, and I can't say that I like all of them. It feels unfair that other people can know more about sides of you than you can. But then I stop worrying if my butt looks big or if my upper arms are too chubby, because I also look happy. It shows in my smile and my eyes and even how I'm standing with an ease I have never actually felt in my bones.

And, also, Jordi is sitting next to me and she looks happy, too. We kiss for a few minutes until there are parent footsteps in the hallway. But the good news is that lunch is ready, and there's something incredibly satisfying about eating something you had a hand in making. Food is Mom's domain at home, but here it feels like something the whole family shares.

After lunch, Mr. Perez loads up a huge Tupperware container for me, and Jordi asks her parents if she can walk me home. (Thank god they say yes.) When we arrive back at my house, I find a note scrawled in my dad's handwriting that says my parents are off to see "Maliah's dad's friend's movie."

"What does that mean?" Jordi asks me.

"George Clooney," I say, but I don't want to explain more because I have an empty house and a girlfriend in it.

CHAPTER 15

When I walk into work on Monday morning—alone because Jordi has the day off thanks to Saturday night's fashion show—there's a big box sitting on the desk in front of the computer.

"Surprise!" Maggie says.

I peer into the box, which holds a sewing machine. "Why?"

"It was just sitting around my house, and it's not heavy duty enough for what I need," Maggie says. "But it'll be a good starter machine for you to make some skirts and dresses."

"Thank you so much." I stare at the machine. I'm not sure anyone's ever given me such a nice and spontaneous gift before. "It's hard to explain to you how bad I was the time I tried sewing, though."

"You hear yourself, right?" She grins. "'The time'? The *one time*? You'll learn. I'll teach you."

"Maggie, thank you. You really don't have to."

"I'll feel selfish if I don't push the girl with the great style to at least try," she says, and I think about the fact that it's how Maggie sees me. I know she's not in high fashion in Manhattan or anything, but this is her world. And I'm not the fat girl or the loud girl or the girl who asks too many questions.

"The fashion show was really fun," she tells me.

"It sounded like it," I say, and then I'm not sure if it's weird I talk to Jordi if we aren't dating, which is of course what Maggie would think. "I mean, from seeing Instagram and everything."

"I'm sorry we couldn't bring you," she says. "But I'm sure you did something more fun with your night."

"Ha!" I say. "Unfortunately, I had to help my parents with Eat Healthy with Norah! stuff."

"Oh no," she says. "Though I'm afraid that's how I'll make Sam spend his weekends when he's a teenager."

"Do you have a kid?" I ask, though that might be way too nosy of a question.

"Yes, I try not to bore you guys with him because I could go on and on forever," she says, bringing her phone over to me. "He's six and he's amazing."

She scrolls through a few photos of an adorable boy who looks a little like Maggie but with darker, curly hair and his front teeth missing. Also, he's dressed a little better than Maggie, but most people are.

"Sam's a good name," I say, and Maggie smiles.

"Why don't you see if Paige needs anything out front, and if she's caught up, we'll go through the basics on the sewing machine," Maggie says. "Sound good?"

I suspect Paige won't need any help, and I'm right. While Laine seems to enjoy having Jordi and I assist her, Paige probably thinks that she can get more done without any teens hanging around. It would bother me more if today it didn't mean that I got more one-on-one time with Maggie.

"You don't have to show me this right now," I say, because while of *course* getting a sewing lesson from one of my favorite local designers is a dream come true, it's not really why I'm here. "I could be working on social media stuff."

"Don't worry about it," Maggie says, as though she's letting me off the hook. I try to relax because, seriously, *I'm so lucky right now.*

Maggie walks me through getting the machine threaded, and then I run scraps of fabric through over and over until Maggie's satisfied. A skirt is probably eons away, and a dress light-years longer than that, but I feel less stupid than the last time I tried this. And, the more I think about it, if Maggie had already bailed on the idea of me winning the job in the fall, she wouldn't be so patient and giving right now, would she? Or is this a bad sign that I'm learning how to sew instead of doing the thing I thought I was actually brought in to do?

Is it terrible how badly I still want the job? I'd be taking it away from Jordi. I'd be winning over *my girlfriend.* (I can't believe I have a girlfriend.) But she'll understand. After all, I'll understand if she's the winner.

Won't I?

I get summoned to the pool again this week, because I think that's potentially all that rich kids do with their time off from school. And, somehow, this is also my crowd now. I ask Maliah if I can bring Jordi if she's free.

Fine. Tell her not to burn down Trevor's house.

I mean, if you're going to be mean, at least be funny or clever about it.

When I get to Jordi's, she opens the door and steps aside. "Are we in a hurry?"

"No, why?"

"My parents are at work and Christian's at his friend's," she says.

I think I actually squeal aloud. "Oh my god, I get to make out with you in the Hello Kitty bedroom?"

"There's not that much Hello Kitty," Jordi says as we race down the hallway. I'm only wearing shorts over my yellow and white striped swimsuit, and now that we're kissing, I'm aware of just how much skin's showing. It's like a wave; my worry starts off small and then as Jordi's hands grasp my sides, it's bigger, except then we keep kissing and my mouth aches and my arms are wrapped so tightly around her shoulders that I'm on my tiptoes. And then the fear's washed away.

"Do you want to sit there?" Jordi asks and nods to her bed. We kissed for a while in my room on Sunday, but we were standing the whole time.

"Yes," I say and wait for her to sit first. "I'm not ready to take off any of my clothes yet."

I wonder if I was thin if I would be. I really hope not.

"Well, me either," Jordi says with a smile, and immediately I feel less like my fatness is some kind of problem for us. "I'm in no rush for anything."

And so we kiss until our lips feel chapped, and then we kiss a little more. Our hands skim each other's arms and backs and sides, but we're still in very G-rated territory with each other. Well, I'm very aware that my boobs are smooshed against hers, but where else would they go? I'm glad that we're on the same page, but I'm also glad I said something to begin with. It's crazy how quickly someone can feel so safe.

When we're at Trevor's gate, I text Jax instead of Maliah, and it feels like he appears in record time. "Hey. Mal said I could bring Jordi."

He shrugs. "There's not a guest list. And any friend of Abby . . ."

Jordi waves. "Hey."

Jax nods at me. "Nice."

"Dude," she says. "I'm standing right here."

"It was a *compliment*," he says. "I'm Jax."

She grins. "Of *course* you are."

"Bam. My reputation proceeds me." He gestures through the gate. "Come on back."

I slip my arm through Jordi's. "Is he as bad as you imagined?"

Jordi laughs. "About as bad. Potentially worse."

Maliah glances over from her spot on the brick wall as we walk into the backyard. "It's about time."

"If you always say that, it's not very effective," I say. "Also, hi."

"Hi," she says coolly. "Hello, Jordi."

"You're the girlfriend?" Trevor asks her. I swear that his bicep is like the size of Jordi's head so it's weird to see him standing near her.

"That's me."

Jax brings us a couple of beers, and I pop mine open without thinking about it. Jordi shakes her head, though.

"I'm cool. Is there water?"

"Anything for Abby's girl." Jax swaps the can for a bottle of water. I will say that the boys are very good at providing beverages to guests. "Abbs, my dad says we're doing good work on Best Blank."

"How is it work?" Maliah asks. "Don't you guys just eat burgers and rate them?"

"It's a five-pronged system." Jax holds up his hand and counts off each one. "Taste, quality, service, value, selection."

"I don't get why you need Abby to do that." Maliah unwraps a popsicle that seems to have appeared from nowhere. I would love a popsicle right now. "Can't you just look up every burger place and guess?"

"This is important," Jax says, and his normal bro tone sounds a bit dialed up. "My dad told me to input real data so when this launches for real, people can rely on it. Also, Abbs and I are having a good fucking time. Why you wanna take that away from us?"

"Yeah, Mal," I say. "Why you wanna?"

"You guys are so weird," she says.

"Does anyone actually get in the pool?" Jordi asks.

"Yeah, you wanna get in the pool?" Jax pulls off his Westglen Prep T-shirt. "Cannonball you."

"What? That isn't a verb." Jordi shakes her head, though she does step out of her shorts and hand them to me. Is it weird that I like being in charge of Jordi's shorts?

Jax races her to the pool, and before long, they're both in and splashing at each other. Also, Jordi looks skilled and strong in the water, and I like that people know she's with me.

"Her suit's cute," Maliah says, which feels like a huge step forward.

But I need to clear up important matters first. "Where did you get the popsicle?"

I find a ton of instructional sewing videos on YouTube, and when I post to Tumblr that I just got my first sewing machine, lots of people comment or message with links to patterns. Maggie gave me some fabric to get started with (nothing as nice as what Lemonberry dresses are made from), but after a few false starts, I make a bag that I wouldn't be embarrassed to use for shopping.

It feels powerful to make something for yourself. I had no idea.

Mom pokes her head into the room. "What on earth is that sound? Oh, wow, you're trying that again."

"I think I might be doing better this time," I say. I don't want Mom to feel like I'm eager to bond with her, but I also don't want her to think my disastrous class at Sew L.A.—that she'd paid for, after all—was repeating itself in my bedroom. "See? I made a bag."

"Honey, that's actually nice," she says. "Can you make me a green one?"

I riffle through the fabric. "I don't have any green, but maybe I can get some."

She sits down on my bed behind me. "You know that I just want the best for you, Abby, right?"

"Is this about me being fat?" I ask.

"Don't call yourself that," she says.

"Why not? It's not an insult, just a thing. A thing I am."

"I just want you happy and healthy and—"

"I'm very healthy. Dr. Misra says so. Remember?"

"Hmmm," Mom says. Every year after my annual physical, it seems she's determined something's wrong with me that could be cured by skinniness. "That's not exactly what I meant."

Adults say things like this when they didn't expect you to catch on to their supposedly subtle coded messages. You're expected to be mature but you're also taken for a child.

"I exercise more than you and Dad do," I point out. "I walk everywhere."

"That's actually what I wanted to talk to you about," she says. "Don't you think it's time you got serious about getting your driver's license?"

"No," I say. "I'm going to New York for college. I'll take the subway everywhere."

"What if you want to take a road trip?" she asks.

"I won't." When we were little, Dad's best friend Andrew lived in San Francisco, so the four of us would drive up every summer to spend a week in a hotel where you could see the Golden Gate Bridge if you looked out the window the right way. And none of that was worth it for the combined twelve hours there and back in the car with my family. "Trust me. Road trips are terrible."

"They're more fun when you're with your friends," Mom says with a smile like she can read my mind. "Can we work on this your senior year?"

I shrug.

"That's all I wanted to talk about," she says. "Okay? I don't know why it always has to turn into an argument with us."

"Seriously?" I ask. "It doesn't seem like much of a mystery to me."

Mom sighs. "I'm sorry that I thought you were going on a date with Jax. I didn't at all mean to offend you, Abby. I didn't realize that you'd . . ."

"Stayed gay?"

She shakes her head. "That's not what I meant either. Abby, I just came in here to see if you wanted to get your learner's permit. That's it."

For a tiny moment, I feel sorry for Mom. I'm no fan of her brand, but I know she works hard constantly. She built Eat Healthy with Norah! from the ground up, and now she's on TV and will have a book. I want to be proud of her.

But I also know that everything about me disappoints her. So the rest kind of fades away.

"I don't," I say.

"Fine, Abby."

Without thinking, I look to Rachel's side of the room, like she'll magically be there and will crack the right joke to perfectly diffuse the tension. But it's just Mom and me and all the same problems between us.

CHAPTER 16

"Is it possible to be romantic without a car?"

Maliah's face is suddenly deep in thought. "Hmmm."

"Yes," Zoe says. "Anything can be romantic if you want it to."

"Oh dear god." Brooke nearly spits out her bubble tea. We're out front of the tiny Boba Loca just down the street from Lemonberry, and my second date with Jordi is only hours away. Brooke and Zoe are pro-boba, but Maliah and I agree that you shouldn't have to chew a beverage, so we're both sipping regular smoothies.

"Zoe's gotten cheesier now that she has a boyfriend," Maliah says. "Much cheesier."

"He's not my boyfriend," Zoe says and blushes. "We're just talking a lot."

"And you *made out*," Maliah says.

The rest of us practically scream as Zoe hides behind her boba as best she can.

"Are you planning a date without a car?" Brooke asks me.

"With your *lady?*" Zoe asks, and now it's me who's blushing.

"Yes. I thought of everything for our second date—Jordi

156

totally planned the first one—but now I'm rethinking all of it. Is it stupid?"

"What else are you going to do?" Maliah asks. "Have your dad drive you?"

"Oh god, no," I say. "Ask her to drive? That just seems . . . I don't know. Ugh, god, maybe my mom is right about one thing."

"Actually, using an avocado instead of cheese is also a good tip," Brooke says. "What? I read her blog to support your family, Abby."

"Don't worry," Zoe says. "Since Jordi really likes you, she'll be fine with walking. She'll *love* walking. I don't think Brandon can drive, and that's fine."

"She'll make Brooke drive them around on dates," Maliah says, and we burst into laughter.

"It seems easier to date a girl," Brooke says.

"I agree." Zoe sips thoughtfully on her drink. "If you have your period, a girl would understand and bring you tea and chocolate."

"And you can trade clothes," Brooke says.

"Trevor gives me chocolate," Maliah says.

"And Jordi and I don't exactly wear the same size," I say. "Or style. You guys make being a lesbian sound like a Hallmark Christmas movie."

"I'd watch that," Brooke says.

"I was remembering something from last year," Zoe says. "We had to do this optic mix project in art class, where we made an image from cutting up other images? It's sort of hard to explain. Most people's didn't look great, but

Jordi's, oh my god. Everyone else just cut out pictures from magazines, but she took a bunch of photos of her own eyes and then made a big image of an eye out of them. I mean, some people thought it was creepy—"

"It sounds creepy," Maliah says.

"—but it was amazing. I thought Mrs. Avakian was going to lose her mind that a student was that good."

"Look at her." Brooke points to me. "She's beaming with pride."

"Get it?" Zoe laughs. "Gay pride."

"You guys are so stupid," I say, but we're all laughing. Even with Maliah being such a drag lately, I realize I'm so lucky to have the friends I do. And when I arrive later to pick up Jordi, right away I feel how little it matters that I'm not in a car.

"This is exciting," Jordi says as I point the way down the street. "Do I get a hint?"

"No way."

"Damn." She grins at me, and it's hard maintaining my composure. She's wearing a very Jordi outfit today, of course—black jeans and a sort of shimmery black tank and black high tops—and how we look together is something I realize I'm starting to like.

"What did you do today?" I ask. "Exciting stuff?"

"Actually . . . I sent some info a while back, and it looks like I'm going to have a photography show at Pehrspace in August."

"Oh my god, Jordi, that's huge! I didn't know you were trying to get a show."

"I didn't want people to know," she says. "In case it didn't work out or go anywhere. But, yeah. It's happening."

"I'm so proud of you," I say, and I worry it's too much for someone I've only been going out with for a couple of weeks. But Jordi focuses her grin on me and leans in to kiss me.

"Thank you, Abby," she says. "You have to be my date, and you have to wear something extra awesome."

"It's a deal," I say. We're making plans for *August*.

"Are we going to Mixto?" Jordi asks as the sign comes into focus. "I love Mixto."

"Yes, and, good," I say. "I just realized maybe it was weird to plan to take you to a Mexican place, because you're . . . Mexican?"

"Well, my grandparents were all born there, but I've been here my whole life, and so have my parents," she says. "So don't worry. I love hipster Mexican food."

"Here's my secret about this place," I say. "I'm sort of obsessed with their kale Caesar salad. But please, please, *never tell my mom*. It would make her way too happy."

We end up getting the salad, a selection of tacos, and horchata and settle in the back corner of the outdoor dining area. We're only about a mile from our neighborhood, but being in Silver Lake is just inherently *cooler* than Atwater Village.

"Hey, Abby," someone says from behind me. I turn around, and it's Lyndsey Malone. "Oh, hi, Jordi."

"Hey," we say, sort of at the same time.

"Oh, hello, ladies." Blake Jorgensen walks up to her. "I see you're enjoying some *horchata*." He pronounces it with what I guess he thinks is an authentic accent, and I notice that Jordi is suddenly staring at the table and blinking. I look away because if we make eye contact right now, there's no chance of not laughing.

"How's your summer been?" Lyndsey asks.

"Um," I say, testing my restraint by smiling at Jordi. Neither of us laughs. "Really good."

"I think our food's ready," Lyndsey says. "See you guys around."

We say good-bye and wait until they're fully around the corner to laugh. It's funny how mere weeks ago, this would have killed me. They were holding hands and Blake was making his I'm Very Serious And Never Smile face and Lyndsey looked happy.

But I don't care. Well, I might care a little. I can still see that Lyndsey is crush-worthy, and no one nice should have to date Blake. But none of it seems like my failing now, and I guess that's because it never was.

After we've finished eating, I direct Jordi across Hyperion Boulevard and a few blocks down to West Silver Lake.

"You don't mind walking, right? Maybe I should have asked sooner."

"Not at all." Jordi lets go of my hand, but since it's to take out her camera, it doesn't bother me. "I should have taken a photo of Blake. It would've come in handy if I ever needed something to throw darts at."

"Oh my god," I say. "That guy's the worst. How does Lyndsey stand him?"

"He seems smart," Jordi says. "He either fakes it or is also smart under his layer of . . ."

"Douchiness?"

"Exactly. She wanted someone smart, and he was close enough."

"I used to have such a crush on her," I admit.

"Me too," Jordi says, which makes me laugh. I don't even stop when I realize Jordi's camera's lens is pointed right at me. The camera has stopped feeling like something separate; it's an extension of Jordi.

"Where are we going?" she asks me.

"It's also a surprise," I say. "Everything's a surprise. You can't get any more info out of me than that."

"You'd be a good spy," she says.

"What are you talking about? I'd be terrible! I always say way too much. You'd be amazing at it, especially because you're usually in all-black."

"You should hear my mom since she met you," Jordi says. "'Jordi, see how nice Abby looks because she isn't afraid to embrace color?'"

I laugh as we turn the corner and Silver Lake Reservoir comes into view. It looks like a lake from far away, but once you're close, you can see that it's concrete-lined. When we were younger, it was a regular thing for Dad to take Rachel and me around it at night. About midway through, you can see the Silver Lake Dog Park, and since Mom's allergies prevented us from having our own dog, it was heaven to spend a little time watching through the fence.

Not that I plan to watch dogs tonight with Jordi. We're just walking past to get to the other side of Silver Lake Boulevard.

"I love it back here." Jordi takes pictures of houses cut into the hills. "My parents say it costs more than I realize to live up there, but after college, it's exactly where I want to end up."

"My parents always say things like that, too. 'Abby, you have no idea how much we could get for this little house in today's market.'"

"Yeah, *today's market*." Jordi laughs. "I hope to god I don't grow up to care about today's market."

"I hope you don't either." I gesture to my favorite ice cream shop, Milk. "I hope this is okay. I love this place."

"It definitely is," she says. "I love it, too."

"We love all the same places," I say. "That feels like a good sign of compatibility."

Jordi pokes my side as we get into the line stretching out past Milk's door. "Were you worried about our compatibility levels?"

"Super, super worried."

"Can you hold this a second?" She hands me her camera and I cradle it, honestly, more carefully than when I had to hold a baby cousin last year at Christmas. Jordi digs around in her black bag with intense concentration. I envision sewing her something new, but I don't know how to create what I see in my head. Maybe Maggie can help me, and if not Maggie, the internet.

"Okay," Jordi says, taking a little black paper bag out of

her bigger black bag. "I made this and . . . I think it turned out okay. But you don't have to like it. Promise me you won't say you like it if you don't."

I hand the camera back to her and then open the bag. Inside is a bright blue acrylic pendant cut into the shape of a pineapple, hanging on a silver chain. "You *made* this?"

Jordi nods while I turn the perfect necklace over and over in my hands. "Do you . . . like it?"

"No," I say. "I love it. I'm obsessed with it. I want to wear it with everything I own."

I take off the heart-shaped necklace I'm wearing it, tuck it away in my purse, and start to put on Jordi's necklace.

"Let me," she says, and now I hold her camera as she fastens it around my neck. The necklace is cool against my throat, but Jordi's fingertips are warm. I know we're in a line for ice cream surrounded by children and older people, but suddenly I want her fingertips all over me.

Obviously I settle for standing in the grass together eating ice cream cones instead.

Jordi, of course, takes photos: the street, the hills, a dog we spot standing on a balcony above. And me, always me. Maybe it should be more distracting, but the photographs are also a record that this is real. And it's still just a little hard to believe that this is in fact what's happening to me this summer.

"Okay, I saved the best for last," I say when our ice cream is a distant memory and Jordi's camera has been silent for a few minutes. "Hopefully. If you've been there before, it won't be that exciting."

"I've been to Mixto and Milk before," she says. "They were still exciting."

We walk back the way we came, but I point us in a slightly different direction once we're past the Reservoir. I don't know why it matters so much to me that Jordi hasn't seen this yet, but my stomach's clenched in anticipation. I want badly to show her something new.

"Oh my god." Jordi stares up at the chandeliers suspended from a tree just off Shadowlawn Avenue. "What is this?"

"It's someone's home," I say. "He just did this because it's beautiful."

Jordi stares up at the different fixtures hanging from the wide-stretching branches. The golden glow glimmers within the leaves. "It's incredible."

I take my change purse out of my bag, because the man who owns the tree and the house installed an old-fashioned parking meter to help pay his electrical bill. I drop in all the coins I have and then Jordi does the same. Since her hands are in her bag, I assume her camera will come back out.

But it doesn't.

"Not yet," she says with a knowing smile.

Then we kiss underneath the glow of dozens of light-bulbs shimmering in a tree. And for just this moment, my world is a fairy tale.

CHAPTER 17

Jax texts me early on my next weekday off from the shop to line up burgers for lunch. I'd been hoping to make plans with Maliah or Jordi, but I realize there's no sense of disappointment waiting outside for Jax instead.

Seriously, weirdest summer ever.

"Met this hot girl last night," is how he greets me over the inescapable sounds of indie rock dudes yodeling.

"Good for you." I buckle in. "Where to today?"

"I dunno, Abbs, the whole city's our playground."

I side-eye him before opening the note on my phone with a list of burger places. "We haven't done In-N-Out yet."

"Bam." He tears off down the street and we slap each other's hands trying to maintain control over the car stereo's volume. "You wanna hear all about this girl?"

"What happened to Gaby?" I ask.

"That was not gonna happen," he says. "Alas. So I move on."

"Hmmm," I say.

"Don't judge me. We don't all get the girl we're after."

"I was actually thinking that sounded pretty mature," I say. "So, yeah, tell me about the girl."

"One, super hot. Two, made a joke at Trevor's expense so she won me over. Three, talked to me for like the last hour of the party until one of her friends made her take her home. Bam, I'm as good as in."

"Sounds like it." I wonder what it would be like to be Jax, with all the confidence in the world as far as girls are concerned. Would I have kissed Jordi a week sooner? Does that even matter now, when my life involves kissing Jordi Perez almost every single day as it is?

"So we gotta figure out my next move," he says.

"'We gotta'? Aren't you the expert on next moves?"

"Abbs, what have I been saying? You know I need your girl guidance."

I watch out the window as the shaded and gated mansions on Los Feliz Boulevard fly past us on our way to Hollywood. It still seems like a miracle I could be someone anyone goes to for girl advice.

"Be nice," I tell him. "Don't pull your weird bro stuff on her."

"I'm always nice," he says, and I laugh and roll my eyes.

"I'm really not an expert," I say. "But being nice feels sort of obvious, right?"

He makes a face but I'm fairly certain he agrees.

"It's weird you can . . . just get a girlfriend, and still it's not like anyone swings by to tell you how it's supposed to go," I say.

"Some lesbian fairy godmother?" Jax asks.

"*Exactly*. Instead I've just got you and Mal, and you're hopeless and Mal thinks Jordi's a criminal."

"I've got *great advice*," he says. "Just be nice."

"It's weird that Jordi and I are, like, competitors," I say. "I mean, I still really want to win and get the job and all of that."

"Yeah, who wouldn't?"

"Someone nice? I don't know."

"You can get the girl *and* the job, Abbs," he says, and I feel good for like a half-second before thinking about the fact that these comforting words are coming from my bro friend, spawn of a Silicon Valley app-running man.

And maybe you *can* get the girl and the job, but can you be nice, too, on top of all of it?

But, also, I don't really have to dwell on it today. Within a few minutes, we're in the long, snaking drive-thru line to the Hollywood In-N-Out, and even though it always looks like it'll take hours to get food, before we know it, we're parked in the lot scarfing down Animal-style burgers with fries and milkshakes. It's sort of a stereotype of a California day, but what a great stereotype.

Since I'm wearing semi-responsible shoes (floral patterned Adidas that look perfect with my bright blue dress), and we're basically over here anyway, I suggest walking around the Hollywood Reservoir. Jax whines a little but then agrees, and before long, we're on the path in Lake Hollywood Park. It's flatter than the Silver Lake Reservoir, which is a lot closer to my neighborhood, but it's longer and I know will take us a big chunk of our mid-afternoon. Maliah and I always manage to talk the entire way around, but I feel less urgency to fill every silence with Jax.

I guess I thought that friendship was something you'd always need in one specific way, but it basically goes without saying that my friendship with Jax is nothing like mine with Maliah, and somehow not in a way that makes it *worse* . . . or even better. It's just its own thing.

I come to Lemonberry the next day with my notebook of ideas tucked into my pocket. (All truly great dresses have pockets.) I've yet to solve the riddle of being a great girlfriend while landing the job, so in my other pocket is a little Hello Kitty sticker. I found it while attempting to organize a pile of crafty stuff Rachel and I had been accumulating for years now. I'd texted to make sure Rachel didn't mind the organization, as we used to fall asleep while discussing our grand plans for our collection of fabrics, glitter, stickers, and other items we deemed spectacular enough to save. But her only response was a delayed *No, why would I care?*

Paige is manning the front of the store, and Maggie's not in yet, so it's just Jordi and me in the back room. I resist kissing her (unprofessional), but I do press the sticker into her palm. Her hand is warm and I think about it against mine, or on my body (also unprofessional, if I'm being fair).

She examines it and smiles her slow Jordi smile as Maggie walks in and directly over to her.

"Good morning, girls."

"Good morning," I say in my brightest, cheeriest voice (professional?).

"Jordi, we got a couple of new pairs of shoes in yesterday," she says. "Would you mind taking some shots for the site and for Instagram?"

She, of course, agrees, and heads out to the sales floor. My hand goes into my pocket and clasps around my notepad of ideas.

"I thought we could maybe do a hashtag of—" I stop myself because it sort of seems like I started in the middle and not the beginning. "I had some thoughts on Instagram, and—"

"That's great, Abby," Maggie says, though does it ever feel great getting interrupted? "I thought you could update inventory for online orders. Let's try to find time to talk about Instagram and everything else later, okay?"

"But . . ." I don't mean to glance toward the sales floor as if I have X-ray vision and can watch Jordi work, but I realize my face is pointed in that direction anyway.

"I know, it seems like Jordi's getting the fun, easy work, but this is so valuable to me, and I honestly always have fun doing it. I love seeing what people are buying most."

"It's not about fun," I manage to say, and it's true. Everything at Lemonberry is pretty fun. Even steaming dresses, potentially the most boring task on the planet, feels like magic when dresses go from wrinkly messes to flowing works of fashion. "I just know that you liked all my social media stuff when I interviewed, so . . ."

Maggie smiles right at me, in that special way that convinces you that you're her whole world. No matter how untrue you know it is.

"I *love* your social media stuff, Abby. But ultimately the internship is about helping out where we need it, and today that's inventory. We'll find time to talk soon, though, okay?"

I nod, not just because I'm still in the glow of her smile, but because I also can see that she's right. Before the summer started, I wouldn't have thought there were so many parts to making a shop great. But Maggie has to think of them all and then make sure they're actually taken care of. Clothes have to hang perfectly and dust can't gather on fixtures and window displays can't appear stagnant and forgotten. And filing isn't, like, *fun*, but obviously, it's essential. And I *like* that I'm a part of it all.

It's true Jordi gets to do the thing that Jordi is specifically very good at, but as I survey our recent orders, I remind myself that what I'm doing matters, too. And if Maggie can look this relieved when I give her the updated report, hopefully she sees that, too.

But of course the truth is that I don't know what Maggie's thinking at all.

Maliah meets me at my house after work, and I'm glad we have plans tonight even though I just lost several minutes inside Jordi's gate with my fingertips on the bare skin of her lower back and her lips on mine. There's so much that I didn't know before, like that you could see someone all day long and yet still feel physically unable to get enough of their kisses, or that someone's hand on the back of your neck could make you feel like you're melting but in a good way.

"Did you have to work late?" Maliah asks with a look to the time on her phone.

"Sure," I say while realizing my lip gloss is probably smudged. "What do you want to do?"

Maliah pats the bumper of the Honda in the driveway. It's covered in more than a fine layer of dust, dirt, and pollen. "Isn't this your car?"

I shrug. "It's technically my mom's. Rachel got to use it, and now I could. If I wanted. Which I don't."

"You have been my best friend my entire life," Maliah says.

"Since fifth grade," I say.

"Ugh, details. Anyway, I know you better than anyone else."

I don't correct her, mainly because I know my connection with Rachel is different. Sisters and best friends are good in a lot of the same ways, but that doesn't make them the same. Of course, maybe I don't even have that with Rachel anymore.

"This is the thing I don't get about you," Maliah continues. "You could have so much more freedom with this!"

"You'll never convince me," I say. "I'm going to college in New York. And I like walking. I have exactly as much freedom as I need. Also, whatever! You're always saying you don't get things about me, like when I said strawberries aren't overrated."

"Oh my god, how can you even think that?" Maliah pauses and then bursts into laughter. "Why do I take that so seriously?"

"I'm terrified to know. Look, I don't want to drive. Does it have to be a thing? Does it have to *keep being a thing?*"

We stare each other down because we are not the kind of best friends who like losing to each other. It hits me that if I were competing against Maliah for the Lemonberry job, I might have strong-armed my way into Maggie's office for a social media meeting today.

Is it bad to know that?

Is it worse to know it and also that I might not do anything about it?

"What?" Maliah asks, because she's right that we know each other extremely well.

"I wish I didn't have to compete for the job at the store," is what I tell her. "Please don't say anything mean about Jordi. You don't want secrets, so there you go."

"You're going to get the job," Maliah tells me. "Don't even worry about it."

"That is not how not worrying works, Maliah!"

She laughs. "Come on. Zoe and Brooke are over at Wanderlust getting ice cream."

"What? We could have already been walking toward ice cream and you took this long to tell me?"

"I'm a monster, right?"

CHAPTER 18

Maliah and Trevor are not exactly my favorite couple—whether or not that makes me a bad person—but one good thing about them is that there isn't any drama. Before my best friend fell in love, that's the main gist I got from overhearing other people's relationship talk at school. There's jealousy, misunderstanding, ignored texts, someone else. But Maliah and Trevor have never been that.

And maybe that's a little why Jordi and I aren't either, but also because I can't even imagine wanting to fight with Jordi. I can't imagine Jordi's tone stern or angry with me. Instead I imagine the year stretching out before us, school and Homecoming and the tree-lighting at The Americana. I don't know which one of us gets the job at Lemonberry but the other one can hang out there, at least the shifts when Laine's working. Laine loves having us around.

Not that I don't want to get the job. Not that I don't still hope that it's me. Not that I don't keep a running tally in my head of our chances. Jordi gets fashion shows, but I get private sewing lessons. Jordi has the air of a professional, but I'm the one who lives and breathes fashion. Photographers are probably more expensive to pay than bloggers—I assume—but does the savings matter when the job is mainly going to be straightening clothes on racks and operating a cash register?

Also, I can't help but worry that it's not, like, morally sound to want to beat your girlfriend at something like this. Shouldn't I want the best for her over myself? I'm not sure how it sorts out. I'll be happy if the job's awarded to her at the end of next month, but also I won't be. So for now I'll just try to do my best and put the rest out of my mind because otherwise I might lose it. My mind, that is, not the job.

Though I guess maybe the job, too.

"Hey, Abby?"

I look up as Maggie walks out of her office, or maybe she already walked in a moment ago while I was running through scenarios in my head. I've definitely been less day-dreamy since my first day, but there's still vast room for improvement.

"I got you a present." Maggie hands me a bag from a fabric store. "That's everything you said you wanted for your project."

"Maggie, you totally didn't have to. I just wanted your advice on where I could find it." I look in the bag and see every single thing I asked about: black canvas, sage green canvas, a shiny gunmetal fabric, and—"Oh my god, Hello Kitty fabric exists!"

"I told you that I'd seen it before," she says. "I also thought you'd want to put a pouch in the bag, so I got you an extra zipper, and hardware for the strap so you can make it adjustable."

"Whoa," I say. "I think that's past my ability level. I just made, like, a couple bags that my mom's using for grocery shopping. Zippers?"

"I think only the Amish are allowed to be overwhelmed by zippers," Maggie says. "And, silly, I'll be helping you. Are you doing anything tonight? You can stop by my house. Wait, I'm sorry. Is that appropriate? I have no idea."

I can't even imagine what Maggie's house must be like, if her workspace is weird piles of paper and her clothing is faded concert T-shirts and expensive but very worn jeans.

I would, obviously, really like to see it.

"I'm free tonight," I tell her. Sure, I've gotten some texts from Jax about getting burgers, but that can wait. Ever since I got the idea to make a bag for Jordi, I've wanted to actually do it, but I knew I wasn't even ready enough to mention it to Maggie much less *make it* before practicing more at home. Mom now has a whole set of green bags of varying quality to take to Gelson's and the Atwater Village Farmers' Market.

"Great. If you don't mind hanging around a little later than usual, I can drive you from here. Sound good? Again, unless it's too weird."

"I don't think it's weird," I say. "Or I don't care, because I definitely need your help on this. You're really okay giving up your evening to help me?"

Jordi walks in from the front, camera in hand.

"Of course, Abby," Maggie says.

I realize I have the bag from the fabric store wide open,

so I quickly close it and roll it so that there's no way any-one could see into it. Maggie seems to notice me doing it, but she doesn't say anything.

"I was going to eat," Jordi says. "If it's a good time for you to break, too."

"It is." I try not to glance at Maggie to survey her face for signs of suspicion. It would be normal for Jordi and me to hang out at work if we were just fellow interns, wouldn't it? Ugh, maybe not, considering that we're also rivals for the job. Hopefully our friendliness just adds to whatever professionalism we're already projecting.

I know my parents are out running errands today, so Jordi and I head there under the guise of leftover zucchini pizza bites in our fridge. But of course we head back hungry, because once we were alone inside, she leaned into me and my hands outlined all her lean curves. Almost like magic, we were on my bed, and now that we're in public again, almost back at work, I feel like we pulled off some brilliant heist. How could a standard lunchbreak compare to making out with Jordi Perez?

"You look suspiciously happy," Jordi tells me as we approach Lemonberry.

"Too happy for getting a burrito at Hugo's?" I ask, since that had been our cover story. But I'm still smiling as scenes replay in my head.

"Definitely out of proportion for burritos," she says, and there's something about her knowing look that cuts right through me and makes me feel all melty.

"It's weird that now you've seen me without my shirt

on," I blurt out, even though *I wasn't even thinking it*, and, also, no no no. "Sorry, I mean—"

We are literally back at the front door of Lemonberry, which would be the wrong place to have this conversation even if it was a conversation we should be having. Also, obviously, I know why I said it and how much I hope Jordi assures me. And why, if something can be completely out of your head as it happens, can it come back to haunt you later?

"*Weird* is not the word I'd use," Jordi says, and then smiles.

"Okay," I say.

"How were those burritos?" Maggie asks, walking up behind us.

"Really good," I say quickly.

"Agreed," Jordi says, looking right at me. I'm melty again.

Inside the store, Jordi's tasked with breaking down a bunch of boxes in the back while I'm reorganizing the jewelry cases. My phone buzzes in my pocket, and even though it's unprofessional, I sneak it out while Laine's talking to a customer and Maggie's nowhere to be found.

not weird. beautiful.

I look up into one of the floor-length store mirrors, trying to see what Jordi sees. I picture her camera pointed at me and the resulting image, but it still doesn't make sense to me.

Maggie's ready to head out tonight at the same time Jordi and I would be getting off work anyway, so I wave good-bye to Jordi and follow Maggie outside to her Jeep. It's surprisingly mostly clutter-free.

"I let Jordi know that I'm helping you with a project," Maggie says. "I didn't want her to worry it was any kind of favoritism."

Obviously I don't mention that I've already halfway explained this to Jordi on our way to my house today, and, even more obviously, the half I left out was that my sewing project is for her. I wish there had been a way I could have completed it before she gave me the necklace, but at least I'm finally getting started.

Maggie's house is on a green and quiet street in Glassell Park, which is about halfway between my part of LA and Highland Park. It's a small house like ours, but inside the chaos seems controlled and not at all cluttered like I'd expected. There are toys everywhere and a few random Lemonberry dresses hung in the kitchen, but it's no episode of *Hoarders*.

"Okay, talk me through this again," Maggie says, and I explain how I want the bag to be color-blocked in black, green, and gunmetal, with the Hello Kitty lining like a secret for the owner of the bag only. Maggie nods, very seriously, and leads me down the hallway to what must be her design studio. This is the room that looks like it's owned by the Maggie I'm used to, because stuff is *everywhere*. Dress forms, sewing machines, a huge iMac, piles of fabrics, and sketchpads lying on every surface. She flips one open, draws something, and holds it up.

"Like this?" she asks, and it's amazing how it's exactly

what I saw in my head. She unrolls gridded paper from a huge roll and shows me how she begins designing her own patterns. Before long we have pieces for each color and the lining, as well.

"Should we order a pizza before we continue?" Maggie asks, and I agree that it's a great idea.

"You're quiet tonight," she says while completing the order online. "You're never my quiet intern. Is everything okay?"

"I'm just trying to learn," I say. "And be professional."

Maggie laughs. "Abby, please never be quiet to be professional. At least not where I'm concerned. I know that Jordi has the silently cool thing down, but it's hardly how I'm evaluating the two of you. God, I really wish I'd never mentioned that on your *very first day*, but I think you've noticed I'm about as loquacious as you are. The last thing I want is for you to feel like it's a constant competition."

"Isn't it, though?" I ask.

"No. Definitely not. This summer is for you two to learn, and for me to get the benefit of having two really talented girls helping out my store. That's it."

"Then I'll try to . . ." I laugh. "Talk more?"

"You talk the right amount, Abby," she says with a serious look in her eyes. "Don't try to be something you aren't."

I nod. "Can I ask a question?"

"Of course," she says. "But let's start pinning the pattern to the fabric while we talk."

I follow her lead and begin attaching the pattern to the

four different fabrics with tiny stickpins. "I seriously love Lemonberry, and I'm not saying that to suck up. I love, like, every dress you've designed, and I love most of the other brands you carry, as well. But your look is so . . ."

Maggie looks down at her ultra-faded Ramones T-shirt. "Glamorous?"

I laugh. "Exactly."

"I love designing dresses for girls like you," she says. "And, occasionally, when I'm feeling fancy, that includes myself. But most days I'm happier just like this."

"Um . . . I really do like everything I'm doing at the shop," I say, because the moment feels so safe. "But I haven't been able to do many social media things yet. I know you're busy, but—"

"You're absolutely right," Maggie says. "Also, you don't have to pretend you like dusting, Abby. No one likes dusting."

"But it's important! The shop has to look a certain way, and that involves dusting." I know I sound like I'm sucking up—which maybe I am—so I laugh myself off.

"I'll find time for you, okay?" she asks, and maybe I'm just caught in the beams of her smile again, but I nod and smile back.

We get the entire pattern cut out before the pizza arrives, and after we eat, we wash our hands free of grease and get back to work. It hits me as the pieces of material begin to take the shape of an actual bag that, ideally, Jordi will be carrying it, and Maggie will see.

But I've put in too much work to turn back. And I

want to give Jordi something I've created myself too badly to keep this hidden from her.

"This will be a nice gift," Maggie says. "Or at least I assume it's a gift. It's not quite your vibe."

"It's a gift," I say. "Yeah."

"Someone special," Maggie says, doesn't ask. I guess that much must be obvious.

"Yes," I say, and I hope I can leave it at that. For now. And lots of people can be special. Jordi's my girlfriend, yes, but she's not the only special person in my life. When Maggie sees her with it, it doesn't have to be a thing.

"Thank you so much for helping me with this," I say. "It's way more complicated than I could manage."

"You're picking it up quickly," she says. "I can tell."

"Still. Without you, it'd just look like a weird black and green lump, probably." I stroke the nearly completed bag with my hand. "I can't believe I thought this up and now it's real."

Maggie smiles. "I feel like that every time I see one of my finished dresses."

I'm not sure I'll ever be capable of designing anything more elaborate than a bag, but it's still nice to have something in common with someone as talented as Maggie. When I sit down at home to write my latest blog post (rompers, even though I am wary of them), I feel less like someone doing the fashion thing from the sidelines. Yes, I just made a bag, and only due to someone else's abilities and equipment at that. But suddenly it's as though I'm finding my way to something, and I'm not just in its approximate area.

CHAPTER 19

Even though I'm anxious to give Jordi the gift immediately, I'm sort of uncertain about what Maggie will think, and so I put it out of my head for the rest of the workweek. Obviously, I'll be seeing Jordi over the weekend, though our plans semi-concern me. It isn't that she hasn't hung out poolside at Trevor's with me, and it isn't that I haven't tagged along to look at art and listen to music at Pehrspace and other spaces like it.

But tonight, somehow, the combined going out crew includes her friends Henry and Evelyn, Maliah and Trevor, Zoe and Brandon—though Zoe won't stop saying things like *it's not a date*—and Jax. Brooke is off on a family vacation, and I guess none of the other lacrosse dudebros were interested—which is fine. The group seems too mixed and potentially volatile as it is, and we're going to *a cemetery*.

It's not as creepy as it sounds. During the summers, a film organization shows classic movies against the wall of a structure within the cemetery. It's always a huge crowd spread out over an open area on beach blankets with picnic baskets. There's nothing scary about it, but Maliah's always refused to come. Until this time—once Jax was going and Trevor expressed interest.

Jordi meets me at my place to wait for Jax to pick us up, since he offered, and also because Jordi's parents each have plans tonight and therefore an extra car is not available. I try to imagine my parents being cool enough to have separate plans on a Saturday night but am unable to.

"Come to my room," I tell Jordi when I let her in.

"Whoa," she says with a grin.

"Not like that. My parents are—just, come on." I take her hand and pull her down the hallway. Okay, we still kiss for a couple minutes, but then I pull myself away from her and pick up the tissue paper–wrapped bag off my desk.

"What's this?" Jordi asks with an eyebrow raised.

"Just open it," I say, though, for the first time, I worry that it isn't good enough or that Jordi doesn't like people picking things out for her or who knows. Suddenly I can't imagine what it'll look like in her hands.

Jordi unwraps the tissue paper and stares at the bag.

"I made it," I say. "If that wasn't obvious. I mean, not *too* obvious, I hope. It's not supposed to look like a sad crafts project."

"You *made* this?" Jordi turns the bag over in her hands. "I love this. And you know mine's in sad shape."

"It's not that sad," I say, and I realize I'm breathing normally again. "Maggie helped me, I should say. I didn't tell her it was for you, but . . ."

"I don't care." Jordi begins transferring the contents of her old bag to this one. "Oh my god, Abby. The inside is Hello Kitty?"

"I didn't even know that material would exist, but it does. Can you believe it?"

She hugs me so tight that I'm back to not breathing normally.

"So it's okay?" I ask, and she laughs.

"You dork," she says, still hugging me. "Thank you."

Mom leans into my doorway. "Jax's car is outside, girls."

Jordi and I pull away from each other.

"Hi, Mrs. Ives," Jordi says while attempting to tame down her untamable waves.

"The fruit's in the refrigerator, right?" I ask Mom, and despite walking in on us in full-body contact, she's smiling. Probably because I volunteered to bring a healthy snack tonight.

"It is. Have fun, girls."

"I feel like your mom hates me slightly less every time I'm here," Jordi whispers to me as we walk to the kitchen. "A few more times and *dislike* will be dialed down to *apathy*."

"And then we have *ambivalence* to look forward to." I take the refrigerated bag out and follow Jordi to the front door. "I'm sorry. Your parents are amazing and—"

"And it's fine."

Jax is out of the car and leaning against the hood like he's the teen dream from some 1980s movie. "Hey, ladies."

"I have the fruit," I say.

"I have four packs of Red Vines," Jordi says.

"*Red Vines?*" Jax's face crumbles. "I thought you were bringing Twizzlers."

"Aren't they the same thing?" I ask.

"*NO*," they chorus.

"Oh my god," I say. "Let's go."

Jordi climbs into the backseat, which leaves me up front with Jax. I turn down his banjo music and check my lipstick in his rearview mirror. I notice Jordi behind me, gazing down at the bag, and I'm convinced that my physical heart feels more like the metaphorical Valentine's one right now. This must be like what it feels like to fall in love with someone, which means that somehow I, Abby Ives, am falling in love at seventeen and without any of my apparent flaws fixed. I'm just me, and this is still happening.

We park in a garage just around the corner from the cemetery and file into the huge line filling the entrance. The movie won't start for hours, but if we don't line up this early, we'll never manage to grab a good spot. Luckily everyone manages to find each other, and Zoe's brought pre-pre-movie snacks for this portion of waiting.

"This is amazing." Maliah selects a pink macaron from the box Zoe's opened for us. "It matches Abby's hair exactly."

"Hold it up." Jordi digs in the new bag for her camera and takes a few photos of the cookie in front of my hair. "It's literally the exact same shade."

"What about this one?" Zoe points to a lavender cookie, and then suddenly everyone wants to suggest macaron colors for me to change my hair to match.

"I'd actually be really sad if you changed it," Maliah tells me. "Not that you aren't practically a grown woman who can make all her own decisions, Abbs. You just *seem* pink."

"I agree with that," Jordi says, though she is taking photos of the rest of the macarons. Now that I associate them with hair dye, they seem less appetizing.

"Don't you think that Abby should put photos of herself on her blog?" Maliah asks Jordi.

"Hey," I say. "Don't do some sort of weird . . . turn my girlfriend against me thing."

"How is that turning me against you?" Jordi asks. "Also, I haven't actually ever seen Abby's blog. She's mysterious with the internet."

"What?" Maliah gives me a look. "You know that my relationship advice is *no secrets*."

"Everyone knows that about you, Mal," Trevor says, which makes me laugh.

"Are you saying . . . it's no secret?" I ask, and he high-fives me.

"You two aren't as funny as you think you are," Maliah says with a heavy sigh, though I can see in her face that she's holding back a smile. "I'm already mad at both of you for dragging me into a graveyard. If we have to sit on anyone's tombstone, I'm going to Lyft a ride out of here."

"No one sits on tombstones," Jordi tells her. "You'll have to walk by some, though."

"I'll protect you from ghosts," Trevor promises her.

"Don't even say that," she says.

"Where's your other friend?" Jax asks, looking between Maliah, Zoe, and me. "Aren't there four?"

"She's on family vacation," I tell him as I notice that Henry and Evelyn are murmuring with Jordi, as well as paying a tremendous amount of attention to her bag. Jordi's smiling in a way I can see is confidential to them, and I try to comprehend that this is about me. When Jordi and I are together, it sorts out in my head. This other part, though, is still unfamiliar.

And I like it so much.

The gates finally open, and we hurry to find a spot on the lawn. We've done a good job at assembling a balanced course of snacks and beverages. We have beers and sodas, Mom's fruit salads, RedVines, a cheese plate (apparently Jax can be fancy), three kinds of chips, more cookies—though of the non-pastel variety—and Maliah actually brought a sandwich platter from Mendocino Farms.

"How much would that make your mom cry?" Jordi asks, nodding at the sandwich selection.

"Probably a lot. Basically everything here but the fruit would make her cry."

"What does your mom think about your little burgers project?" Maliah asks.

"I think she's still holding out hope that, over burgers, I'll fall in love with Jax," I say. "So she can overlook some buns."

"Some *buns?*" Jax asks.

"Hamburger buns," I say, which makes everyone laugh. The art kids and the lacrosse dudes and my friends. We don't actually feel like three separate teams here.

"I'd be so sad if you fell in love with Jax," Maliah says.

"Probably not as sad as me," Jordi says, and Maliah grins at her. If the two of them become friends, I feel as though my whole life would get easier. I'd at least be less tense when they're in the same proximity.

The movie starts at about the same time we've all had our fill of snacks, and it's an old classic in black and white that I worry everyone else will get bored of. But the team holds together, even though once we hit the second hour of sitting on the ground it's not the most comfortable film ever watched. Jordi and I trade off leaning against each other, and she even takes off her jacket and covers our bare legs with it once the sun is down and the night air is cool.

After the movie's over, we stretch and gather up our things, and people start making plans for what's after this. I love this group, but honestly all I want to do is be somewhere warm and comfortable and *alone* with Jordi.

That said, there's a good chance we'll go see some bands play at Pehrspace, and that's okay, too.

"Man." Jax nods his head at the group clearing out behind us. "Those women all look like my mom and they *killed* some wine."

"Moms can drink," Trevor says, which makes all of us laugh, except that my eyes catch on something familiar, and I drop Jordi's hand.

"What?" she asks, but then she sees too and steps away from me.

And then we're clearly making eye contact with Maggie.

"Shit," Jordi says.

"Let's go," I say.

"What happened?" Maliah asks, and her eyes aren't suspicious but kind. I don't have time to rejoice over how much better things are, though, because I feel careless and unprofessional. Up until this moment, I thought the worst outcome at Lemonberry would be that Jordi gets the job instead of me, or even that I do and it makes us awkward.

But obviously the actual worst scenario is that neither of us do.

We sit on my tiny front porch once Jax drops us off, sipping leftover sodas.

"Is it bad?" I ask. "Really? We didn't get an employee manual or something that said *no dating*."

"I don't know," Jordi says with a sigh. "I've just been trying to follow every possible rule I can this summer. My dad told me that lots of businesses have policies about employee 'fraternizing'—" she uses airquotes— "and to be careful."

"Ugh, I thought your dad was cool. That sounds like something my dad would say."

She grins. "Sorry to burst your bubble. Miguel Perez is not cool. Anyway, we can tell Maggie we're just friends, but she probably saw me smelling your hair."

"You were *smelling my hair?*" I pretend to squirm away from her. "You're so weird."

"If we get fired," Jordi says, and her voice is shaky, "I don't regret you."

"I don't regret you either," I say very quickly.

I try to continue being serious but instead we kiss until one of my parents flicks the porchlight on and off and we have to say goodnight.

CHAPTER 20

On Monday, Jordi and I walk to work as separately as two people who live within blocks of each other can manage. Laine lets us inside, and we stay very quiet as we begin getting settled for the morning. It's always easy to find work to do on Mondays, and hopefully if I'm in the midst of steaming a bunch of dresses, Maggie won't find me particularly suspicious or unprofessional.

"Hi, Abby."

I spin around to see Maggie behind me and hear a bunch of water splosh on the floor near but thankfully not on my feet. "Hi. Sorry. About the water. Hi."

Jordi's standing just a bit behind her, and she looks too nervous to be amused by any of this.

"Come on back to my office, girls," she says with a wave. It doesn't feel serious, except that I know it is. I know there probably was some mention of an employee manual or set of rules that I daydreamed my way through or forgot about as they wouldn't have applied to me. At the beginning of the summer, I never would have imagined dating anyone, much less someone here. Everything about Jordi's been the best kind of surprise.

Oh my god, am I seriously daydreaming again? Right now?

"We're sorry," I say as we sit down across from her at her desk. "If there's a policy and we violated it."

"What policy?" Maggie asks.

"My dad said . . ." Jordi lets herself trail off and shakes her head. "Never mind."

"Girls . . ." Maggie looks back and forth between us. "I'm going to let you tell me what's going on."

"It's not unprofessional," I say, even though I may not have enough business knowhow to qualify if that's true or not. "At work, we're just . . . working."

"I take this internship really seriously," Jordi says.

"She does," I say. "She would never, like, smell my hair here. I mean, I take it seriously, too. We both do."

"*Smell your hair?*" Maggie takes a huge sip of coffee. "I called you both back here because we're going to have a table at a local designers' show this coming weekend and I think I can get you both included if you're free to help. So I have, literally, no idea what's going on."

"Didn't you see us on Saturday?" I ask.

"No . . . ?" I've never seen Maggie look so confused. Maggie's cluttered piles of random paperwork might make her seem like a disaster, but she does have a firm handle on everything. Usually.

"At the cemetery," Jordi says.

"Oh! Were you guys there? Did you have fun? I could live without sitting on the hard ground for four hours at my age, but some of my friends love going." She takes another sip of coffee. "You're allowed to socialize outside of here, you know."

"We, ummm . . ." I start, but even with my big mouth, it's hard to keep going.

"We've been doing more than socializing," Jordi says in her very professional tone and, I can't help it, I laugh.

Thank god, so does Maggie.

"Abby's the girlfriend!" she says. "I had no idea. Is this new?"

"New-ish," Jordi says. "Yeah."

"The bag!" Maggie says. "Clearly that bag was for Jordi, wasn't it? Oh no—shit. Did I spoil the surprise?"

"No, I gave it to her this weekend," I say.

"Girls, between us," Maggie chuckles. "I was pretty drunk on Saturday night. It was one of my first nights out with my friends since Cory and I split up. We could have had an entire conversation and I might not have remembered the next day."

"You guys did have a lot of empty bottles of wine," I say, though immediately I wish I hadn't. Luckily Maggie's still laughing.

"This has been . . ." Maggie shrugs. "Not my favorite summer. It's been easy for me to tunnel vision and proclaim that love and hope are dead. So knowing that you two . . . well, it's nice."

"So we're not in trouble?" I ask.

"No one's in trouble. Let's talk about this show on Sunday, because I'd love to have help if you're free." Maggie laughs some more. "I hope you two are never in serious trouble for, uh, anything, because you'd both crumble under investigation immediately. It was sort of incredible to witness."

"No lives of crime for us," Jordi says.

"Definitely not." She fishes around in her purse and takes out a ten-dollar bill. "Go down the street, get yourselves Frappuccinos or whatever, and take a moment to recover from . . . all of this. We'll chat about the show then. Sound good?"

We agree and take off as quickly as we can get out the front door.

"I can't believe you actually said *smell my hair*," Jordi says.

"I can't believe *you* actually said *we've been doing more than socializing!*"

We both laugh, and I feel the heaviness that's been upon me since Saturday night finally lift.

"I really like Maggie," I say.

"Me too."

And then we're quiet because I think we're both wishing that we'll be the one to win the job. At least, that's what I'm doing.

It would have sucked to have the internship cut short if it turned out that relationships were against the rules. But this small part of me, I realize, wishes at least a little that it had happened.

Because at least then we both would have been out of the opportunity together.

I go over to Jordi's on Tuesday because she's responsible for Christian and therefore can't take off anywhere without him. I bring my laptop with me to work on +*style* if there ends up being a lot of brother/sister bonding and I need to keep myself amused.

"I have a date," Jordi greets me when I arrive.

"What? With who? Not me? What—"

"I meant, a date for my show at Pehrspace," she says. "It's officially August 11. It'll keep running for about a couple weeks—depending on what else comes in—but that's the date everything goes up."

"It's soon," I say. "Like a month. Less than a month."

"Less than a month," she repeats. "I have so much to do."

"Can I help?" I ask as Christian runs into the room.

"Hi, Abby," he says. "What are you helping with?"

"No one's helping with anything," Jordi says. "I just want to spend some time today sorting through all my photos."

"I can sort through photos," he says.

"Just me," she says. "Are you guys cool with that?"

We are cool with that, so Christian plays a video game and I get out my laptop. My recent post about summer accessories has had a lot more interaction than usual—maybe since it wasn't plus size specific, so a few other blogs than usual linked to it—so I spend some time thanking people and answering questions before starting today's post about summer party looks. I finish it quickly, and when I peek in on Jordi in her room, she doesn't look up. I'd love to say I go right back to my laptop, but instead I watch her for just a bit. Her eyes are scanning her screen while she's scribbling notes in a Moleskine notebook, and I feel so *proud* watching her work.

She grins without looking up. "What?"

"You're cute when you're serious," I say.

"Oh my god." She shakes her head but she's still grinning. "Hey, is your blog secret from me?"

"It's not secret," I say. "It's just . . . I don't know. You're out there making art. I'm talking about rompers and quality strapless bras."

"Come here," she says, making room in her desk chair for me.

"Christian's out there alone," I say. "Is that okay?"

"Jesus, Abby, he's thirteen. He's not going to choke on his Xbox controller." She minimizes her photos and places my hands on the keyboard. "Let me see your blog."

"That sounds so creepy!" But I type the URL and wait for it to load. "See? It's nothing exciting."

Jordi leans in to read my latest post that I just wrote from her living room. I expect it to end with that, but she keeps scrolling down. She reads the rompers post, and the strapless bras one, and every other thought I've had about clothes for months.

"This is really good," she says finally, and I exhale. I couldn't have been holding my breath this whole time, could I? I would have suffocated. "You write like you talk. Like you're walking me through all of this."

"It's just clothes," I say.

"It's not," she says. "You're making people feel good about what they want to wear. And you make it really easy and fun."

"Do you think it's bad I don't have photos of myself?" I ask. "Mal clearly thinks it's like the end of the world."

"I don't think it's bad," she says. "And I get it. Who wants to be on the internet where anyone could say anything? But you write about all these great dresses to wear to parties, and I know you have dresses that would make your point for you. And if you wanted to do that—which, yeah, I know right now you don't—obviously there's probably someone who'd take those photos for you."

"I know," I say. "Thank you."

"If it's about privacy, I'm with you," she says. "But if it's something else . . . I guess I'm with Maliah. Is that the worst? I could take some really fun shots, if you wanted me to."

"It *is* the worst," I say, though I kiss her. "Do you need to get back to work or can I stay in here?"

"I have to get back to work," she says. "But will you think about it?"

I say *yes* but I don't mean it at all.

Jordi keeps working, and I spend the late morning looking at social media for other shops like Lemonberry. I'm not sure how much of that I'm supposed to be doing at work—yes, I'm scoping the competition, but maybe Maggie wouldn't see it that way. It feels a lot like she'd rather have me doing general shop stuff like steaming and folding than spending time on my phone or the store laptop.

THE SUMMER OF JORDI PEREZ

Other shops of the same-ish size seem to be doing better at all of it. There are more likes and faves and shares and comments, even for stores that I don't think are as good or even as ultimately successful. Lemonberry seems to have shoppers constantly, which I can't say for some of the other local stores like Timeless Vintage.

I rotate between tabs and study each. And even though I know nothing's an exact science on the internet, the longer I look, the more I see it. We look—especially since June when Jordi took over the photography—sleek, professional, to die for. But the other stores look *real*. The photos are casual and easygoing and I can picture myself in these shops hanging out with these girls, even the ones in other cities I've never visited.

Jordi's pictures are *better*, but they're set apart. They're not inviting. Lemonberry seems like it's for girls like Laine, who are beautiful and styled and confident. I love everything about Lemonberry, but if I had to judge based on these accounts alone, I never would think it'd be a place for someone like me.

Maggie wants my expertise, and I know it. And I want the job, and I know it. But there's no way to explain this without either making Jordi sound at fault—which she isn't—or taking her off a significant portion of her duties—which maybe she should. It's not that Jordi wouldn't have other things to do and have a million more ways to be valuable to Maggie. I guess she could adjust how she photographed, but wouldn't she need a person to direct those shots for her?

I'm proud of my analysis, though, even if I'm not sure I should share it. Mom might have thought of me as a dumb kid who thought she could handle a grownup job. Right now, though, I feel I have proof that I know what I'm doing, at least a little.

"Sorry I'm so boring." Jordi walks into the living room and flops down on the sofa next to me. "Do you guys want to do something?"

Christian immediately has seven ideas, none of which are particularly doable without a car, but at least it gives me a chance to close all my tabs and then shut down my computer. I'll do my best to get the job, but I'm not sure this is how I want to do it.

CHAPTER 21

I don't mention anything about photography to Maggie the next day at work, and then it's easier to do the same on Friday. Instead of asking if I can, I just start creating promotional post drafts and graphics using Jordi's photographs. Maggie likes every single one of them, and so I feel less weird about holding anything back from the job.

Also, yes, it is way more fun than dusting.

The show over the weekend is too busy to talk about much at all. I'm helping customers and trying to keep up our Instagram presence at the same time now that Maggie seems to have more faith in me. Before I know it, our shift's up. And instead of dwelling on Jordi's photographs, I spend the rest of the day scouring the other booths for myself. (I score a new skirt, new shorts, and a set of bright Bakelite barrettes.) And then by the time next week rolls around, nothing's so heavy on my mind.

We have so much to do anyway. The fall line actually hits the store in mid-August, so we're already accepting pre-orders. Jordi and I are both spending time tracking the dresses selling best and relaying the info back to Maggie. But Maggie's less available than usual, as launching this season's looks is a bit more important than carefully tallying the interns' contributions.

Though maybe that means the tally's already been finalized, and I'm being way too quiet, for once, for my own good.

With Jordi using most of her free time getting her photography show ready, my summer hangout place has switched from Trevor's backyard to the Perez house. Which, obviously, is more than okay with me. Maliah's mentioned my absence a bit, but I can't imagine she minds. Inviting me was an easy way to include me but as long as she's with Trevor, would she miss me much?

Obviously, I miss how things used to be, even if there isn't much I enjoy more than hanging out in the same place as *my girlfriend*. When we were little, best friends could be your everything. So I don't even always know if it's Maliah I'm missing. Maybe it's the time in my life before I knew that wouldn't always be the case, before boyfriends and girlfriends and arson rumors.

I've gotten back into updating my blog more often, as Jordi's productivity is a bit contagious. Researching posts does take a while, from visiting online stores and other fashion blogs to compiling a selection on a theme, to putting it all together in a way that looks interesting and not like I just listed out a bunch of preexisting stuff. Whenever I schedule or post my latest, my brain feels nice and exhausted.

Then I think about scientists working to, I don't know, cure cancer, and I feel silly. And I'm only spending some of my time doing that anyway. Christian forced me to learn to play *The Last Guardian* with him, and I'm slowly making my way through an epic book involving dragons because he wants to discuss it with someone and Jordi's too busy.

I'd never really pictured myself dating anyone, it's true, but I guess I still had this little corner in my mind tucked away even from myself about what it would be like anyway. Maybe you can't help but lock away a little hope, no matter how improbable that possibility might be. Dates and kissing and love.

But then there's also this. Being happy to know someone's working one room away from you. Hanging out with their little brother because he's somehow part of your world now, too. Knowing where the glasses are in the cupboard and that the water on the door of the fridge isn't as cold as the Brita pitcher inside it. It's funny how I feel romance in all of it.

I feel Jordi in my whole summer.

"Hey." Jordi walks into the living room while I'm leaving comments on a few other blogs and Christian is reading a long dragon novel I assume I might have to read next. "Are you bored?"

"I'm not . . . not bored," I say, and she laughs.

"Come on," she says, and I follow her into her room.

"Do I get to see your show pictures?" I sit down on the swivel chair at her desk. "Have you picked them all by now? How many are you showing? Are they printed yet?"

"Abby." She squeezes in next to me and takes my hand off the touchpad. "I love your questions but . . ."

"Not now?"

She smiles. "One at a time, at least. I know what I'm showing. They're being printed now. And you can see them at the show."

"Has anyone seen them?" I ask.

"You've seen plenty of the photos," she says. "But not in this arrangement. I just want everyone to see them to-gether. If you want to just look at more photos in general, obviously they're all here."

I look at the multitude of folders in the window onscreen. They're in alphabetical order, and the first one is *abby*.

"Wait, so all the photos of me are in one folder?" I'm not sure why that makes it more overwhelming than the photos existing in different folders, but it does. It's a lot of Abby, all together.

"I have things organized a few different ways," Jordi says, scrolling around in the main photography drive. "But, yeah, I have an Abby folder. It's one of my favorites."

I don't ask, so I'm relieved that she clicks on it, because not knowing is weirder than being confronted with what feels like a million pictures of myself. But I've gotten used to it—even if it's been in piecemeal before—and so I don't hate it.

"You're quiet," Jordi says, still scrolling.

"It's a weird experience," I say. "Seeing so much of me. Seeing me like you see me. It's still kind of foreign."

"So much of you," Jordi says with a laugh. "You make it sound like I'm taking naked pictures of you."

I blush and she looks away, and if that's not enough, suddenly Mrs. Perez is home and in the doorway.

"Are you two okay in here?" she asks. "Anyone need a beverage refill?"

"We're fine, Mom," Jordi says, and I nudge her knee with mine because obviously parents only check in on your beverages to make sure you aren't making out. There are plenty of moments where it's hard keeping my hands off Jordi, but open doors and proximate family members are pretty much guaranteed mood-killers for me. But I don't think it would be helpful sharing that with Mrs. Perez.

"You haven't shown anyone these, have you?" I ask as the photos of me continue. I learn what I look like mid-laugh.

"Like my mom?" she asks.

"No, just . . . anyone. When you submitted stuff to get your show at Pehrspace or showing Maggie your work or anything."

She tilts her head at me. "Why?"

Her tone is cooler than I want it to be.

"Just . . ." I consider my words carefully. People get so worked up when I'm honest about not wanting the world to see me, even though I don't know why that isn't a normal accepted attitude. I'm so tired of hearing that there's something beautiful about me when I'm not arguing that. Of course my girlfriend thinks I'm beautiful, of course Maliah thinks I look great when I spend so much effort on my looks, of course Jax thinks I'm *fuckin' cute*. They have something invested in me while the world doesn't. And it's

okay that the world doesn't; I don't need it to. I'm lucky
with how things stand, even if no one in my life believes
it. I like how I look, usually, but people—especially people
on the internet—can be so mean when you're fat. As if fat
makes you stupid or dirty or irresponsible. As if fat makes
you anything other than . . . fat.

"It's just that anyone who saw these would know that I
love you," I say, instead of the truth, and then it—a bigger
truth—is just out there. It's a moment I would have planned
for Griffith Park or the Chandelier Tree or even walking
the shady sidewalks between our houses. Definitely not
sitting at her desk with an open door and a billion photos
of me open on the screen and a desperate need to change
the subject from my size.

I hadn't even said the words to myself yet. Not in that
order.

Jordi closes out of the photos and sits back from her
computer. "I haven't shown anyone," she says, and her tone
hasn't warmed at all.

"I mean, Maggie has to think you're a professional,"
I continue. "Not that you just take pictures of your girlfriend. Not just stuff you'd put on Instagram or whatever."

"I'm glad that's the quality you think I've mastered,
Abby," she says.

"No, no, Jordi, your stuff's amazing, just, the subject of
those, not exactly something you'd want people to see."

She stands up from her desk.

"I feel like I explain everything badly," I say.

"You explain everything fine." Jordi flops back on her

bed. I don't join her because I'm pretty sure she's mad at me, I don't want her mom to walk by and get the wrong idea, and also because it hasn't escaped my notice that she didn't return my *I love you.*

"Should I go home?" I ask.

"No." She sits back up. "Come here."

"Your mom . . ."

"She can't literally expect that the only place we'll sit is sharing that stupid swivel chair," she says, and I laugh.

"You know I think you're amazing," I say. "Not because we're together. I think you're amazing because you're amazing and take amazing photographs."

"The word *amazing* has ceased to have any meaning now," she says as I sit down next to her. "Thank you. Seriously."

I lean my head on her shoulder, and she slips her arm around my waist. We still seem to fit together, but I don't think I'll ever like the Abby folder as much as she needs me to, and also it's very possible that Jordi Perez doesn't love me.

But we of course walk to work together the next morning, and while I expect it'll feel different, it doesn't. I love seeing my bag strapped over her shoulder, and I'm wearing my blue pineapple. Henry invited her to see an art show and a few bands play at The Smell downtown, and she shows me the message where he typed *bring your pink-haired lady,* which makes us both laugh.

"What's going to happen next year?" I ask. "I mean, next month, really. Whose lunch table are we sitting at? How do people decide that?"

"It's a new year," Jordi says. "We'll start our own. Whoever's cool can just join us."

"Ugh, but then I won't see Maliah at lunch," I say, and Jordi laughs, and I only feel a little guilty. I don't know if we'll all fit together or not, but I'd sort of rather put the responsibility on Maliah than shoulder it all myself.

At work, there's a new shipment, so I get to work steaming everything while Jordi brainstorms photo ideas, and then once I have one of each style ready, she begins shooting. I get the rest of the stock ready to display before sitting down to survey all our social accounts. Since Maggie's working in her office, I feel safe pulling up the ModGirl and Timeless Vintage pages to see if my hypothesis continues to hold.

And it does. Their casual photos are doing better, period, and then when they do post sleek professional photos, people react in a different way. I know there are a million factors involved, and we wouldn't just automatically replicate their success if we copied what they're doing.

I glance Maggie's way. She's flipping through paperwork but doesn't look stressed or any more frazzled than usual. It seems like there's finally a breath to take in between the fall line announcement and the upcoming release. Jordi will be occupied with photographs until it's lunchtime—and even then we'll probably have to make her stop working for a bit—so it's a safe time to have this discussion.

THE SUMMER OF JORDI PEREZ

One big reason Maggie brought me on is clearly that I know how to handle this. So these sorts of conclusions are exactly what she expects from me, or at least what she hoped for when she called to offer me the internship. I'm not betraying Jordi and I'm not setting aside my own relationship just to get ahead in this contest—it's not even a contest, for god's sake! I owe it to Maggie and Lemonberry to do the very best job I can. Also, I think I owe it to myself. Falling in love might be changing my whole life, but that doesn't mean I shouldn't also be working toward my dream career.

"Hey." Jordi leans into the back room. "What are you doing for lunch? There's a ton of leftover pozole at my house. And also, no people for once. Christian's got plans all day."

I close all the tabs that aren't directly related to Lemonberry. "Then I guess for lunch I'm . . . making out with you. There doesn't really have to be pozole."

She laughs. "There really is pozole. I'm not bringing you into my house under false pretenses."

Maggie walks out of her office. "Jordi, I meant to ask you the other day, how's your prep for your show going? Is there anything I can help with? I know you're taking on a lot."

"Thanks," she says, and I see how something in her shoulders tightens. "I'm not sure there's anything to help with. I just hope that people like it. I keep second-guessing myself."

"Trust your instincts," Maggie says. "The first time I did a show, one of my friends said that my work all looked too retro, and so the week, before I ripped up a ton of my work to modernize it." Maggie shakes her head. "It didn't even look like me anymore. And all the feedback I got that day said I should have fully embraced the vintage looks that had clearly inspired me."

"So from then on you did?" I ask, even though I'm not sure I'm technically in this conversation, just in the room.

"Exactly," Maggie says with a smile. "Learn from my fashion disaster."

"Jordi's stuff is all amazing," I say. "She seriously has nothing at all to be worried about. People will love it."

"It's very hard putting yourself out there, Abby," Maggie says gently. "Especially for the first time."

I feel chastened. Jordi looks smug, or at least smug for Jordi.

"But listen to your girlfriend," she tells Jordi. "Abby has a great eye. She wouldn't believe in you if she didn't really see something special in your work."

Jordi makes a frustrated noise. "This would probably be easier if you still thought we were just colleagues."

Maggie laughs. "Too late. You'll have to deal with my undying support of your work and your relationship now."

We excuse ourselves for lunch, but once we're at Jordi's house, we forget all about the pozole.

Jax picks me up on the early side the next day so we can head all the way across Los Angeles to eat at the Apple Pan. It's a tiny diner with no booths or tables, just stools all the way around their giant counter, which practically fills the entire restaurant.

"We only have to do the Eastside," he says for the millionth time while we're studying menus.

"I know, but this place is a classic," I say. "Jordi and I were looking at some articles about the best burgers in LA and—"

"You're planning burger stuff with Jordi?" Jax asks. "Abbs, I thought what we have is special."

"Have you tried mentioning this to anyone else?" I ask. "*Everyone* has an opinion on where we should be getting burgers. Jordi is no exception."

"You could invite her," he says. "I guess. If you want."

His tone sounds a lot like when I'm not feeling casual but really want everyone to think I am.

"I thought what we have is special?" I ask, and he grins. It feels a little like Jax is glad to have me to himself, a lot like how grateful I am to hang out with Maliah without Trevor. Can that be true, though? Sometimes it's hard for me to remember that I guess boys have feelings, too. I seriously don't know how straight and bi girls manage.

"How's it going?" he asks as the counter guy serves us our sodas. They're actually soda cans served with little paper cones filled with ice and fitted into metal holders. This is how I suspect they've served soda here since they opened way back in the 1940s. On one hand, I think we've really evolved into better drinking options, but on the other, I also love when L.A.'s history is still right in front of you. Even with something small like soda.

"You guys ready?" the counter guy asks, and I order the Hickoryburger while Jax chooses the Steakburger. I convince him to split an order of fries so we have room for pie later.

"Things are good with Jordi," I say to Jax once our order's in. "I guess. I mean, they are for me. I assume they are for her. It's so weird someone could like me this much."

"Oh, shut the hell up," he says. "You know your girl likes you. We all do. She watches you like you're the most interesting thing on the fucking planet. Like she's gonna jump your bones the second you're alone. Which, ya know, if you want to give any details . . ."

"Stop," I tell him, though I also feel myself smiling. If other people can see it, too, it must be real. "It still feels like maybe it's magic. Sci-fi and not a documentary. You know?"

Somehow our food is already up, and so Jax doesn't respond right away. I even assume he's forgotten the thread of conversation as we wolf down our burgers and fries and then input our judgments into Best Blank.

"I was gonna yell at you about your self-esteem," Jax says. "But maybe when it's really good, it's supposed to feel like it's sci-fi. Aliens and laser beams and shit."

"Has it been like that for you?" I ask.

"Shit, Abbs, I'm still waiting for it. But since you brought it up, I gotta tell you about this new barista at Proof."

"Nope," I tell him, but we both crack up and I lean in for the story.

CHAPTER 22

I change outfits five times the night of Jordi's show. I start with loud and then try to go neutral and then I wonder if I should look artsier to be a better pairing with Jordi and then I think I should complement her instead so I'm back at loud. That seems too loud, so I find everything in my closet that looks sophisticated. But I don't look like myself so I pull on my birthday Lemonberry dress, my pineapple necklace, and step into my yellow sandals. I'm not sure that I look like the girlfriend of an amazing photographer, but since that's exactly what I am, maybe I do after all.

"Whoa," Dad says when I walk to the living room. He's sitting on the floor surrounded by printed recipes, and I'm not sure, firstly, how this happened since I got home, and, more importantly, how I'll manage to get out. "You look great, kiddo."

"Thanks," I say. "Does everything have to stay on the floor, or . . .?"

"Just skirt the perimeter," he says with a laugh. "Big plans tonight?"

"Jordi's show is opening," I say. "It's a big deal."

"Very cool," he says. "Tell her congratulations for us."

"I might be out late," I say. "I'll call if it's super late."

"If what's super late?" Mom walks back into the room. "Oh, you look very colorful, Abby."

I tiptoe around the edge of the room. "Jordi's photography show. I told Dad I'd call if it's really late."

"How late can that go?" Mom asks. "You look at some photos. It can't take too long."

"Mom, god, could you be nice about like one thing?" I know that I should stay and make sure she's not offended and that Dad's prepared to smooth things over, but I don't want to. I feel my heels stomping at my frustration or hurt or whatever all these horrible things in my chest are, but then I reach Jordi's gate and ring the doorbell, and it's already lifting. It's Jordi's night and that kind of makes it my night, too.

"Hey, Abby, come on in." Jordi's dad holds open the door for me. "I think she's almost ready."

"Thanks."

"Do you want some water or lemonade?" Jordi's mom asks. "Anything?"

"I'm fine," I say. "But thank you. Are you coming tonight?"

They look at each other and laugh.

"We are, but later," Mr. Perez says. "Jordi wants us to—"

"I want you to what?" Jordi walks into the room, and I am pretty sure my heart and brain explode. She's wearing a silky white and black striped top over black tuxedo pants and shiny black leather Vans. Her hair looks extra purposefully mussed, and her eyes are smudged with black liner. Jordi looks like a goddamn rock star.

"Oh my god, you look amazing," I say and throw my arms around her. I normally try to act like a restrained and tasteful person in front of Mr. and Mrs. Perez, but how can I stop myself tonight?

She smooths her shirt. "So it's good?"

"Perfect," I say.

"We'll see you later, honey," her mom tells her. "No earlier than nine-thirty sharp."

"We've synchronized our watches," Mr. Perez says.

"Stop," she says, but with a smile. "I just want to get settled and make sure everything's right. And Pehrspace is always really disorganized, so . . ."

"We're teasing," Mrs. Perez says. "Go get settled. We'll see you two soon."

We say good-bye and head outside to Jordi's dad's car.

"Do you want to borrow my lipstick?" I ask her as I buckle my seatbelt. "I know you never have any with you. Or maybe at all."

"I'll just take yours," she says and kisses me. Of course it's just a line, and one that makes me melt at that, but the truth is that when she sits back to start the car, her lips are flushed with my favorite Urban Decay shade of pink. I feel like it would be so boring to date a boy and not be able to share makeup, but maybe that doesn't feel like a big deal to most girls.

"Are you nervous?" I rest my hand on her shoulder as she drives down to Glendale Boulevard. "Because you shouldn't be. It's going to be amazing."

"I'm allowed to be nervous," she says. "Which, yeah, of

course I am. But I did everything I could. Hopefully it'll be okay."

"It won't be *okay*," I say. "It'll be awesome."

"I'm worried your friendship with Jax is rubbing off on you," she says, but she smiles. "I'm glad you're coming with me."

"Why wouldn't I? Ugh, I feel bad you have to drive yourself to your own show. This is the sort of thing I should be doing for you."

"I'll teach you to drive," she says. "Which might not be completely legal, but I will. Now that this is finished, I'll have time."

"Okay," I say. It's the first time the prospect of driving hasn't sounded scary to me.

Jordi finds parking right away on the curvy street that swoops off Glendale, and even though my photos look like the work of a child next to hers, I make her stop in front of the street to take her picture with my phone. Then she swoops me over and takes a selfie of both of us, and even the selfie looks like a work of art. I make her send it to me immediately because we've never looked fancy together before. I envision our future will be full of these occasions.

"Oh, god, people are already here." Jordi grips my hand and shoves her hair out of her face with her other hand. I notice her standard black nail polish has little flecks of glitter in it tonight. "Do I look like I'm freaking out?"

"I'm pretty sure you aren't capable of that," I say. "Come on. People are going to be so excited you're here."

We both assume that people are just early to see Murphy Gomez, the band that's playing later tonight, but as the guy taking money waves us through, I can see how the crowds are clustering around the framed photographs. Maybe people aren't here for Jordi, but now that they're around her photography, of course they're drawn in.

But, wait.

"Jordi," I say, dropping her hand. I feel like ice and fire together. "Jordi."

There's a wall of me.

"Surprise," she whispers, and I physically pull myself away from the word.

There's a wall of me.

"Why would you . . ." I stare at the images. Me in front of Jordi's gate. Me in the Del Taco parking lot the very first night we hung out. The back of my head and my hands straightening dresses at Lemonberry. Me with a cookie the color of my hair. Me looking freshly kissed in my own bedroom.

"I knew you would worry," she says. "But see? You look so beautiful up there."

"If you knew I'd worry, why didn't you ask me?" I feel people's gazes whip from the photos to me. I feel larger than life. I feel the size of an entire photograph. I'm taking up so much space in the frame of each picture and now I'm taking up too much space in this building and I have to get out.

There's a crowd right beyond the doors, smoking cigarettes and pot and drinking beers out of paper bags. The combined smells turn my already-turning stomach, and I keep walking, but where am I supposed to go? Jordi drove me here. Jordi's done everything tonight.

"Abby." She races to me, her hair bouncing with each step. "Abby. I'm sorry. I'm *so sorry.*"

"You didn't think about me at all," I say. "No, you *did* think of me, and then you decided it didn't matter? And I don't even know why. You could have a whole great show without me, but you did it anyway, and now I'm . . ."

"Those are some of my best work," she says.

"Fuck your best work," I say. "I'm a person. I'm your *girlfriend.*"

"That's why I love those pictures so much, because you—"

"No," I say. "Don't come out here and tell me why the pictures are so great when you know you should have asked me. And you know I would have said no, and that's exactly why you didn't."

Jordi is silent.

"It's so . . ." I search for words that capture how broken my heart is. "*Intimate.* We were on my bed and now that moment's on a wall and later people can see it while Murphy Gomez is playing that song about pants."

"I'll talk to them," she says. "Pehrspace, not the band. I'll see if I can take them down right now. I'm—"

"Oh, just leave them up. I should have known if you'd burn a house down to get a good shot for your portfolio that I'd have no chance of escaping unharmed."

It isn't a fair thing to say and we both know it.

"Please let me fix this," she says.

"I don't know how you can," I say. "Just go back inside to your show. I'm sure you'll get into whatever art school you want now."

"I care more about you than art school," she says.

"Now there's definitive proof that actually you don't at all. You don't even love me." I turn from her and walk further, and when I don't hear her footsteps following me, I keep walking. I stop in front of the gas station above Temple Street and take out my phone. How had I even managed to switch my lock screen to the selfie Jordi took of us only minutes ago?

I call Maliah and literally cross my fingers that she'll answer. And she does.

"Hi," I say. "I'm sorry. You're probably out with Trevor but—"

"Abbs," she says. "Are you okay?"

"Oh, god, am I crying?" I touch my face. I'm crying. "Can you come get me?"

"What happened?" she asks. "Abby, please tell me you're okay."

"Jordi and I broke up," I say.

"I'm on my way," she says. "Send me a pin."

I click to my maps app and message my location to Maliah. To kill time, I go inside for a Diet Coke, and I know I'm still crying when I pay for it but I pretend like I'm not. My phone vibrates in my hand, but I go back outside before checking it.

the photos are down, Jordi has texted.

i fucked up so bad.

please come back, abby.

Maliah's Mini screeches up to me, and I practically fall inside.

"Thank you so much."

She looks me over. "Hi."

"I know you want to say it, so go ahead."

"Say *what?*" She reaches over and smooths my hair. "Girl, somehow you look wrecked and better than ever all at once."

"Thank you?" I lean into her. "You can say *I told you so.* About Jordi."

She shakes her head. "You didn't say anything when I went to that snobby country club party with Trevor, even after it was horrible in that really clichéd country club way. You even helped me pick out my outfit and let me complain for days."

"We're friends," I say. "Of course I did."

"Exactly." She hugs an arm around me. "Seriously, Abbs. Where the hell even *are we?*"

I direct Maliah back to the familiarity of our neighborhood, and we end up at her house. I text Mom and Dad that I'm here, and that they can even call the Joneses to verify.

My phone gets three more texts while I'm holding it.

where are you?

abby, are you okay?

please, can we talk?

"Come on." Maliah gently pulls my phone out of

my hand. "This won't do any good right now. Tell me everything."

I finish drinking my Diet Coke, and I tell her the whole story. By now, Jordi's parents should have arrived at Pehrspace, and I wonder what they think about my absence and the empty wall of the exhibit. I wonder where they stacked all the photos of me, of my life, of my relationship, of my body.

"Did she apologize?" Maliah asks.

I nod.

"But it's over?"

I nod more.

"Okay," she says. "What do you want to do? What are all the breakup things? I can't believe I'm doing this for you. I just always thought it'd be you for me first."

"Me too," I admit, and then we both laugh.

"Ice cream?" Maliah asks. "Chocolate? Why are all break-up clichés food?"

"It's dumb," I say. "But also . . . okay. If you have those things."

"If we don't, we'll get them," she says. "Abby, I'm sorry."

I nod.

"Not just . . . that you and Jordi broke up. I don't feel like I've been very . . ."

"Supportive?" I try, and she laughs.

"It's true I didn't like Jordi at first," she says. "But you've been really cool to Trevor, and so I should have tried more. I'll try more with the next girl, okay?"

"Oh, like there'll be a next girl," I say. "It's a miracle there was one girl!"

"It's not, and you have to stop saying things like that," Maliah says. "There will be more girls. There'll be some girl you marry while wearing the most amazing dress. Though instead of wedding cake, your mom will probably make something out of a melon."

I laugh despite, well, everything. "Oh my god, that's horrible. A wedding melon cake is literally the saddest thing I've ever heard, and I just broke up with my girlfriend."

I just broke up with my girlfriend.

If I keep saying it maybe I can understand how the last hours even happened.

The Joneses are all up early the next morning to take a family hike in Griffith Park, so I thank Maliah a hundred times and then head home. I'm still in my dress and heels though my hair's all flat and my makeup's gone and I left my pineapple necklace at Maliah's.

"Oh, good, you're home," Mom says without looking up from her computer. "I thought you might be able to— Abby, what happened?"

"Nothing," I say. "I spent the night at Maliah's, and had to sleep in this dress because I can't fit into any of her pajamas, and yes, I know if I were thin then I could have and all my other life problems would be solved, too."

"Hey, kiddo." Dad walks into the room. "What's up?"

"Jordi and I broke up. I'm going to my room."

I push past him, lock my door behind me, and pull my

dress over my head. It looks wilted on my floor but that's exactly how my insides feel, so I kick off my shoes and leave everything as it falls.

My phone buzzes and I guess I expect three more messages from Jordi, but it's magically Rachel.

Are you okay? Mom just told me to check in on you.

When people ask if you're okay, it always sounds like they want you to do anything in the whole world but say *no*.

But it's Rachel. Finally. So I tell her the truth. It actually takes me ten separate texts to tell her the full truth.

Then I hear from Jax. *how was jordi's thing?*

I tell him everything, too.

Shit abbs. That sux.

Yeah. It sux indeed.

CHAPTER 23

I want to sleep for the indefinite future, but my phone makes a bunch of noise on Sunday morning. Maliah, Brooke, and Zoe have all texted about brunch, and so I guess I have to face the world. I have to face Modern Eats and my friends, at least.

Maliah picks me up and glances my way as she speeds off down the street. "You look better than expected."

"Thanks a lot." I did manage to take a quick shower and pull on a dress that requires no effort or accessorizing. My neck feels bare without my pineapple necklace and I wish I'd put something else on in its place. Or should I make myself feel this emptiness around my neck, too?

We get a table right away at the restaurant, and I stare at my menu instead of at my friends' sad faces. I feel like I've let everyone down. This is our first real breakup.

"If it makes you feel better," Brooke says, "Henry tagged Jordi in some photos last night, and she looked *miserable*."

Why doesn't that make me feel better?

"We'll figure out who else likes girls," Zoe says. "It can't just be you and Jordi in the whole school, or even the whole class."

"I don't care," I say. "I don't want to go out with anyone else."

"Well, not *now*," Maliah says. "Eventually. This is our senior year. We're all going to prom."

"I'll take you to prom," Brooke tells me. "Even if I have a boyfriend by then. He'll have to understand."

"Same," Zoe says. "You'll have the best dress of anyone there anyway."

"You're both screwing up my point," Maliah says. "My point is you'll feel better at some point. And by that point, we'll have figured out who's available. And hopefully whoever it is . . ."

"Likes me?"

"Oh shut your face," Maliah says. "Is good enough for you. Unlike Jordi."

I open my mouth to defend Jordi. And then of course I don't.

No one can decide what to get, so we order four things (pancakes, waffles, an omelet, and a vegan breakfast burrito) with the plan of splitting everything. But just like last night, no matter how good comfort food sounds, I barely take a bite of anything.

"Do you want to go shopping after this?" Maliah asks. "I can clear my whole day."

"Me too," Zoe says.

"I have nothing to clear," Brooke says. "Let's do it."

"I can't believe I'm saying this, but . . ." I try another bite of pancake. It tastes like nothing. "I don't want to go shopping."

"We'll do whatever you do want," Zoe says. "What sounds good to you, Abby?"

"Nothing," I say. "Thanks for making me come to brunch, really, but now I just need to go back home and collapse. Okay?"

They look at each other like they don't know if it is.

"It's only been like thirty-six hours," I say. "I'm allowed to want to lie in bed and feel like crap. I have to see her tomorrow at work and . . ."

My voice breaks, and Maliah puts her hand on my shoulder. Being visibly shattered is a strange feeling; I would have guessed it would be horrible, but I don't even have any control right now. Everything's ruined so who cares if everyone knows that?

"Can you skip work?" Zoe asks. "Say you're sick?"

"They're not even paying you," Maliah says. "You should absolutely play sick."

"No, I . . . I should get it over with. And I really can't let Jordi win now. If she did this and gets the job . . ."

"You're brave," Brooke tells me.

But that is one thing I don't feel at all.

I leave early on Monday morning so that there's less chance of running into Jordi on my way, and luckily I make it safely to Lemonberry. Laine sees me and runs over to open the door.

"You're early," she says. "How was your weekend? How did Jordi's opening go?"

"Fine," I say. "I think people really liked it. And it was crowded."

"That's great! I think Maggie and I are going tomorrow. Will we be the oldest people there? By decades?"

I force a smile. "No, it's not all people my age. I'm going to get some coffee."

It feels safe in the back. I'll have at least a few moments before Jordi could reach this room and I have to see her again. I don't understand how I could ever again see her eyes, her neck, the way her hands are so delicate but hold her camera with all the world's strength.

I guess a small part of me always knew we might not last forever. I might not get my happily ever after. But in these worst-case scenarios, it was always the job that would end us.

Somehow, I never saw this coming.

"Hey, Abby." Maggie walks into the room with a coffee carrier full with cups. "I needed caffeine before I made it in, and I thought everyone might appreciate something better than my sad old coffeemaker's best efforts."

"Oh, thanks." I take a cup from her. "That was really nice."

"It's too bad about Jordi," she says.

What? "What?"

"I hate being sick during the summer," she continues. "The worst."

"So she's out all day?" I ask.

"She is, sorry. Want to sit with me to think about this week's orders?"

226

Of course I do, and by the time we're debating if cardigans will keep selling as well as they have been, I feel a little more like myself again. Maggie even takes my advice on which print of a dress to order. And then I tweet how excited we are about our upcoming orders, and people start asking nearly immediately what we're getting in.

And then I realize this is the perfect time to bring it up.

"Um, so of course Jordi's photos are amazing," I say. "She's really talented. But when you look at a lot of really successful Instagram accounts, like corporate ones?"

"Oh god." Maggie laughs. "Am I corporate?"

"Well, you know. Not personal accounts. Anyway, they still post things that look a little . . ." I shrug. "Amateur? Maybe that's not the right word. But not like something you'd see in a fashion shoot or an official lookbook."

Maggie nods. "I get what you're saying. Like something you'd take with your phone."

"Exactly. And maybe since Jordi's sick today, I could try something? Just to see if it makes a difference. And if it doesn't, I'll delete it."

"Sure. Just let me see it first. I don't want it to look *too* amateur."

Maybe I've gotten ahead of myself. I'm a little afraid that *too amateur* is all I can manage. But after lunch (Mom's leftovers because my life isn't sad enough) I try a bunch of different shots and finally settle on one of the jewelry display case with a caption about the current sale.

"Is this okay?" I bring my phone back to Maggie and let her review it. This is the most I've pushed myself to fully do what I think I'm good at here, but I try not to imbue this moment with *too* much meaning.

But luckily Maggie nods her approval, so I post. I'm not sure how much of a betrayal it really is; I should have brought this up a while ago, but I didn't even want to chance hurting Jordi. It's not as if Maggie won't still need photos of clothes for the web site and a million other promotional things, though. But if my assessment is right, I was smarter about this, and it'll be quantifiably certifiable. Sure, Jordi could switch from her fancy camera to her iPhone, but would she know what works best for the brand? Would she know just how to phrase a post about new styles?

Seriously, she can't have done what she did *and* get the job. My heart can't take it.

"Abby?" Laine leans into the back room. "You have a friend out here."

I walk up front and find Jax examining a rack of crinoline skirts.

"What the hell are these?" he asks. "Old-fashioned underwear?"

"Why are you here?" I ask. "Aren't you supposed to be in San Francisco?"

"I just got back and thought I'd see how you're holding up." He looks me over. "You seem okay. Not your best, not your worst."

I don't even want to know when Jax saw me looking worse than two and a half days out from my only breakup.

"When do you get off?" he asks. "Let's get fucked up and talk shit about crazy girls."

"That sounds terrible. Can we just do the opposite of that?"

"I have no idea what that would be, but, sure. Anything you want, Abbs."

We end up going to Patio Burgers because Jax says his dad is getting anxious about the app. I wonder how this would even work if Jax hadn't teamed up with the daughter of someone currently anxious about a cookbook. I feel like most people have parents who worry about normal things.

"I'm pissed because you're pissed," Jax says. "But I don't think it sounds that bad."

"Are you serious? It was the worst. It was the hugest violation."

"She wasn't taking secret nannycam pics of you or whatnot," he says. "Right? Every time I saw that girl she had a camera pointed at something. Usually you."

"But I thought that was private," I say. "Just for her."

Jax shrugs. "Feels like the danger of going out with a photographer. You date Taylor Swift, she writes a mean song about you. You date Jordi, your picture's gonna be on a wall in some gallery."

"First, you have to accept that you're never, ever going to date Taylor Swift," I say. "Second, no. People shouldn't assume you're a public person just because they are."

"Have you talked to her?" he asks.

"No, and I'm not going to," I say. "It's bad enough I'll

have to see her at the store on Wednesday. Luckily she faked sick today."

"It's gonna be okay," he tells me. "I see Tina Pang plenty, and she broke my goddamn heart."

"I have no idea who that is," I say. "But it's interesting you have a heart to be broken."

"*Had* a heart," he says with a grin. "Once upon a time. Just like you."

Sometimes I literally hate myself for how happy I am that Jax is my friend.

Mom's still at her computer when I get home, and she actually pauses what she's doing and glances up at me. "Hi, Abby. How're you doing?"

"Fine," I say.

"I'm really sorry to hear about Jordi," she says.

"Are you?" I walk into my room and flop on my bed. Unfortunately, Mom's followed me in.

"Of course I am," she says. "I'm not sure why you always assume I don't . . ."

". . . don't dislike everything about me? Just paying attention, Mom, that's all."

She sits down next to me on the bed. "That's an unfair thing to say."

"Seriously? You hoped I was going out with *Jax*. You wanted me to lose weight so I'd be *pretty*. Like if only I was a thin straight girl, you could love me. But I'm neither, so."

I shove my face into my pillow so that hopefully she can't tell I'm crying. I really had no idea just how much I could cry. It's sort of gross. Can my head lose too much moisture? And if it does, will that hurt my brain? Considering how stupid that sounds, I worry this process has already begun.

"Of course I love you," Mom says.

"Well, then *like me*."

"Oh, Abby." She somehow gets me to turn my face to look at her. "I just want your life to be easy."

"Can't I just be me? I feel like that's the easiest option."

She watches me for a few moments. "I was seventeen when I went through my first breakup, too."

"You had a boyfriend in high school?" I ask.

"Two. One my junior year—that was the breakup—and one senior year. That one took me to prom."

I remember seeing Mom's prom picture. When I was little, I thought she looked exactly like Cinderella, and so I did think for a while the guy might have been a prince. It now seems unlikely this was the case.

"What happened?" I ask.

"He kissed my best friend at a bonfire," she says.

"*No.*" I stare at her. "That's horrible. Jordi didn't do anything that horrible."

"That doesn't surprise me," Mom says. "She's always so polite."

I guess my heart is still a little behind on recent news because I feel a warmth in me that Mom thought something nice about Jordi.

"I'm sorry about your boyfriend," I say, which makes Mom laugh.

"Well, I'm over it now! That took a while, though."

"Did you forgive your friend?" I ask.

"Eventually. Sort of." Mom strokes my hair. "What if you tried a nice strawberry blonde? That would look so cute on you."

"I like it pink," I say. "Pink's my favorite color. Why can't my hair be my favorite color? That's the thing you always do! You try to change everything about me. I know you wish I was more like Rachel. I'm just *not*. I'm not going to be."

"Honey, no." She sighs. "I don't know why things always come out like that."

"Well, because you say them." I turn over so I'm facing the wall instead. My bulletin board looks ransacked because I pulled off every photo of or by Jordi. It's strange how in just a couple months, one person can become so much of your world.

Which means when your world's been expanded, when that person's gone, it feels like mass extinction.

"I'm better with food," Mom says.

"Than with people?" I turn back to her, and I feel bad that I laugh when she nods. "Mom, that's not a thing."

"Well, with you then. I always seem to say the wrong thing. When I'm writing for this book or for my site, my meaning always seems to come across correctly. With us . . ."

I think about how easy it is to be myself as I'm posting style photos of other people. Easier than this, for sure.

"Mom?" I look down at my hands. "I really thought you were going to ask me to run your social media this summer."

"Oh, Abby . . . honey, that's a big job. I was aiming to get this book deal, and we've had so many near-offers on a Food Network show."

"I guess I get it," I say. "At least why you needed it to be . . . not a teenager. But—"

"I never meant to hurt your feelings. I thought—we're just so different, honey. When I was your age, I thought if I wasn't like my friends the world would end."

"The world did end." I look over to my bulletin board. "But not because of that. And my friends and I are all different. I know you see it as the skinny straight ones and then *me*, but that's not how they see me, you know."

Mom nods, though I don't think she believes me. "I promise things get easier after a breakup. You just need some time."

I nod, too, though I don't believe her either.

CHAPTER 24

I'm early again to work on Wednesday, but Jordi was earlier, because she's already chatting with Paige when I walk in. I try not to make eye contact but her gaze sweeps over me. I can't find my way out of it.

"Hi," she says.

"Hi. Good morning." I walk to the back to get coffee and hope that Maggie's already here so that I have a reason to stay back here. Since she's not, I just make this the most thoughtful cup of coffee I've ever poured or mixed.

I guess this is why people say you shouldn't date in the workplace. It just sounded like a thing that affected business executives, not Jordi or me.

"Abby." She walks into the backroom. "Please. Can we talk?"

"I seriously have no idea what you want to talk about," I say. "I just want to work. Okay?"

Maggie walks into the room. "Hi, girls. Jordi, are you feeling better?"

She shrugs while staring at the floor. Jordi looks so small and frail, and it's hard not to want to do something about that. Something I guess I hadn't foreseen about falling in love with someone is how much your heart can ache to take away their pain. You hear about the inability to think about anyone else or how happy you can be just to be near someone and of course how mind-blowing the tiniest bit of physical contact can be. But the safety you can feel and you can *be* while in someone's arms is something I didn't anticipate.

So it almost doesn't make sense that I can't provide that to Jordi right now. Which is nuts! She's upset because I broke up with her, and I broke up with her *because of her.*

I still do my best to avoid looking at her for the rest of the day. Of course we have to walk in the same direction after we're off. Sometimes I'd wondered, if we hadn't had time alone before and after Lemonberry, if we would have ended up together when we did. Then, it felt like a gift.

Now, less so.

"I know you don't want to talk to me," Jordi says. "Can you at least listen?"

"I can't stop you from talking." It's something I never could have pictured myself saying. Quiet, steady Jordi. Her words had been everything in the world to me.

But now she can say whatever she wants. She won't get my words in return.

"I never would have . . . Abby, I thought if you could just see the photos, you'd see."

"See what?" Ugh, not talking is so hard. "See that you didn't really care about me? Not like you said, at least. Not if it doesn't ultimately benefit you."

"Why won't you believe me?" Jordi stops walking, and I do, too. "I made a mistake and I know that, Abby. Why don't you have any faith in me?"

I stare at my feet. Today I'm wearing pink flats decorated with white leather flowers, which I clearly remember wearing when we sat on a blanket together at Hollywood Forever.

But that feels like a long time ago. So I walk home without another look back to Jordi. When I watched romcoms and saw main characters storm off from the person they once loved, I sometimes couldn't handle it. It always seemed so silly not to just give someone a chance. I had no idea how this could feel, though. I didn't know that the thing that would seem silliest is the idea of giving someone the chance to hurt you again.

Jax makes me go out with him to lunch on Thursday even though I still don't quite feel like a normal day is what I need. Maybe if I did know what I'd need I'd just go do that, but it's not as if anything else feels right either. My time feels too big and unfillable, which is exactly how I felt in June, too. And I guess I was making it work or at least getting there.

And then I didn't have to, because there was Jordi.

"You still look like shit, Abbs," Jax says while I'm looking over the menu at Fusion Burgers. "What the hell is aillade?"

"Garlic puree," I say, and he raises his eyebrows. "When your mom's entire life is cooking and weird food combinations, you learn a lot."

"Oh yeah, the great Norah of Eating Fancy with Norah," he says.

"It's Eat Healthy with Norah, exclamation point," I say. "The exclamation point is very important to the brand."

"'*Boschetto a la tartufo remolade*,'" Jax reads. "I literally don't understand one word I just said."

"I thought you were smart," I say, and he cracks up.

"Seriously," he says. "You doing okay?"

I shrug. "Seriously? Probably not. I lost my only chance to be in love."

"Shut the hell up," he says. "There's a new chance to love every goddamn day. Look at me, no luck at all this summer, and I'm not worried. Going to a party tonight, who knows what could happen. Hey!"

I rack my brain for an excuse before he even asks.

"Come with," he says. "We'll find you a new girl. And me. We'll find me a girl, too. You'll wingman—wingwoman me. It'll be awesome."

"Jax," I say. "Can I have at least, I don't know, a week? Two? Until school starts? I still feel . . . I don't know how I feel. Not good. Not party-ready."

"The best days of your youth are passing right by you," Jax says.

"I find that very hard to believe."

So I go home after rating the super spicy Dan's Inferno and sweet salty Mexican BBQ burgers that Jax and I split.

I convince Jax to head off to the party on his own, and I spend the evening in my room. The photos and cut outs from magazines that used to decorate my bulletin board, pre-Jordi, are still in my desk drawer, so I take them out and fill the empty space. Before long, my room looks just like it used to, and between that and the burgers actually tasting like something today, maybe I'm doing better.

Jax texts while I'm slowly putting together a post about maxi dresses for +style. *wuts the deal w ur friend brooke.*

Even after all this time, his flexibility with the English language really pains me.

What do you mean by 'the deal'? I respond, and then go back to posting photos from my usual collection of shops. It feels foreign doing this in my bedroom and not on the Perezes' living room couch. It's weird that my soundtrack is one of my favorite playlists, not Christian playing *The Last Guardian.*

she's cute, & i assume u have good taste in friends.

Oh, this is just what I need.

What about that barista? I text. *Weren't you just concerned about her deal very recently?*

I try again, very hard, to concentrate on prints versus solids instead of watching my phone. But of course it buzzes again.

that went nowhere. new plan. And then: *ur girl is here. she looks like shit too.*

It offends me that Jordi's ready to be at a party less than a week out from our breakup. And what offends me more

238

is that that's a thought I have. *Forget about Jordi, forget about Jordi, forget about Jordi.*

As a compromise, I picture how terrible she must look, and then I try to put whatever party stuff is going on completely out of my mind and focus on *+style* instead. It only sort of works, but for now, *sort of* is more than enough.

Maggie's already in when I arrive at work the next morning, and she greets me by holding her arms out to her sides. Hopefully I'm not supposed to hug her? The gesture is vaguer than she must think.

"Why didn't you tell me?" she asks.

Oh, no.

"You were absolutely right about Instagram," she says. "We had so many new comments and followers since Monday. I can't believe you didn't mention it Wednesday."

Oh, yes, Wednesday, the day I tried not to look at or think about Jordi. That must have taken up more of my brainpower than I'd realized. Why am I letting my professional responsibilities slip by me yet again?

"I'll chat with Jordi once she's here, but, yes, absolutely, effective immediately let's try to post as many candids as possible. Keep checking in with me, but, Abby, this is really in your hands. I'm so impressed with your analysis."

"Thank you," I say. "I'll come up with more today, and we can even schedule things to run when I'm not here, if that helps, and—"

"Absolutely," she says with a smile. "Really great work. Also, we got the Bella dress in a new print, and I made sure there was an extra in your size for you."

"Oh, thanks," I say. "I can't really afford to get a new dress right now but—"

"It's a gift." Maggie digs through a nearby box and pulls out the dress. It's a tropical old-school floral—something that would fit in at a tiki hut—and even has little hibiscus flowers that match my hair. It couldn't be more Abby if it tried. "I wanted to guarantee you'd have it."

"Thank you so much, I—"

Jordi walks into the room and flicks her eyes in my direction for the briefest of moments. "Hi."

"Jordi, come on back to my office for a moment," Maggie says, and I realize it's going to happen now. Jordi will have less to do for Lemonberry, and there's no way I won't at least right now seem like a more viable candidate for the fall job.

A more viable candidate? Who even am I?

Jordi walks past me a few moments later. Somehow she seems even smaller than Wednesday when she stood on the sidewalk down the block from her home. "I guess you're taking pictures now."

"Just for social media," I say. "The rest are all for you to do."

Wait, why am I trying to make her feel better?

She takes her camera out of her bag, hangs her bag on the usual hook, and heads out to the storefront. This is, no contest, a round I won.

But I think back to Jordi's proposal. *Proposal.* Now there will definitely be no Ives-Perezes or custom dress made by Maggie or fight between Maliah and Rachel for who would be my maid of honor. Obviously none of those things were guaranteed or in the imminent future, but back then they felt like a dream I wanted to have.

And now the dream is over and, even if I deserved to, I'm the one who violated our terms.

That said, I spend all morning taking pictures until I settle on one of the new Bella dresses with Laine in the corner of the shot. There's something about her smile that seems to capture her energy. I think of Jordi telling me that taking a photograph means that you can make everyone else see the world the way you do.

I don't know why, but I walk back and hold out my phone to Jordi. "Do you think it looks okay?"

She looks up from whatever she's doing in Photoshop. "The framing's good, the lighting . . . could be better. Do you want me to show you?"

"I don't want to interrupt you," I say. "I'll figure it out. Thanks."

I tell Dad about my work success when I get home because he seems likeliest to be impressed by it. Mom comes in during the midst of our discussion with two hangers that hold two really beautiful dresses I've never seen before. For a moment, I'm hopeful, but they're tiny. These are definitely not for me.

"Abby, I'm so glad you're home," she says.

"Abby was just telling me about her big social media

triumph at work," Dad says. "We should get the full household involved in this operation."

"Greg, not now, this is an emergency," Mom says with a sigh and then looks back to me. "I'm having photos taken by the *LA Times* tomorrow morning, and I'm not sure which of these will look better on camera. If either of them even will."

"The green and white one," I say. "Your hair will look better against it, and I think the print will be good on camera, not too distracting."

"Thank you, sweetie," she says. "What's that?"

"Oh my god, Maggie gave me this," I say. "I mean, I heard you end up getting something free with the internship, but . . . I guess I thought it might just be something extra lying around that no one wanted to buy."

I show Mom the dress but of course I hold my breath that she won't ruin one of the only good things to happen this week.

"Wow," she says, which doesn't sound like the most hopeful of beginnings. "That's really fun, Abby. The flowers match your hair."

"I thought the same thing!" I decide to hurry to my room instead of chancing the moment any further. But then I have another smart thought and lean back into the hallway. "Mom? Can I be your stylist?"

She walks down the hallway. "Well, it's not exactly a full-time job, but, sure."

Now I definitely have to halt all contact with my mother

because there's no way she won't somehow screw up before the day ends.

Jax insists on going out for burgers the next day. I'm still really not feeling up for so much socializing, so we compromise on driving through Fatburger in Los Feliz. Jax pulls his BMW into a parking spot and rips open the bag.

"You could just open that like a normal person," I tell him.

"Nah, let's get to the good stuff fast." He hands me my Small Fatburger and fries. "How're you doing or whatever?"

"Your concern is overwhelming." I bite a fry in half. "I'm fine or whatever."

"Hey, I'm concerned. I let you trap us in this car with all your feelings."

I realize I'm smiling.

"You get the job yet?" he asks me.

"No, but . . ." I shrug. "I did some good work this week. Hopefully it wasn't unethical."

"Nothing's unethical in business," Jax says. "Or so Jackson Stockton the First says."

"Gross," I say, and then, "I'm sorry."

"You ready to meet new girls yet?"

"Emphatically no." I decide not even to bring up how unlikely that possibility seems. Even if there were girls who'd be interested—which by no means feels like the reality I live in—what does it matter when my heart is this broken? Can hearts stay broken forever? Is that me from now on—just broken?

"Are you crying?" Jax asks with a horrified edge to his voice.

"No!" I am lying. Lying *and* crying.

He sort of scatters extra napkins near my face, which—despite my tears—makes me burst into laughter.

"Why are boys so scared of girl feelings?" I ask.

"Abbs, I'm a feminist," he says. "I'm equally scared of all feelings."

CHAPTER 25

Someone taps on my door on Saturday morning while I'm still in bed. I try ignoring it, but it keeps getting louder. I turn to face the wall, because Mom and/or Dad should know better, but then I hear footsteps in my room.

"Get up, lazy butt," says a voice so familiar I can't believe it's even real. But I turn around and Rachel's in my room.

"I took a red eye." She flops onto the bed next to me. "Surprise."

"Oh my god." I sit up in a flash. "I can't believe you're here. I haven't seen you *since Christmas*. Did you come home because of my breakup? Is it that big of a disaster? Also, did you just say *lazy butt?*"

"No, I just . . ." She rolls her eyes. "I missed you. I even missed Mom and Dad. And the internship's . . . fine."

"How's Paul?" I ask. I'd like to say that after falling in love this summer I'm more understanding about the choices people make in relationships, but I still think that Paul's a goober. Hopefully this doesn't make me overly judgmental or hypocritical.

"He's fine," she says. "I don't know. Relationships are hard, Abby."

"Tell me about it," I say, and she laughs.

"You're my baby sister. You're not allowed to be the jaded one." She stretches her arms out above her head. "I need to finish sleeping. Wait, what's on my bed?"

"Tote bags," I say. "Eat Healthy With Norah! branded tote bags."

"I've definitely been gone too long." She settles under my covers. "Move over. You're taking up too much space."

"You're in my bed!" But I shift closer to the wall. "Actually, I don't even care if you came home because I'm sad and pathetic. I'm really glad."

Rachel smiles with her eyes closed. "Your being sad and pathetic is just a lucky coincidence."

"I'm so glad you're home," I say. "It's been so weird without you here."

Somehow, she's already asleep.

Mom and Dad force us up at a reasonable hour, and Mom makes a huge welcome-home breakfast. I'm set to mutually eye-roll with Rachel over whatever *solution* Mom's invented today, but there are mixed greens and a fruit salad and the most delicious egg white frittata I've ever had. Okay, potentially it's the only egg white frittata I've ever had, but I can't imagine any others would even be in the running.

Mom's cooking doesn't feel like *a solution* today, even though everything's healthy. For a moment, I think about the day in Jordi's family's kitchen, racing to seal empanadas, but I shake loose the memory.

I know Rachel being home is for a very limited time, but having all four of us around the table makes a lot feel right again. Maybe some stuff has been going right anyway, but it's easier to feel it with Rachel in the house. Of course, after next year, I'll be away, too, but right now that feels a very long time from now. I have to get through the rest of August, after all, before I can even think about next year.

Maliah meets me at Lemonberry when I get off work on Monday. Jordi has to walk by her to leave, and for once I look forward to the glare I expect from my best friend in Jordi's direction. But for once, it doesn't come.

"I always thought this would look cute on you," I tell Maliah, holding up a short white dress with an asymmetrical neckline. "And it's on sale!"

She takes the dress from me. "When I'm successful, I'm hiring you as my stylist."

"If you can even afford me," I say, which makes her laugh. "Do you want to try it on?"

"Next time," she says. "Or whichever time I'm not wearing neon red underwear."

"I didn't even realize that red could be neon," I say and wave good-bye to an unimpressed Paige before walking out into the late afternoon sunshine. "Where are we going? Did you plan something?"

"Who am I, *Jax?*" She points to her car. "I'm not the one who has weird elaborate little activities lined up."

"They aren't weird or elaborate," I say. "They're literally eating burgers at a bunch of places. If we do anything else it's because of me, because I don't want to die of a heart attack at seventeen from all these burgers. Hikes and walks are necessary."

"I think it bothers Trevor that Jax didn't ask him to eat all those burgers," Maliah says. "But he's being such a *boy* about his feelings and not wanting to admit it."

"I think Jax was the same way about all the time Trevor spends with you, though," I say. "I don't know if it's just a boy thing, though. Sometimes talking about your feelings is really hard."

Maliah shrugs. "You know my opinion on that."

"Yeah, but . . . some stuff's private. It's not about keeping secrets, it's about . . . I don't know. Sometimes I need things to exist in my own head for a while."

"I guess," Maliah says. "Do you want to take a walk around the Reservoir and then get a snack at LAMILL?"

"Perfect. I'm even wearing comfy flats today."

"Oh, please, like I haven't seen you walk a mile in heels," she says with a smile. "Your feet are tougher than mine."

Maliah drives over to Silver Lake and parks the car down a side street near the dog park. We take off on foot and I do my very best not to think about being here with Jordi. It's crazy how much of LA now reminds me of her, even though it's been my city since I was born.

"So . . ." Maliah puts on her sunglasses. "Have you talked to Jordi?"

"No more than necessary at work," I say. "Why?"

"I just thought maybe you'd calm down a little," she says.

"What? What are you talking about?"

"Abbs. She just took your photo. God knows I'm not Jordi Perez's biggest fan, but I really feel like you have to give her another chance."

"I don't *have to* do anything," I say.

"She thinks you're hot," Maliah says.

"Did she tell you that? When did you even talk to her?"

"Anyone with eyes could see that, Abby. So she took photos of her hot girlfriend. And, I'm sorry, I actually support what she did, and I wish I would have been there to see the show. Because the way you are about yourself, no one understands it."

"The way I *am* about myself? What does that even mean?"

"It means that you talk a great game online," she says. "You talk about being happy with how you look, no matter your size, and that health and confidence are way more important than dress size. You spend all your spare time telling other girls to like themselves, but then the second someone suggests you're worthy of that, you shut it down."

"I can be confident without putting my picture everywhere," I say.

"Sure. But you won't put it *anywhere*. Even on your super locked-down Facebook account, everything's just your face. And I know it doesn't matter if I tell you that you're gorgeous, or if Jax says he'd want to do you if you were straight, or that your girlfriend basically worships you. Until you believe the stuff you tell everyone else, I guess it doesn't matter."

"That's not—I don't—Mal. Come on."

"I think Jordi was trying to force you into seeing it," she says. "And maybe she didn't pick the greatest way to do it. But considering how annoyed it makes me, and I'm only your best friend . . ."

"Don't say *only*. Best friends mean a lot."

She sighs. "I don't know. I've been worried ever since you went all googly around Jordi that this would be over."

"What are you even talking about?" I ask, and I'm so confused that I forget to keep walking and then have to sprint to keep up with Maliah. "I'd never do that."

"I'm not saying it's something you'd *do*," she says. "But it must be different from Trevor and me, because I really still need my girls. I need you, Abbs. But if you have a girl you tell everything to and do everything with and then also get to make out with her, I don't see how I'll be necessary."

"Oh my god, Mal, seriously?" I grab her arm to make her stop walking. "I needed to talk to someone about Jordi as much as you do about Trevor. I just haven't been because you were so convinced she was a criminal."

"Marji saw her getting into a cop car," Maliah says. "And the aftermath of a fire."

"It's a much smaller and less dramatic story than you'd think," I say. "She's not a criminal. She just maybe cares too much about her art."

Except that I hear my words aloud and wonder if it's even possible. Art is life. How can you care too much about life?

"Fine," Maliah says. "Moving forward, I'll be less judgmental about Jordi Perez."

"Moving forward, it won't matter," I say. "But on the extremely off-chance that I go out with anyone else, I'll want to tell you so much, as long as you're open to them. Okay?"

"Only if your taste doesn't continue to be criminals," she says but with a huge smile. "I really am sorry it didn't work out, Abbs. I know you were happy."

My phone beeps, and I check it to see that of course it's Jax.

"Ignore him," Maliah says. "And I will say there's one positive thing to come out of your breakup."

"This conversation where you lectured me?" I ask, and she rolls her eyes.

"No, it's just made me extra grateful for how good things are with Trevor," she says. "We're really open and honest with each other, and so I always feel that we're on the same page."

I want to be offended that she's made this about her, but, actually . . .

"Oh my god," I say. "That's so great. It absolutely proves everything."

Maliah wrinkles her nose. "'Proves'? What are you talking about?"

"It's like in movies," I explain. "The heroine always has a cool sassy best friend—that's me—whose life's specifics don't really matter, because the epic love story is the heroine's. That's you, obviously. And this is always how it works! Late in the movie, the best friend has some sort of experience that makes the heroine see her own relationship more clearly. Which for us is my breakup and you with Trevor. Seriously, it maps out *perfectly*."

"Uh, Abbs? Life is not a movie. It's just . . ." She shrugs. "Life. I'm no more a heroine than you are. You are the sassy one, but I'm the one who's invisible at parties if you and your incredible style's around. I have plenty of sidekick in me, too."

I stare at her. "I never thought of it that way."

"Oh my god, Abby." She laughs and shakes her head. "This is why we shouldn't have any secrets. I could have fixed your thinking long ago."

The boys join us after we snack at LAMILL, and we spend the evening walking the neighborhood hills. When we reach a particular landing, even cool as hell Trevor has to admit the view of the city below is pretty breathtaking.

"Don't hit me," Jax whispers to me. "But I wish your girl was here to take a picture of this."

I guess I still believe a little in secrets, though, because I don't tell him that I'm wishing the same thing.

CHAPTER 26

Maggie emails me on Tuesday night that she's taking me out to lunch the next day so that I won't bring any "bread-free leftovers" from home. I barely sleep because I assume Jordi will be there too *or* I'm finding out earlier than expected that her decision's been made about the fall job.

But when one o'clock rolls around on Wednesday afternoon, Maggie pulls me aside on my own.

"Ready to head down?" she asks quietly, and I nod. We make our way down the block to Bon Vivant. I examine the menu, but Maggie practically has her face pressed up to the glass of the pastry case.

"How many macarons do you think you could eat in one sitting?" she asks, and I'm so surprised at the question that I laugh. "Every flavor here, for sure. Perhaps two of every flavor."

"The weird thing is that even though I eat against my mom's beliefs all the time, I really can only eat so many sweets now," I say. "But macarons are so light and perfect. Maybe I could eat all of them, too."

"I actually made one of your mom's recipes the other night," Maggie says. "I started to worry that with all my stress this summer over the fall line and of course my ex moving out that Sam was going to think all food came from a delivery guy."

"Which recipe?" I ask. "And was it good?"

"It was a coconut chicken salad," she says. "And it was honestly really good. But then we ate ice cream for dessert, so does that still count?"

We step up to order, and then Maggie looks over every empty table before settling on one right in the middle of the restaurant. I think back to lunch with her our very first day of work, and if magic were real, I'd will myself back there right this second.

I guess if magic were real, a lot of things would be different.

"Before you worry this is going to be some *big talk*," Maggie says, "I want you to know I haven't made my decision for the fall yet."

I nod.

"And, honestly, I hate this," she continues. "If there was a way that I could hire you both, I would. Absolutely. Please know that, okay? No matter how this works out."

"So Jordi's getting the job?" I ask. "Or it's at least leaning that way?"

"No, no, no," Maggie says. "I truly am undecided until after we talk, Abby. And then probably even for a while longer."

"Jordi should get the job," I say, because it feels like the right thing to say.

"Really," Maggie says, her voice full of surprise.

"Really. Her photos are amazing. And she works really hard."

"You work just as hard," Maggie says. "And you must know how great you are on, you know, all of our social media. You come up with *strategies*. You know I'm too old to know what I'm doing there, Abby."

I shrug. I don't even know why I'm saying what I'm saying. Obviously I have strategies. I could write an essay about my Lemonberry contributions.

"I don't know what's going on with you girls." Maggie raises her eyebrows. "Because this is just how my talk with Jordi went, too."

"Jordi said I should get the job?"

Maggie sighs and takes a sip of her iced tea. "Is there something I should know?"

Well, Maggie, I thought I was finally going to get my epic love story, but instead everything fell apart. And I don't trust Jordi anymore but I don't know if that's right of me, and all I want is for things to be okay again and not to feel like I'm missing a part of me that I didn't even know I had.

"No," I say. "I just think that Jordi deserves it more. That's all."

"Okay," she says. "Abby, I know that I'm your boss, and that I'm one trillion years old, but . . . do you need to talk about anything?"

"You're not one trillion years old," I say, even though I'm not certain of Maggie's precise age. She's definitely younger than my parents, and even they aren't a trillion. "And no. I might have been unfair to Jordi about something and . . . and I just don't think she should have anything else bad happen to her."

"Okay," Maggie says, and suddenly her voice is drenched in kindness. I wish it were appropriate to throw my arms around her and cry. "We can talk about something else now."

"Thank god," I say, which makes Maggie burst into laughter.

"Promise me, okay, that if Jordi ends up with the job, that you'll still keep in touch with me?" Maggie smiles right at me, even as a waiter drops off our food. "I'm really invested in knowing how your future turns out."

Something settles over me, and for once it isn't anxiety or a million questions to ask. I feel myself smile. "I'm pretty invested in that, too."

When I get home, the living room looks halfway organized, and Mom's sitting in the kitchen with a man her age who looks vaguely familiar. I assume he's been on her segment on the news or might be from Food Network. Considering that I overhear a few words like *nutrition* and *branded content* and *gluten-free*, my guess seems to be correct.

"Honey, come on in," Mom calls to me, which is unusual for a business meeting. I'm wearing one of my less crazy dresses—solid purple and no extreme flare to the skirt—so I guess she feels I can make a good enough impression.

"So this is the famous Abby." The man stands and holds out his hand to shake mine. He's wearing a T-shirt I don't recognize by brand but hangs like something expensive and jeans that fit the same category. It's funny how sometimes a lazy, casual outfit can signal *rich* just that quickly.

"Oh, you two haven't met?" Mom asks, which, why would I have met this man? "I guess with you living in San Francisco, you can't keep up as much as you'd like, huh."

"Definitely not," he says, and then I see it in his face, how it's the same shape as Jax's, and how his eyes are the same, too.

"Mr. Stockton?" I ask, and he laughs.

"Good to see my reputation precedes me," he says. "I really owe you a thank-you, Abby."

I wait to hear about how much work we've done this summer on Best Blank.

"It made it so much easier to connect with your mom," he says.

"It was a great idea," Mom tells me. "Your dad's really right that you have a lot of business savvy."

I'm confused about this entire conversation, and also, *business savvy?*

"I'd mentioned to Jax a few months ago that I wanted to partner Best Blank with some leading food experts and celebrities and chefs," Mr. Stockton says. "Your mom's brand is a great fit."

A few months ago.

"So you told Jax to get to know me to talk to my mom?" I ask, and he and Mom *laugh* while my pulse switches over to what feels like a blaring alarm clock inside my veins.

"Nothing that structured," Mr. Stockton says. "You

guys clearly got to know each other, and Norah and I set up a meeting."

"I'm going to choose my five favorite healthy meals in the city," Mom says. "How fun will that be?"

"Fun." I can't even manage to dredge up any sarcasm right now. It's like I'm broken. "If you can please excuse me, I have a few things I need to take care of."

"Of course," Mom says.

"We need to get back to talking shop anyway," Mr. Stockton says.

I get to my room and close the door before I realize Rachel's lying in my bed. "Could I please have some privacy?"

"Sorry, Abby, Mom's doing some business deal with that tech guy. You're stuck with me."

I actually say *argh* aloud and walk out of the room and into our tiny backyard. *What's going on with your dad??* I text to Jax.

As usual, his response is fast. *Y? did he say something stupid? whuts up.*

I cannot have this conversation with any more *y*s or *whuts*, so I call him.

"Aaaaabbs," he drawls. "Sorry you have to meet Jackson Senior. He can really be the worst."

"Jax," I say as calmly as I can manage, "did you seriously use me just so your dad could run co-branded Eat Healthy with Norah! content on Best Blank?"

This is the grossest reason I've ever been angry with someone.

"Define *use*," he says.

I pull my phone back from my ear and stare at it. And I tap to hang up. Unfortunately, it rings again immediately.

"Dude," he says. "I was *kidding*. Do you really think Fancy Eating with Norah's so famous my dad can't just email her?"

I think about that for a moment.

"I'm sure he dropped some whole 'since our kids are friends' line to her, but he's got major investor money, Abbs. Why would he need to gain some upper hand? Jackson Senior's all hand."

"Gross," I say. This whole thing is gross.

"It has nothing to do with anything."

"It has to do with why you wanted to hang out with me, and—"

"Are you listening? It goddamn *doesn't*. It's because . . ."

He trails off so dramatically I check my phone to make sure we're still connected.

"Why is it because?"

"Abbs, you're fucking cool, okay? It was a good excuse to hang out with you. And I'd rather eat all those burgers with you than go on dates with Trevor and Mal."

"You just wanted to be my friend?" I ask. "For no reason?"

"I said the reason! You're cool! I think you're, you know. Funny and shit. I'm not friends with any girls, but . . ." His voice gets softer and a little maybe sheepish. "I just wanted to hang out with you. This was a good excuse, okay? Can we stop discussing it?"

"Emotions aren't actually bad," I tell him. "You won't fall apart because you're having some right now."

"Don't make me take back the cool thing," he says, which makes me laugh. "The app thing was just . . . Ya know. A bonus or whatever. I know you think I'm some rich guy with a rich dad and an awesome ride, but . . . my dad sort of sucks, Abbs. When he asked me to help out on Best Blank, it was the longest conversation we'd had in like a year. So I just wanted you to think it was really important work we were doing."

"I get it," I say. "Trust me."

"But if we're gonna be honest about emotions and shit . . . You're my friend and maybe shouldn't jump to the worst-case scenario about me," he says.

"Ugh, fine. Fair point. Sometimes you're right about things."

I think about Maliah's only-honesty-no-secrets lifestyle, and while I do think there will always be things that are just for me, I can't deny that this is good, too. There is a certain amount I might owe the people in my life. The ones I care about, anyway.

"So is your dad happy with the app so far?" I ask. "Is he done with the initial testing?"

"No way. A lot of burgers to get through, and Dad says we can also switch off to a different food if we want to next. Best fries in LA."

"Ooh, best milkshake. Or taco."

"Tacos are too clichéd," he says. "What are you doing now? The burger role's still ours for the present. Wanna hit something left on our list?"

Actually, I do.

Rachel's still in my room when I get back from hanging out with Jax. I can't believe we shared this tiny area until just the other year. Now it feels like very little space for two people.

When this summer started, it seemed as though all I needed was to get Rachel back. Everything would be fine with Rachel sharing my little room in our little house. But the summer happened anyway. I became an intern and I fell in love and I made a new friend, all with Rachel about three thousand miles away.

"When are you going back?" I ask. "Not that it's not good to have you here, and it's exciting that the tote bags are in a box now and not all laid out on a bedspread. I just figure you can't take off too much time from your internship."

She shrugs. "I don't know. I actually . . . well, the company I had the internship with closed down. The danger of throwing all of your efforts into a startup."

"You should have said something! I've been whining about Jordi while you were dealing with this, and—"

"And I'm your big sister, and I was here for you," she says. "It's your first breakup. It's my job."

I sit down on my bed. "You haven't even had *your* first breakup yet."

Rachel makes a muffled sound, somewhere between a laugh and a sigh. "Well, it's not going *great*, Abby. He

261

doesn't seem that supportive about me losing the internship, and—"

"You should talk to him," I say, even though I've been secretly hoping for the day this particular news came. I imagine Paul twirling his mustache one last time and then disappearing into the sunset. "Maybe he doesn't know you even need support. I mean, you didn't tell me. I could have been being supportive instead of making you pack up those tote bags yourself."

"I was saving you from extra drama," Rachel says.

"I don't need to be saved. And Mustache Paul probably doesn't either."

"Oh my god." She throws a tote bag at me. We both learn very quickly that empty tote bags are not built for flight. "Do not call him Mustache Paul."

We laugh until we cry just like we used to years ago when, in a lot of ways, Rachel was my whole world. It's weird to realize it's okay that she isn't anymore.

"Come on," Rachel says, and I can tell from the look in her eyes that she has An Idea. It feels good to be the little sister ready to follow her again, no matter where that leads.

I sit in the passenger seat of her Honda and watch out the window as she drives down our street and to the edges of our neighborhood. My mind's awash with possibility: music, art, snacks?

But, no. We're in an empty parking lot.

"Switch with me," Rachel says once the car's in park. I can't even process what she's saying before she's outside and opening the passenger side door.

"Did Mom put you up to this?" I ask. "Did Maliah?"

"No one put me up to it," she says. "I know you're scared, and that's fine. But fear doesn't always mean that something's wrong, you know."

I give her a look. "You're the one hiding out here."

"Touché."

We continue our staring contest.

"I know you want to move to New York," Rachel says, "and hopefully you will. But sometimes life goes in other directions. Also, you have a whole year until then. Don't you want some freedom?"

Who doesn't want freedom? But why does it have to be tied so closely to this one freaking activity?

"Come on," Rachel continues. "Obviously it would be horrible getting your first driving lesson from Mom or Dad. But it's me. I'd never lead you astray."

"Oh, *really?* You just drove me to an abandoned parking lot in industrial wherever in the middle of the night."

"It's seven-thirty, Abby."

We both laugh. It's crazy how you could go months without seeing a person and have everything fall right back together this easily.

"Just around the parking lot," Rachel says. "One loop. If you hate it, we'll go home and never speak of it again."

"I find that really hard to believe," I say, but I unbuckle my seatbelt and get out of the car. It's jarring to sit down in the driver's seat, like a mirror image of how things are supposed to look from the front seat. And there's stuff in the way of everything—my feet and my boobs and my arms. Rachel so calmly explains everything, though, that I can't deny that nothing feels quite as scary. And before long, I carefully shift the car out of park, take my foot off the brake, and watch the world slowly roll by us.

"You're doing it!" my sister says, and it hits me that I am.

I make the entire loop around the parking lot, and it sort of happens so quickly that I decide to do it again. We keep going until we're almost dizzy and then switch spots again for our drive back home.

"I think I'm going back in a few days," Rachel says as we pull into the driveway.

"You can't! I have to learn driving on real streets!"

"I promise we'll do that before I go," she says. "But you're already becoming a pro. Now a few lessons with Mom or Dad won't kill you."

"But I need you here," I say, though as the words leave my lips, they don't exactly ring with truth and urgency. A lot happened without Rachel here, and I survived. It's funny how having someone back can prove what's true without them. I hope Rachel's always sort of my actual *bestest* best friend, but I also hope that it's because she wants to be and not that she *has to* be.

"You'll be fine," she says, and then I'm sort of annoyed that she's older and wiser and has figured all of this out already on her own.

Dad looks up as we walk into the house. "Is this an okay time? Not secret girl stuff going on?"

"If there was, would we tell you?" I ask.

"Excellent point, Abby. So I know we haven't done

this in forever, and you're both grown up and probably don't want to spend any time with your dad, but I was thinking about taking a night hike. You guys probably don't remember, but we used to do that all the time."

"Dad, that was literally about four years ago," Rachel says. "I was sixteen. I can remember things from when I was sixteen."

"I want to go," I say. "Rachel?"

"Despite my supposed diminished mental capacity, yes, I want to go, too."

"You're very funny," Dad says. "Let me put on my hiking shoes."

Rachel and I look to each other and burst into laughter. Dad has this ugly pair of brown sneakers he insists are *hiking shoes*. (They aren't.)

"Should we ask your mom?" Dad asks, ostensibly, us, but looks right at me.

And I say yes.

CHAPTER 27

Jax wants to go to some random party on Saturday, and I decide it doesn't sound like the worst thing in the world. I could stand to see people beyond my normal circle, but it's safer at a Westglen party than a Village Community High one. I'm still too freshly post-breakup to see too many people from school.

"I told Maliah to bring everyone," Jax tells me in the car. "Ya know, everyone as in Brooke."

"I hope you specified that to Maliah," I say. "Because *everyone* has never actually meant that."

"Mal gets me," he says.

"Uh huh. So why do you even like Brooke anyway? And you have to be specific."

"One, she has a really good laugh. I goddamn love it when girls laugh at my jokes."

I widen my eyes. "Girls laugh at your jokes?"

"Abby, I'll have you know I have been *very* successful with the ladies," he says. "You'd be surprised."

"Fine." I grin at him. "What else?"

"She's cute, she's smart, and she's funny as hell," he says. "She's kind of like you but less . . ."

"Gay?"

Jax almost howls laughing. "I was gonna say *diffi-cult*. You're a lot of work. I need approximately five to ten percent less work in a girl."

"Jax, I say this with all the love in the world, but . . . You're the worst."

I expect him to turn west in pursuit of fancier parts of town, but he's still following Glendale Boulevard. Maybe someone's parents live in a posh loft downtown.

"Thanks for making me go out," I say. "I think I might occasionally need to be bullied into doing the right thing."

"That's what I'm here for, bullying. And, speaking of . . ."

He pulls the car off the street into a red zone. "This is actually weirder to do than it seemed when I helped plan it, but . . . You've gotta get out of the car now."

"What?"

"Just trust me. You love me and I want the best for you."

"I can't go to the party?" I ask. "What's happening? You're just dumping me in . . . wherever we are?"

Actually, I know where we are.

"C'mon," Jax says, though gently. "Get out of the car."

I can't believe I do, but I do. I regret this decision almost immediately, so I knock on his window. He rolls it down but doesn't unlock the door.

"Give her a chance," he says. "I'll wait here."

"Can't we just go to the party?"

"Abbs, there's no party. This is your party. Bam. Outfoxed you."

Then he rolls up the window so I basically have no choice. I walk toward Pehrspace.

Jordi's standing right in front, but there's no crowd tonight. It's just her. "Hey."

"Hi."

"Will you come in?" she asks, and I nod. The usual guy's at the door, but he just smiles and waves us through. The place is empty besides us.

Jordi's photos are still on the wall. I caught such a quick glimpse of the ones that weren't me, but I think they're all still up. In place of the ones removed are photographs I haven't seen before. Each frame holds somewhere I know, though. Lemonberry's back room. The Chandelier Tree. The sidewalk outside of Folliero's.

"This was after you," Jordi says. "My summer without Abby. It looks the same, but . . . it isn't."

"The photos look good," I say quickly.

"Abby, I'm sorry," she says. "I should have asked."

"Yeah," I say. "You should have."

"I fucked up," she says. "I wanted to have the best show possible, and . . . those were my favorite photos I've taken. And, yeah. I knew what you'd say if I asked you, and . . . I couldn't have used them if you'd actually said no."

"These pictures are just as good," I say with a shrug. "Better."

"You're the only one who thinks that," she says, and a smile slides across her face. I missed that slow smile in my life. "You're beautiful, Abby. I just wanted to capture that."

"And have a good photography show," I say.

"And that. I'm sorry. I'm sorry times a million."

"I'm sorry I didn't let you explain," I say, and something in her expression softens. "I feel like maybe I owed you that? I don't know. I don't know any of this."

"Me either," she says. "Obviously."

"It's hard to think of myself as beautiful." I'm saying more than I would have imagined sharing with her, with anyone. "People *hate* fat girls. The way people talk online. The way people will just *stare* sometimes . . ."

"That doesn't make you ugly," Jordi says. "Fuck those people."

"I wish it was that easy," I say. "It's not always that easy for me."

"I should have realized that," she says. "But it's hard to when I look at you. None of that makes sense when you're this cute."

"I feel weird saying that what happened is okay." I shrug some more. Suddenly it's all I know how to do. "It wasn't okay. But I guess it is now. Or I want it to be. Or I'm over it. Or I get it. Or I don't think you could ever be mean to someone who didn't deserve it. Or—"

"Abby," Jordi says and laughs.

"Don't make fun of me," I say, but I find myself smiling. "I missed you! I have like a million things to say."

"Oh, god, me too," she says. "My parents actually apologized to me."

"About the arson?"

AMY SPALDING

"Jesus, Abby, it wasn't arson," she says, but then she laughs again. "About the fire and the cop, yeah. Honestly, I don't know what changed. They just finally saw me."

"I'm really, really glad that happened," I tell her, and she nods in her understated Jordi way. Did you know you could miss how someone nods?

"I drove a car!" I tell her, and she looks a little disappointed. "What? Aren't you excited for me?"

"I wanted to be the one to teach you," she says. "But, *yeah*. I'm excited for you."

"I still might not get my license," I say. "But I'm not scared anymore."

We watch each other for a few moments.

"Are we okay?" Jordi asks. "If there's even a *we*. Should I ask that first?"

I reach out and wind my fingers through hers. "I don't want to pretend like what happened didn't happen."

"Of course not." Jordi pulls me closer. It's hard to think with her brown eyes looking right into mine, with her lips so close.

"But I feel bad for not believing you either," I say. "Or letting you screw up without just ending stuff. Especially after your parents jumped to conclusions about you this summer. I didn't want to add to that."

"I'm okay," she says. "I'm okay if you are."

I nod. "I'm okay."

She untangles her hands from mine and then clasps my face. "I love you, Abby."

"Oh my god," I say, and it's a terrible reaction, and then

I laugh, which is even worse. "I'm sorry! I just didn't know if you'd ever—"

She presses her lips to mine. It fills me with relief that she tastes the same. I don't know why I thought she wouldn't. I don't know why I thought that one mistake would alter everything. People make mistakes.

"I should have said it when you did," Jordi says. "I was worried about the show—and you—and I was surprised, and—"

"I love you too," I say, and I kiss her. It feels like before; her hair brushes my cheeks and her fingertips touch my face with just enough pressure that I feel held and when I slide my arms around her waist, we curve together as if we were built for each other.

But there's something new, too; I know that Jordi won't always have the right thing to say and she knows that I might freak out when she doesn't. You don't fall in love with just the good parts, and I know that now.

"Hey, um, you're probably going to think I'm stupid," I say. "But maybe now that we're back together, you should take down the 'summer without Abby' photos."

"Oh," she says, and I can practically see how hard she's thinking about what she'll be able to replace them with.

"And this will make you think I'm even *more* stupid, and it's your show and not mine, but . . . I have an idea of what you should put up in their place."

Jordi puts all the original photos back up at Pehrspace. She invites everyone again, and I invite everyone else: Maliah and Trevor, Jax, Brooke and Zoe, and even my parents. Rachel's already back in Boston, posting annoying selfies with Mustache Paul, and I've liked every single one of them on Instagram.

The photos of me aren't actually as big and wall-covering as I remember. They take up a normal amount of space. Maybe even the right amount of space. I don't look the way I do in mirrors, or in my own selfies. Jordi's forcing the world to see me as she does, and I realize that in her eyes I'm beautiful.

And I guess it's possible that it's not just her. It's possible I look this way to other people, too. It's more than possible that I recognize the girl looking back at me in the photos myself.

"Thank you," Jordi tells me, in the midst of this crowded room. "You didn't have to."

"I wanted to," I say. "I wanted to see your whole show the way you intended it."

"The way I intended it was to also have a photo of the fire." She nods in her parents' direction. "But I figured I shouldn't push my luck."

It's hard to keep it just the two of us when the room is full of people who know us. Our hands stay clasped while we're inundated with people.

Jax tells Jordi her photos are *dope* and then hits on Brooke.

Brooke rolls her eyes but I don't see them apart for the rest of the night.

Jordi's parents invite me over for dinner next week.

My parents don't say anything stupid at all, and Mom even asks Jordi if she's ever worked in food photography.

Maggie asks Jordi and me if we just want to split the part-time hours in the fall. We'll both barely make any money but we all feel silly that we didn't think of this solution sooner.

Laine says that I have to reconsider being in some photos for Lemonberry.

I tell her that I'll consider it. It's scary, but maybe girls like me should get to see Maggie's beautiful dresses on someone who looks the way they do.

"Hey, are you guys still doing that app thing?" Jordi asks, looking between Jax and me.

"Hell *yeah* we are," Jax says.

"So what's the best burger?" Maliah asks.

Jax and I glance at each other.

She and Jordi exchange a little glance.

"How do you guys not know?" Jordi asks.

"I dunno," Jax says. "Haven't really thought about it."

"It's honestly just been really fun eating burgers," I say. "I wasn't, like, interested in data."

We both get out our phones and tap on the Best Blank app.

"Is it just In-N-Out?" Maliah asks.

We nod. "It's literally just In-N-Out."

"Will your dad mind?" I ask Jax.

"Nah. Who is Jackson Stockton Senior to challenge cold, hard, Animal Style data?"

"Animal Style is overrated," Maliah says, and Trevor makes such a dramatic face that I pray their love survives.

"Can we get in on this?" Brooke asks, and it's such a good segue for Jax that I shoot him little eye daggers until he turns directly to her. Suddenly it seems like everyone's arguing over burgers and secret menus and rating systems, and so I lace my fingers back through Jordi's and pull her away from the crowd.

I kiss her like no one's watching, because who cares if they are? Tonight, the story isn't about anyone else.

Tonight, the story is us.

ACKNOWLEDGMENTS

Thank you so, so much to my editor, Nicole Frail, for believing in and loving this book. Thanks as well to Emily Shields, and the rest of the Sky Pony team for your hard work.

As always, thanks to my agent Kate Testerman for your tireless optimism!

Thanks to early readers and cheerleaders: Christie Baugher, Jen Gaska, Jasmine Guillory, Riley Silverman, Sarah Skilton, and Eliza Tiernan. Thanks for everyone who participated in burger research, especially Suzanne Casamento and Marisa Reichardt. Thanks to Jessie Weinberg for cool art! Thanks to Audrey DuBiel and everyone at Audrey K Boutique for all the shop talk! Thank you to my local crew of L.A. YA writers for their friendship and support, including—but not limited to because I know I'll leave someone important out—Robin Benway, Kayla Cagan, Heather Cocks, Charlotte Huang, Jeff Garvin, Maurene Goo, Aditi Khorana, Kathy Kottaras, Gretchen McNeil, Nicole Maggi, Morgan Matson, Jessica Morgan, Isabel Quintero, Lilliam Rivera, and Zan Romanoff. Thank you to the Fight Me Club for the venting and the wisdom. Thanks to my mom, Pat Spalding, for all her support.

And to all the girls who worry they take up too much space: you don't.

ABOUT THE AUTHOR

Amy Spalding has a B.A. in advertising and marketing communications from Webster University, and an M.A. in media studies from the New School. Amy studied longform improv at the Upright Citizens Brigade Theatre. By day, she manages the digital media team for an indie film advertising agency. By later day and night, Amy writes, performs, and pets as many cats as she can. She grew up in St. Louis, but now lives in the better weather of Los Angeles.